trusting
in forever

Enjoy!
Ali Holt

TRUSTING IN FOREVER

Cover | Character Artwork by Brianne Wright

Cover | Design by Annalee Thomasson

Photo | Author Photo by Felicia Hall

Edit | Dune Press & Co.

Paperback | 978-1-7377904-3-3

EBook | 978-1-7377904-4-0

DEDICATION

This book is for all the "Emmas" out there.
May you guard your heart but not lock it up forever.

ACKNOWLEDGMENTS

Whew. I still can't believe I've published my first book, and that this is my real life. But none of this would have been possible without the love and support of so many.

First, and most importantly, Darrin and the boys. I wrote Trusting in Forever while also working a full-time job, so there were many Sunday afternoons that Mommy would sit at a coffee shop and write all the words while the three of you were at home or out doing something without me. I will forever be grateful to my husband and sons for allowing me that time—and never being anything but excited for me in this adventure.

As a little girl, my mom always told me I could be whatever I wanted; that I could do anything I put my mind to. It may have taken a few years longer than either of us would have liked for that lesson to sink in, but, thank you Mom for always believing in me and encouraging me to follow my dreams.

To the most amazing tribe of women I've ever met —Ashley, Desire, Felicia, Lisa and Stephanie. Where would I be without the most badass of all the bitches supporting and encouraging me daily? I'll never find words to express what that means to me.

And to Annalee, my publisher, all I can say is thank you. Thank you for encouraging me. Thank you for believing in me. Thank you for lighting a fire under my bottom when I needed one lit.

You may also notice as you read this book that uncles play a big role in the lives of their nieces and nephews. It wasn't something I did intentionally, but having the most amazing uncle in my corner for my whole life clearly spilled onto the page without me realizing it. So one final thank you to Ball Ball for, well...for everything.

trusting
in forever

CHAPTER ONE

"This cannot be happening." Nick Ewing tightened his white-knuckled grip on the steering wheel of his Suburban as he raced through Boone Heights, Maryland.

"I'm sorry, Uncle Nicky." Teddy's voice peeped from the backseat. Strapping his crying and bleeding five-year-old nephew into the car seat had already broken his heart, and Teddy's sweet apology shattered the pieces that were left. Nick worked to control his panic as they drove down Main Street, passing *A Novel Idea* (the town bookstore) and *Knit and Stitch* (the craft store owned by the Kipling sisters.)

"How's it going back there, buddy?" Nick looked into the rearview mirror, thankful that his brother had recently switched Teddy into a front-facing car seat. If he'd had to drive to the clinic without being able to see his nephew's face, it would have haunted him in his sleep.

"Okay, I guess," he sniffed. "It hurts, though, and I think it's still bleeding, but I can't tell too good."

Nick brought Teddy with him to work that day, something they loved to do together. The pair would usually find themselves knee-deep in a dirt pile, checking on projects and looking at all the tools and equipment. They'd never ended up in a situation quite like this one.

This time, Teddy found a shovel in one of the piles and grabbed at the blade without realizing that it was broken. The jagged metal sliced into his skin before Nick could even call out a warning, and there was only so much he could do to handle such an injury without a proper first aid kit. An active construction site without a first aid kit infuriated Nick, and he made a mental note to deal with that problem later. He had pulled a clean tee shirt from his gym bag and wrapped it around Teddy's hand in a quick attempt to stop the bleeding, which also worked to hide the wound from the boy, helping him to calm down.

As if an injured nephew wasn't stressful enough, Nick was also rehearsing the ways he might explain the whole thing to his older brother. He was going to have to admit that Teddy got hurt on *his* watch, and Nathan was going to kick his ass. Then again, he was already beating himself up—what were a few more blows?

Nathan—Nick's older brother, his partner at Ewing Brothers Construction, and a single father—left for Baltimore early that morning to pick up some custom supplies for a project, leaving Teddy with Nick for the day. The Ewing siblings were all blown away when Stephanie walked out on Nathan and Teddy and had done their best ever since to help care for Teddy and fill the boy's life with enough love to make up for the fact that he didn't have his mom. A boy needed his mom in a situation like this—bleeding and afraid in the backseat of a car.

"Hey buddy, I heard you met Aunt Sarah's new puppy yesterday." Teddy desperately needed a distraction, and Uncle Nicky knew that talking about his sister's new puppy was his best shot. Sarah was the baby of the family and worked as a veterinary technician for Dr. Krenshaw—the Boone Heights' one and only veterinarian, who had to be close to one hundred years old by now. It was the perfect job for her; Sarah was a total animal lover and was always bringing home strays.

"Uh huh," Teddy said, perking up a little to talk about the newest Ewing. "Sadie was so tiny! All she wanted to do was lick my face and try to sit in my lap."

"Puppy kisses are sweet." Nick shot up a thankful prayer that his distraction technique worked. A few minutes away from the clinic, he realized he hadn't called ahead and wondered how long the wait would be. Then again, how busy could a small town doctor be on a Wednesday morning?

As they pulled into the parking lot of the Boone Heights Family Clinic, he was relieved to find the place mostly empty—except for one car with a Massachusetts state license plate. An out-of-state plate would normally have sparked some curiosity in him, but not today. He had other things on his mind.

Nick unbuckled Teddy and lifted him from his seat. "Let's try to keep that shirt wrapped up tight, okay, buddy?" He carried the boy inside quickly, but not so fast that he might scare him even more. Teddy was starting to look a bit pale, and Nick was worried about blood loss and other horrific things that might have caused the color loss in his nephew's face. A mind could drift to crazy places in times of stress, especially when it came to an injured child. He'd seen plenty of accidents in his time working in construction, but nothing compared to his own nephew being hurt.

"How can I help you?" A petite blonde welcomed them from behind the reception desk, wearing bubble gum pink scrubs that seemed to match her personality.

"I got a boo-boo," Teddy said.

"Yeah, we had a bit of an accident this morning. Little man needs to see Doc about this cut on his hand," Nick explained. "He's been so brave today, and I'm so proud of him." He hoped that Teddy would hear his words and feel encouraged.

"Go ahead and fill these out," she said as she handed a clipboard over the counter. "I'll go back and get a room ready. Just give me a minute." Nick sat down with Teddy on his lap and made his best effort to fill out the paperwork. Parents deserved a hell of a lot more credit for these things.

"Holy hotness," Katie said, walking into the exam room where her best friend Emma sat charting notes from their last patient.

"What?" The doctor asked.

"The most beautiful specimen of a man is out there with the cutest little boy." In true Katie form, she dropped her shoulders for dramatic effect. "Why are all the good ones taken?" She paused. "Come to think of it, I didn't see a wedding ring. He could be a single dad. We'd be okay with that, right?" Katie went on and on, never stopping to make sure that Emma was even listening.

"I still have no clue what you're talking about." Emma tucked her falling curls behind her ear, still laser-focused on the computer screen in front of her. She'd tossed her hair into a loose elastic that morning, running late to get to the office. Now, her natural curls did their best to break free. "Is there a patient out there?"

Katie turned to Emma with hands full of gauze, tape, and antiseptic wipes. "Aren't you listening to me? Yes, there is a patient—an adorable little boy with some sort of cut on his hand. Dad is filling out paperwork now."

"Just bring him back. If he's already a patient, we probably have all the information we need." Emma loved her best friend but hated the way an attractive male could grab her attention so quickly and completely. "No need to make a kid wait."

Katie had always been boy-crazy, and Emma never understood why. Surely, a girl should have outgrown that phase by thirty—not that Emma ever had a boy-crazy phase of her own to outgrow...not one that she could remember, anyway. As the only child of a doctor and a lawyer, she spent most of her time studying and squeezing in some quality time with her parents when their schedules allowed.

The girls grew up in Boston, graduated from high school together, and even went on to share a dorm room in college. When Emma moved on to medical school, Katie went out "to sow her wild oats"—although Emma never thought that Katie's oats were as sown up as they should have been. In that time, Katie managed to finish her nursing degree, which proved to be an added blessing when Emma moved to Boone Heights to take over a clinic that happened to be in need of a physician *and* a nurse.

Emma's life blew up—seemingly overnight—just a few months before, leaving her with no clue what would be left of the medical career she'd worked for her entire life. On top of the professional chaos, the grenade seemed to turn her love life into shrapnel. When a teenage delivery boy arrived on the steps of her parents' front porch with an envelope—a certified letter that required a signature—Emma never would have predicted what would come of it.

Standing in her parents' wide-open gray and white kitchen, she pulled a stack of papers from the manilla envelope. On top was a handwritten note that looked like a chicken scratch at best, signed by one Milton Oliver—a name that she had never heard before—that simply asked her to read through the enclosed documents with an open mind. So, she did.

Milton Oliver turned out to be a doctor in Boone Heights, Maryland, and—according to him—Emma's long-lost uncle. She never knew the man even existed, and all of a sudden, he was writing to ask that she come to Boone Heights to run the "family clinic" while he tended to some personal matters—none of which were explained in the paperwork, of course.

After consulting with an attorney who decided that the contract seemed above board, she called and spoke with someone at the Boone Heights Family Clinic who lightly mentioned that they were also in need of a nurse. Desperate for a change of scenery, Emma signed on the dotted line agreeing to become the doctor of record at the clinic. Her first task would be to convince her best friend, Katie Zeigler, to make the move with her to fill the vacant nurse position.

Emma snapped back into the present as Katie walked into the exam room, followed by a frantic-looking man who carried an adorable little boy.

"It's okay, Uncle Nicky. I'll be alright." The word *uncle* forced Katie's eyebrows into an excited arch, which Emma seemed to feel too.

Uncle Nicky was distractingly handsome and—as Katie mentioned—was not wearing a wedding band. Emma usually didn't find his type of ruggedness to be so swoon-worthy, but his dark brown wavy hair seemed a little longer than he might have intended for it to be, the scruff on his face made it seem like he'd just crawled out of bed, and his brown eyes reminded her of her favorite dark chocolate filled with caramel. The tight jeans and flannel shirt—while usually not her thing—completed the package.

"Um, hello there," Emma said. Her parents hated when she began sentences with 'um' and had forced her to break the habit years before. Apparently, a little scruff on a handsome man caused her brain to malfunction.

"Good morning. I'm Doctor Cunningham. What happened, buddy?" There it was—the professionalism she prided herself on.

"Hi, Dr. Cunningham. I'm Teddy, and this is my Uncle Nicky. I had an accident at his work. I know I shouldn't have picked up the big shovel without asking, but I wanted...well, I just wanted to help." Emma looked at Katie with a smile, knowing she was just as captivated.

The tall, dark, and handsome man—*oh, what a cliche she was*—spoke up. "Yes, hey. I'm Nick Ewing, and this is my nephew, Teddy. He's hanging out with me for the day while his dad is out of town. We were going to stay at the office, but something came up, and I had to take him over to one of our construction sites—which I know wasn't the best idea. He found an old shovel and somehow cut his hand. I don't know why we don't have a first aid kit in the office—but don't worry, I'm going to fix that as soon as we leave here. I found a shirt in my gym bag to wrap around it to try and stop the bleeding. It's a clean shirt, I promise. It was just bleeding so much, and I didn't know what else to do. So, I just wrapped it up and got him here as fast as I could." He finally took a breath. "Wait," he said as if a lightbulb went off in his head. "Where is Dr. Oliver?"

Holy shit. When did I become such a rambler? And who is this woman? Where is Doctor Oliver? Why is my brain not working?

Dr. Cunningham didn't seem phased by his rambling. While she listened, she unwrapped Teddy's hand to take a look. A tear dropped from Teddy's eye when he saw the blood, and Nick's heart sank. How was he ever going to make this up to Teddy?

"Alright, kiddo. It looks like the cut isn't very long, but it is pretty deep. After we clean it up, I think you'll need a couple of stitches." Dr. Cunningham stood and turned to Nick. "Has he had a tetanus shot?"

"I don't know. I mean, I assume so. My brother is really on top of things. He's like a super-dad...but I don't know that stuff. Maybe I should just call him and ask." Nick reached into his pocket for his phone.

"No need for that," Katie waved. "I can go and check his records. I'm assuming Dr. Oliver has seen him before?"

"Yes. Doc has taken care of our family for as long as I can remember. Where is he, by the way?"

"I'm here for a few months while he takes care of some personal business," Dr. Cunningham answered before turning to her nurse. "Katie, go ahead and check his vaccination records while I get ready for sutures. Uncle Nicky, would you like to hold Teddy's other hand? Unless, of course, blood makes you feel faint or something."

"I'll be fine," he said rather abruptly. He wasn't about to let the doctor think he was afraid of a little blood.

"Is this going to hurt?" The fear in Teddy's voice pulled at Nick's heart.

"Well, kiddo, I won't lie to you...it doesn't feel *good*. I'll give you some medicine to hopefully make it hurt less, but I can't promise you that it won't hurt at all. I always like to tell my friends the truth—and we're friends now, right Teddy?" Dr. Cunningham had the most soothing voice Nick had ever heard. He wasn't sure where this woman came from, but she was stirring something up in him that he hadn't felt in quite some time: feelings that certainly shouldn't have been stirred up while his nephew was hurt.

"And, you know what? Since we're friends, how about you call me Emma." Teddy nodded again, and Nick found his head bobbing along as well, wanting to be friends with Emma Cunningham in a big, *big* way.

"I'm going to need you to be super brave for me, and we'll get this over with as fast as possible, okay?"

Katie returned with a large tablet in her hand. "It looks like the youngest Mr. Ewing is up to date with that tetanus shot."

"That's good news," Emma smiled while she managed her tools. On a tray, she handled a syringe with a needle that made Nick shutter. She laid out the gauze, tape, and antiseptic wipes that Katie had prepared earlier and approached Teddy with a kindness in her eyes that would help anyone feel calm. She laid his arm out and set his hand down on the rolling tray she'd pulled from the corner of the room, and draped a new cloth over it.

"This part might sting a little, Teddy," she said as she opened a package of antiseptic wipes.

"That's okay, I'm really brave," Teddy said.

"Of course you are," Emma said. "I just wanted to give you a warning. And remember, even when you're brave, you can cry, or tell me that it hurts—okay? You don't have to keep anything hidden to be brave." Emma always hated the idea that by crying or letting on that something hurt, a child would be viewed as any less brave. She wanted to teach every child out there that bravery wasn't the absence of emotion but facing something through that emotion. Emma knew all about bravery.

When she started to clean the cut, Teddy gasped at the sting of the antiseptic. As a family physician, Emma loved being able to treat and help patients of all ages. While she knew that what she was doing was exactly what Teddy needed, it was still hard to help someone heal in a way that was painful for the patient—especially a little kid.

She pulled a liquid into the syringe. "Okay, Teddy. Now, this is going to pinch, but after that, you won't feel anything, and I'll be able to stitch up your cut without it hurting."

Teddy's eyes widened at the sight of the needle, and the grip on his uncle's hand turned his little knuckles stark white. Nick rubbed his nephew's back in slow, calming circles.

Hearing Teddy wince at the needle prick felt like salt in Nick's wounded heart, but Emma quickly finished with the numbing injection and worked on stitching up his cut. When she wrapped the gauze around his tiny hand, Nick finally began to relax.

Family was everything to the Ewings. Ross and Nell still expected their five grown children to return to the Blue House every Sunday night for a family dinner—and there was an active group text with constant participation to remind them of such things. Even their father—who hated the idea of cell phones in general—was in on the group messages, although he only did so to please his wife.

Nick was actively avoiding the group text message for now. He would need to tell them what happened eventually, but he was still beating himself up over the whole situation. He wasn't ready for the wrath he would get from his younger brother Tyler or for the way his older sister Natalie would come to his defense. He didn't deserve her defense. Besides, the first person he needed to talk to would be Nathan, and that wouldn't be through a family-wide text. Teddy's father at least deserved a phone call to hear that his child needed stitches.

"Excuse me, Mr. Ewing," Emma interrupted his thoughts. "Mr. Ewing? Teddy is all ready to go. Katie is going to print out some instructions for you on how to take care of the wound, but for the most part, you just need to keep it clean and dry. If it's easier, you can just have your brother give me a call. He'll need to bring Teddy back in ten days so we can take those stitches out."

"Okay. Thank you," Nick said.

Katie returned and handed the paperwork to Nick. "I'm sure Dr. Cunningham already explained, but you'll need to change the dressing every other day—so I put some supplies in this bag for you. Otherwise, just keep his hand clean and dry. Of course, if you need any help, just give us a call." She topped off her flirty smile with a wink.

Katie was attractive, no doubt about it, but Nick wasn't interested—not in her, at least. He was more interested in Emma.

"Thanks," Nick said, taking the brown paper bag from the nurse. "Alright, Teddy, time to go. I need to call your dad and then Grams and Pops. We can go wait for your dad at the Blue House." Teddy hopped down from the table, putting a bit too much pressure on his bandaged hand.

"Ouch," he cried. Tears welled up in his eyes, and Dr. Cunningham sprang back into action.

"Alright, buddy," she said as she lifted Teddy back onto the exam table. "Let's ice that hand. You might want to rest it for a while, okay? Maybe you can ask for help with things—like getting down from an exam table." She wiped the tear that fell down his cheek and rested a hand on his shoulder. "Let's go find that ice pack."

Katie stayed behind to clean the room for the next patient while Emma took the boys to search for an ice pack. With an extra dose of her kid-friendly personality, she had Teddy join in.

"We've got to crush this up to get it cold. Do you think you can help me out with your good hand?" Teddy was eager to help, and Emma loved seeing the joy he got from crushing and shaking the ice pack, noticing as it went from room temperature to ice cold as he worked.

"This feels so much better. Thank you, Emma." Teddy leaned into her for a hug, and her heart nearly burst. "You know, I like Dr. Oliver, but I think I like you better. Plus, you're way prettier. Isn't she, Uncle Nicky?"

Emma held her breath until he answered, wanting to know if Mr. Tall Dark and Handsome agreed. She mentally chastised herself for thinking that his opinion mattered but perked up when she heard his reply.

"Yes, Teddy," Nick said. "She's very pretty. I mean, prettier than Dr. Oli-yes, she is pretty."

"Well, thank you," she said with a smile. "I think you're both very handsome as well." Nick smiled back, sending butterflies through her stomach and a rose blush to her cheeks. "Ah...alright, you two. It seems that you have some calls to make and a...blue house to visit?"

"That's Gram and Pops' house," said Teddy. "It's bright blue. Pops says he hates that color, but Gram loved it, so that's the color it is. My dad says it's because Gram and Pops have a *forever love*."

"That does sound like true love," Emma agreed, turning to Nick. "Don't forget to have your brother call me for that follow-up appointment." She pulled a notepad from her pocket and a pen from a nearby table. "Here's my cell phone number, so you can reach me anytime. I know Teddy scared you today, but you did the right thing—bringing him here. He'll be perfectly fine. Don't let Gram and Pops spoil him too much tonight."

"Thanks," Nick said, reaching for the paper and sliding it into his pocket. "And I...uh, I really appreciate your help. I guess we'll be seeing you around—at least until Dr. Oliver gets back."

"See you around." She waved and smiled as Nick reached to open the door.

"Bye," Teddy said as they walked outside.

When the door closed, Emma let out a long breath. Meeting Nick Ewing made life in Boone Heights seem a bit more interesting. It was too bad that he couldn't possibly fall into her list of priorities. She wouldn't be here forever.

CHAPTER TWO

"The bachelor auction? You're serious?" Nick glared at his older brother while he reached for his beer.

"Hey, man. You're the one that said you'd do anything to make up for my kid needing stitches today." Nathan settled into the seat next to Nick's. "You're in no place to negotiate, and I plan on taking full advantage of it."

"Clearly," Nick muttered. "How did you get roped into a bachelor auction in the first place?" The brothers sat on the front porch of Nathan's restored Victorian farmhouse—one of the first projects they'd worked on together. That house was the one material thing Nathan would have fought for in his divorce had Stephanie cared enough to fight for anything—including her son.

Nathan laughed. "You know Mom—she just can't accept that I'm happy with the way things are. So she signed me up and told me about it afterward. She knew I wouldn't back out on a benefit for the library." He stretched his legs, resting his dirty work boots on the porch railing and his arm behind his head. "But you, my brother, have just given me the perfect out." The content mischief in his eyes would have been understood by siblings everywhere. Nick just laughed, knowing his brother was right. He had zero desire to be auctioned off, even if it was for a fundraiser, but Nathan had him dead to rights.

Nick never liked the idea of dating in Boone Heights. He hadn't dated anyone local since Kelsey Mitchell in the tenth grade. An event like this came with the risk of tongues wagging and things becoming a circus for him. Deep down, he hoped that someone like Mrs. Keller, the retired librarian, would outbid everyone for a date with him. He'd been wanting to repair her fence anyway, and if she promised to make him some of her famous sweet tea, their date would be as good as done.

"Mom isn't going to like this," Nick said. Although, everyone knew that Nell Ewing would be satisfied with any one of her sons settling down.

"Why not? Getting you married off would give her just as much—if not more—joy than me settling down...*again*."

"Just send me the details—and you get to tell Mom. I refuse to have her fawning over me because of this." They sat in companionable silence for a few minutes, drinking beers as brothers do.

Nick's mind returned to Dr. Cunningham—to Emma. He was shocked to see her in place of Dr. Oliver at the clinic and hoped he'd played it off well. He couldn't remember the last time a woman made him feel that way. Hell, he didn't know if a woman had *ever* made him feel that way in the entirety of his thirty-two years—not even Kelsey Mitchell in the midst of the hell that is puberty, and that girl made him feel all sorts of things.

It might have been her thick dirty-blonde curls, her smoky gray eyes, or the way she looked at Teddy with so much concern, but something drew Nick in. She even tried to get him to forgive himself for letting the boy get hurt on his watch. Since then, he couldn't stop thinking about her. When he asked about Dr. Oliver, Emma seemed to keep a bit of detail to herself. As far as he knew, Doc didn't have any children or even a wife. So there was no way to tell how long Emma would be there—not that it mattered.

Clearly, it had been far too long since Nick had been with a woman. Given the way she made him feel and the reactions his body had to just being around her, he could have been convinced that he'd been a one-man band for decades. But it was more than just the way he felt. The piece of paper with her phone number on it was burning a hole in his pocket. It was intended for his brother, and he knew that Nate would want to talk to Emma about the accident; yet, he hadn't given it to him just yet. Nick wasn't ready to part with her phone number, and a part of him thought Nate might reach out about an appointment and end up finding some kind of connection with Emma. He'd never withheld anything from his siblings before, and that alone was enough to show him that something about her was different.

Nick cleared his throat and tried to shake it off, reaching for the paper in his back pocket. "Dr. Cunningham gave me her phone number in case you wanted to speak to her directly. I told you Doc wasn't there, right? Apparently, he's taking some time off."

Rather than reach for the paper, he shook his head and took another long pull from his beer. "First of all, you told me about Doc twice already. And second of all, I spoke with Dr. Cunningham when I called the office to make Teddy's follow-up appointment, which is in ten days..." Nathan paused and stared his brother down. "...if you'd like to come with us."

Nick put the paper back into his pocket and polished off the rest of his beer. "What are you getting at?"

"I think you ought to hold onto that phone number for yourself."

"What?" Nick shot off, flustered. "It's not like I need to talk to her about Teddy." He tried to make his argument and keep his cool.

"Maybe you could ask her if she has any plans on Friday night," Nate suggested.

"Why would I care about that?"

"Because you'd probably like for her plans to include you."

"Are you being serious right now?" Nick wasn't one to get defensive, and he knew that Nathan would pick up on his frustration sooner than later. "Why would I want her plans to include me?"

Nick grew more and more frustrated at his brother being such a pestering ass. Nathan laughed so hard his chest shook, and he had to sit up to gather himself.

"What in the hell is so funny?" Nick's tone was a bit harsh. Then again, he *was* curious about Emma's plans.

"You are just so easy to read right now." Nathan adjusted the hat on his head and leaned back in his chair. "Tell you what. I'll tell Mom about the bachelor auction—not because I want to save you from her wrath, but because I'm a decent brother. If I were you, I wouldn't even *think* about that doctor in front of Mom. You'll be interrogated on the spot. She must be something, though. I'm not sure when I last saw you in such a fit over a lady."

Nick realized his protest was useless. Nathan was the oldest and had always taken it upon himself to be involved in his siblings' lives. As the middle child, Nick had mastered the art of blending in, but Nathan always managed to know everything that was going on.

"I don't know, man. She was good with Teddy—a little closed off, but good. And she's beautiful. Like...effortlessly beautiful." Nick ran a hand through this hair. "Fuck. Forget I just said all of that." Nathan laughed, and Nick reached over to punch his shoulder.

"Why don't you hold on to that number for a few more days," Nathan suggested. "You know...just in case."

He always appreciated his brother's advice and knew that he was right. He decided to let it sit for a bit, have a few more beers, and go home. He needed to spend some time that night on his grand plan to ensure that Mrs. Keller kept him from being bought by any of the other ladies at the auction.

CHAPTER THREE

Katie sat cross-legged on the couch in Emma's rented cottage, sipping on a glass of the ruby-red merlot they were trying that night. She watched her best friend closely as she walked back into the kitchen for the charcuterie board she'd made for their Girl's Night In—a fancy name for their usual Wednesday night.

"If you stare at me any harder, you're going to pop a blood vessel in your eye, Katie. What is it?" She set the food between them on the marble end table she grabbed at an estate sale in college.

She knew exactly what was on Katie's mind. Emma was still reeling from her reaction to Nick Ewing, and her best friend could certainly tell. She'd managed to remain completely professional while she treated the boy in the office, and she was fairly confident that he hadn't found anything about her behavior to be odd. But Katie—her longest and closest friend—had undoubtedly picked up on the way Emma felt around him. If history had taught her one thing, it was that lying to Katie would get her nowhere. Still, she didn't know where to start or what to say.

"You know exactly why I'm staring, and I don't need to ask anything. I know you'll talk eventually." Her cheerful confidence was aggravating. Emma hated when Katie was right. She needed to talk this through before it consumed what was left of her mental energy. They picked at the brie and crackers and sipped their wine.

Emma cleared her throat. "I honestly don't know what to say. I was flustered today. That man had me all out of sorts."

Katie sat silently, waiting for more. *She is infuriating*. Katie was the person who had always encouraged Emma to let down her hair a little as a counterbalance to her rather uptight and conservative parents. When everything exploded with Kyle less than six months before, Katie was there for her every step of the way. But damn, the way she could read her was irritating at times, mainly when Emma was trying to avoid answering the questions Katie was asking, or, in this case, not asking.

"It's been a while...if you know what I mean. And he is certainly handsome." Emma shrugged her shoulders in an effort to be nonchalant about the whole thing, all the while knowing this answer wouldn't satisfy her best friend or herself. She struggled with the fact that Nick made her stumble in her otherwise rigid tracks. After barely surviving Kyle's mess, she'd vowed to think rationally when it came to men. She would never let herself foolishly trust or follow someone ever again.

Kyle Walker came into her life during her first year of medical school. He was a few years older and was beginning his residency. At first, she had looked up to him like a mentor or even a big brother, but it wasn't long before those feelings turned into more—mostly due to his constant presence in her life and the way he looked at her with those dirt brown eyes. *Nick's eyes were more like milk chocolate.* Emma certainly hadn't wanted to get involved with anyone during her first year of medical school, but Kyle made it so easy. He understood the demands of a medical student; he had them himself. Over the next two years, Kyle became someone she leaned on and trusted, a welcome source of calm from the crazy.

After four years of medical school and a residency in Boston, Emma followed Kyle's guidance and matched in family medicine. As soon as her residency was over, she joined his practice. *How was that less than a year ago? Why had so much happened in such a short time?*

The chaos she'd survived could explain her reaction to Nick Ewing. Then again, she knew—somewhere deep down—that wasn't the reason she had felt so drawn to that specific man just moments after meeting him. Maybe it was time to try and talk it out with Katie after all, even if she didn't know where to start. Blowing out a defeated sigh, Emma picked up her wine, took a large gulp, set the glass back down, and looked at Katie.

"Okay, I have no clue what happened today." She stopped to inhale and center herself. "I've never reacted to a man like that before—not even Kyle. It was so confusing and it really threw me off. God, I hope he didn't notice." Once she started, she couldn't stop her rambling. "Not that I would have let it impact my work. I mean, how cute was Teddy, right?" Emma threw that last bit in hoping that Katie would take the bait and move on to talking about the kid instead of the man, but it didn't work.

"Well, that was easier than I thought." Katie reached for a green olive on the tray Emma had set up and popped it into her mouth with an entertained smile. "It's not a bad thing, Emma. He was insanely attractive. I'd be more worried about you if you weren't affected by him, but let's be honest—this is *you* we're talking about." Katie grabbed another olive. "And nice try. You can't distract me by talking about the boy."

Nick was so overwhelmed with taking care of his nephew. The way he paid so much attention to someone other than himself was easy to notice and hard to forget. For as good of a doctor as Kyle was—or pretended to be—he never could have faked that kind of genuine concern for another human being. On top of that, Nick accepted full responsibility for Teddy's accident—another trait Kyle seemed to lack. *Stop thinking about Kyle.*

Accepting her uncle's offer to move to Boone Heights was supposed to be a fresh start. Maybe Nick was part of that fresh start, like some cosmic gift of karma.

"So now what?" Emma asked.

"What do you mean?"

"Let's be honest; I've never really been in this kind of situation." Katie tried and failed to stifle her laughter.

"You mean you've never been so attracted to someone that you were desperate to know if they felt it too? Or do you mean that you have never actually had feelings for a man?"

"Both. I mean, what do I do now?" Desperation was a new feeling for Emma, too.

"Whatever you want," Katie said, brushing her off.

"How about some actual direction and guidance instead of your Yoda-like riddles?"

"Emma, do whatever you want. Pursue him. Casually run into him somewhere. Spend all day pining away and writing his name in your notebook. It's up to you." Katie polished off the last of the olives and burst out in laughter at the confusion on Emma's face as she paced around the living room, looking like she could have crawled right out of her own skin. Tears streamed down Katie's face as she tried to pull her laughter under control.

"Girl, you need to chill out—you have a crush. It's just a crush! Something people have had since forever. I understand that this is a new sensation for little Miss Focus, Drive and Prepared, but I promise you'll survive. Besides, you've got me, and I could write a book on how to crush on a hot guy."

With the reminder that her best friend had her back, Emma stopped her pacing, and her thoughts began to quiet. She collapsed into a chair and reached for her wine.

"Clearly, Nick Ewing has gotten under my skin. You know, at thirty-one years old, it's embarrassing that I feel this way. I like him. I mean...I think I like him, but I'm not even sure I'm ready to like anyone again. It's probably best not to even think about it." Emma sat up in a hurry. "Oh my gosh! What if he has a girlfriend? Or a fiancé? Did I just spend the whole day obsessing about someone who isn't even available?"

"Oh, he's single," Katie said casually. Emma could have thrown a pillow at her, sitting there so calm and unbothered by the situation. If Katie hadn't been holding a glass of red wine, Emma just might have.

"How do you know that?"

"It was pretty obvious to everyone—except, of cours,e the smartest person in the room—that he was totally into you, too." Emma glared, desperate for her friend to continue. "Also, I asked Mr. Higgins about him when I stopped by the bookstore after work."

Mr. Higgins was a retired journalist who had opened up the cutest bookstore and juice bar several years before. He never could retire the traits of a journalist, though, and he seemed to have made it his mission to know everything about everyone in Boone Heights—something Katie and Emma had learned the hard way when they stopped in during their first weekend in town.

"You what?" Emma's parents could have heard her scream all the way back in Boston. "Why would you do something like that?"

"Because it's my duty as your best friend to see to it that—while you're still working on getting over Kyle—you pursue other available bachelors and move on with your life. So, before I went on encouraging you to chase this Nick Ewing, I wanted to make sure that he was actually available and worth chasing—because that's what friends do." The satisfaction on Katie's face told Emma that another argument would not be heard.

"So, *27 Dresses* good for you?" Emma picked up the remote and pressed play on the rom-com they had watched together one hundred times before. A soft smile settled across her lips that had nothing to do with the movie and everything to do with the fact that Nick Ewing was *available*.

CHAPTER FOUR

Nick pulled into the driveway of his small, dark gray house tucked into the woods at Boone Lake, replaying the conversation he'd had with Nathan. He was annoyed that his brother managed to rope him into the bachelor auction but thankful that the payback didn't go any further. He would have done anything to make up for Teddy getting hurt on his watch, and his brother was well aware. He sat back and thought about paying Mrs. Keller a visit the next day to make sure she had enough money to bid on him—and win.

Then, his thoughts returned to Dr. Cunningham—to Emma. He couldn't figure out what to call her. They were adults, and she was a medical professional. He should refer to her as Dr. Cunningham.

Since meeting her at the clinic, she'd consumed nearly all of his thoughts. He meant it when he told his brother that the doctor was effortlessly beautiful and seemingly unaware of it. On top of that, the way she cared for Teddy was wholesome, pure, and sexy as hell. Of course, he'd kept her phone number. What man wouldn't have? It kept her within reach.

He parked his truck, turned off the ignition, and ran a frustrated hand through his hair. He couldn't get past the part where she'd kept so cool around him—not reacting to him like women usually did, all giddy and ridiculous.

Nick wasn't full of himself, but he'd never had trouble finding a woman. In fact, most women made it clear that they were interested in him rather quickly. He was used to the many subtle—and not so subtle—clues that women gave him. But Dr. Cunningham barely seemed to notice him, let alone show any signs that she was interested. The nurse on the other hand...

Still, he was attracted to her like a magnet looking for metal. Inside, he tossed his keys on the entryway table and admired the exposed beams he'd spent weeks restoring. He stopped in the kitchen for a bottle of water before letting Bo, the sweet chocolate lab Sarah had convinced him to adopt a few years before, outside. Nick waited patiently while Bo finished his business, called the dog back inside, and walked up to his bedroom with the taps of dog claws following right behind him.

At his nightstand, he triple-checked that he'd set his alarm for five the next morning to run with his younger brother. He pulled the handwritten phone number from his back pocket, set it on his nightstand, stripped down to his briefs, and brushed his teeth. He turned on the industrial-style ceiling fan over his bed and crawled between the sheets, mind racing with thoughts of her. He wasn't going to be able to shake this one. He was already in deep.

The next morning, their feet hit the pavement in a soothing rhythm as Nick and Tyler ran the trails behind the house. The physical activity barely helped to take his mind off the girl.

"I talked to Nate last night. How in the hell did he get you to take his spot in the bachelor auction? He's been hounding me about it since Mom signed him up," Tyler said between breaths.

"Man, after what happened with Teddy, I'm just glad that's all he's making me do. Besides, I have a plan."

"A plan?" Tyler laughed.

"I'm going to go and see Mrs. Keller this morning. Her fence needs some work. Sounds like a good date for her to win at the auction, doesn't it?"

"That's not a bad plan, actually. Nathan should have thought of that."

"I'll give her enough money to make sure she isn't outbid. And since the whole thing benefits the library, I doubt she'll fight me on the idea."

With just enough air left in his lungs, Ty let out an appreciative chuckle. "Damn. That's genius." Tyler had always admired his older brothers.

At thirty years old, Tyler was their mother's twin—aside from his piercing blue eyes. Nell Ewing was the family matriarch: fair-skinned with emerald-green eyes and honey-colored hair that she kept in a simple bob cut—matching her no-nonsense yet loving personality. Nick, Nate, and Sarah favored their father with heads full of dark hair, dark brown eyes, and olive skin. And Natalie, who fell between Nate and Nick in birth order, often called herself the "odd sister out," with her deep red hair and freckles. She was also the only sibling to share Nell's green eyes.

Tyler was the tallest of the brothers at nearly six-foot-four. He was also the most creative of the bunch and owned a woodworking business where he regularly worked on projects for his brothers' renovation projects and new builds. He had a sensitive side that few got to see, but the admiration in his eyes when he spoke about any of his siblings was clear.

"It's a middle child's survival mechanism," Nick said. "Outsmarting the rest of you was all I ever had to do. Some things never change. Besides, I've needed to fix that fence for a long time. This is the perfect excuse and a great way for me to avoid the single ladies desperate for a husband."

"Like I said, genius. You've got the brains, but how about the brawn? Race ya back," Tyler yelled, sprinting ahead in an unfair head start.

Kicking into high gear, Nick raced for the last half-mile, knowing full well that his brother would beat him but appreciating the sudden endorphin high nonetheless.

A smooth aroma of coffee, vanilla, and maple syrup welcomed the girls like old friends as they walked through the front door of The Roasted Bean.

"Who knew we'd become so dependent on this place," Katie said before taking a deep breath.

"Me," Emma laughed. "It's the only coffee shop in town. I knew we'd be regulars here." They both loved their coffee as much as they loved their wine—cliché but true. A maple latte from Luke was a morning dose of pure magic. As if on queue, Luke Brewer set two large iced maple lattes on the counter—one with whipped cream for Katie—and flashed a quick smile.

"Morning, ladies. Here are your lattes, and I've got a bag of that dark roast for the clinic."

Falling right into his flirting, Katie flipped on the charm and batted her eyelashes. "You're a doll, Luke. A total doll." Emma left her friend to flirt and went to the register to pay.

An older lady in line ahead of her turned to Emma. "Did Luke say that coffee was for the clinic? Are you the new doctor I've heard about?"

"That's me," Emma reached to shake the woman's hand. "Emma Cunningham. I came in from Boston a few weeks ago. It seems Dr. Oliver didn't let anyone in town know that he'd be gone."

"That doesn't surprise me," the woman laughed. "Milton is a wonderful physician but doesn't know the first thing about social norms."

Emma added that bit of information to the short list of what she knew about her supposed uncle. "Well, that explains why everyone seems so shocked to see me." The look of an idea crossed the woman's face and then quickly disappeared.

"You know, I might have a way for you to introduce yourself to the town rather quickly."

"Do tell," Emma smiled. The woman seemed to be a bit of a small town busybody. Katie joined the duo just in time to hear the answer.

"Why don't you come to the fundraiser this weekend? It's for the library. Most of the town criers will be there. It's the perfect place to meet people and the quickest way to spread the news. Although if I had to guess, I'd say most of the town knows you're here, they just want a chance to come and meet you without being too obvious about it.

"Our first town event," Katie smiled. "We have to go!"

The woman laughed. "Looks like your friend will be there. Can we count on seeing our new physician as well?"

"Temporary physician," Emma corrected before turning back to Katie. "And why do we have to? There's nothing wrong with a quiet night in."

"Come on, Emma. It could be fun. Let's embrace the small town life." Katie was practically vibrating with excitement. Saying no to that would feel like walking away from an abandoned puppy.

"It seems I'm outnumbered." Turning to their new friend she asked, "So how do we get tickets?"

"Just call the library, or stop by and ask for Norma. You can let her know that Nell sent you." She started to leave but turned over her shoulder to add, "Pleasure to meet you Dr. Cunningham. I look forward to seeing you at the fundraiser." Nell stepped out of the cafe quickly, seemingly afraid to give Emma enough time to change her mind.

"Oh, I'm so excited! This is going to be so much fun. Our first Boone Heights event...I can't wait. Just leave the tickets to me. I wonder if there is a theme. Maybe it's a formal event—wouldn't that be fun?"

Walking back out to the car, Emma began to regret driving Katie to work that morning. Katie went on and on about the fundraiser as Emma glanced at her watch—only seven forty-five. It was going to be a long day.

Nick followed Crabapple Lane all the way to Mrs. Keller's house, resolved in his plan to make it through the auction without a real date. Ten years ago, a room full of single women bidding on him would have been exciting, but it didn't hold the same appeal these days. Settling down sounded better and better as he neared thirty-five. A few months back, he'd ended things with Sally—a restaurant marketing executive in Baltimore—and he'd made no attempt since then to get otherwise entangled.

He'd never been into one-night stands or hooking up, but typically after ending a relationship—a term he used loosely—he would move on to something else just as casual a few months later.

A bachelor auction was no place to find a *Forever Love*—a term his father used to describe his marriage to his mother. Each of the Ewing siblings had been taught by example that a forever love was the most magical relationship of them all. In fact, during a drunken night with his brother, Nathan had confessed to marrying Stephanie even though he knew that she wouldn't be *his* forever love.

The women of Boone Heights were each wonderful in their own ways. Nick had known them all for years but never found one worth breaking his *no dating in my hometown* rule. No one even came close.

Nick parked at Mrs. Keller's modest two-bedroom home, happy to find her outside tending to her flower garden. Having the fence in question in sight during their conversation would make it easier to get her to agree to his plan.

He tucked his navy blue Ewing Brothers Construction polo into his jeans, straightened his belt, and fixed his hair. He saved the pomade for special occasions, and this morning he'd used enough to hold his style in place. He reached for the muffins he'd picked up from Luke's place. They were her favorite.

Edna Keller looked up from the flowers as Nick closed his door. "Nicky Ewing! To what do I owe the pleasure?" She stood from her gardening knee pad with more grace than most seventy-four-year-olds would have, brushed the dirt from her gloves, pulled them off, and tucked them into her apron. Nick couldn't help but smile. This woman was pure sunshine and light. She had managed to foster a love of reading in every person in town in her years as the head librarian and still had a way of making you feel better just by saying your name.

"Good morning, Mrs. Keller. You look lovely as always." Nick walked up from the sidewalk and gave her a small kiss on the cheek. The Kellers never had children of their own but always had a yard full of little ones...and bigger ones. They were almost like pseudo-grandparents for the entire town.

"I brought your favorite: blueberry crumble." He raised the bag and the scent of blueberries, vanilla and sugar rose with the steam. "Luke pulled these out of the oven just as I was getting my coffee. I had to resist the urge to eat one the whole way over here."

"You're a doll, Nicky," she said as she peeked into the bag. "Let's go share one on the porch, okay? I'll refill that coffee for you, too. I could use another cup, myself." Edna spoke to Nick with the same tone she used when he was nine years old. Her smile brightened as

Nick handed her the treats before they settled into the white rocking chairs on her front porch.

"You're a growing boy, sweetie. You should have eaten one." *The perpetual nurturer.* Convincing her to let Nick fix the fence would be tough. This was the same woman who still cut her own grass. Of course, she used a riding lawn mower, but she did it on her own. She was never one to ask for help, and rarely accepted when it was offered.

Nick laughed and spread out two napkins while Mrs. Keller dove into the muffins, and refilled his to-go cup from Luke's.

"So what brings you by today, Nicky? And tell me the truth. While I'm grateful for my favorite treat, I know you didn't come out here just to share a muffin with me."

"Can't get anything past you," he smiled and shook his head in defeat. "I do love getting to share a muffin with you, but I was also hoping to talk to you about that fence." Edna raised her eyebrows, ready for more. "That, and I was going to ask a favor of you."

"A man with a plan," she said before taking a bite of her muffin. "These are so good. You knew I couldn't say no to you if you came armed with muffins. You've always been the Ewing with the most brains."

Nick couldn't contain his laughter. He loved any excuse to spend a little time with Edna and truthfully, it had been way too long since he last had a chance. The need to fix her fence was merely a well-timed opportunity.

"Yes, ma'am. Let's get down to business then." Nick cleared his throat. "It's time to fix that fence." Edna waved him off, ready to argue. "No, no. Now, listen. I drive past this house a few times a week. I know just how much work you put into that garden of yours. Why don't you let me take care of the fence?" Knowing he hadn't won yet, he added, "Of course, then, I could really use some help of yours, too." She looked up to him with a grin. "I was thinking that you could bid on me at the auction. I'll even grab us lunch from the deli. It will be a proper date—with a meal." He flashed her the smile he'd been told would melt the panties off of a nun and crossed his fingers that she would accept. But Edna had no intentions of letting him off the hook so easily. She took a slow sip of her coffee, thinking long and hard—just to make him worry.

"Nicky, that's quite an offer, but I'm not sure an old widow stands a chance against all the pretty young ladies in town. Besides, you're single. And you're quite a catch. Why don't you go find yourself a young lady to spend some time with?"

A deep blush crept over his face. He'd never admit it, but he agreed. He was a catch—though, having a seventy-something-year-old retired librarian remind him of it was less than comforting.

"That's very kind of you to say, but that's also...part of my point. I don't really want to be won by any of the single women in town. It wouldn't be fair to them anyway; it's not like an auction date would lead to anything else. And, I know you've got many good years left in you, but I thought my offer to fix that fence might be enough to keep you away from the other eligible bachelors in town." He threw in a wink to seal the deal, using the last bit of charm he'd tucked away for her. "Of course, I'll cover the cost of the bid too—you can take that bid as high as you want. It's the least I can do. You know better than anyone how much time I spent hiding in that library." He wasn't above begging but hoped he'd made his case.

"You always enjoyed the peace and quiet."

"You don't get much of that in a house with five kids."

"Oh sweetie, you had me at *favor*. Of course I'll bid on you. Your mother is not going to be happy about this, though. Nathan already escaped her master plan, and now you're avoiding her matchmaking, too. This certainly is not what your mother imagined when she pitched this fundraiser idea to the board."

"She did what?"

"Oh, I think I just spoke out of turn," Mrs. Keller said, taking another bite of muffin to avoid having to answer.

"Our secret," Nick said, pretending to zip his lips closed and toss the key. "But you'll do it, right? You'll make sure I don't get stuck with any of those girls, and I'll build you a new fence. Right?"

"With lunch—don't forget lunch from the deli. You promised," she replied. With that, all of Nick's concern melted away.

"Lunch. Of course—anything you want. The most expensive meal they serve is yours. You are a peach, Edna. Never let anyone tell you otherwise."

"I never do, my boy. I never do." They laughed and finished their coffee and muffins in silence on the porch. For a few minutes, it felt like nine-year-old Nicky and Mrs. Keller were young again, just listening to the sounds of the birds nearby, and the leaves blowing in the wind.

"I guess I should be going," Nick said a few minutes later.

"Of course, dear. Oh, but tell me. How exactly did Nathan get you to take his place in the auction? What did you do to owe *him* such a favor?"

Nick hung his head and exhaled with guilt. "I messed up with Teddy. I had him with me at a job site and he cut his hand. It was pretty bad. He needed stitches and everything." Without thinking, he continued, admitting way more than he intended to. "I took him to see Dr. Oliver at the clinic. Did you know he has someone filling in for him for a while? Emma—I mean Dr. Cunningham. I was surprised to see her. Although, her blonde curls were a quick giveaway." He felt the blush come back to his cheeks. "She was so good with Teddy, though. She seems like a...a very capable doctor—for stitches." He stuttered over his words and cleared his throat. "I mean...for Teddy—who is okay, by the way."

He stopped rambling to take a deep breath. What was it about Emma Cunningham that made him feel like a preteen boy on the verge of puberty who'd never even held hands with a girl before? A woman never had that effect on him, and it was driving him crazy.

Well," Mrs. Keller laughed. "That's quite a story. I'm glad Teddy is okay." She reached for Nick's hand and stood from her seat. "You know, I may have heard something about a new doctor in town. I didn't know her name—or that she had blonde curls." She waved her eyebrows, and a grin crossed her lips at the chance to poke fun at him.

"Well, now you do." He laughed. "I've got to get to work, but I'll come over to measure the fence for materials. And remember: you bid as high as you want. Outbid them all. If you need more than this, you let me know." Nick pulled an envelope full of cash from his pocket and turned back toward his truck. He could feel Edna Keller's eyes on him, but he didn't dare to turn back. She was a smart woman and likely wouldn't forget how much the new doctor in town had gotten to him. He left, hoping a day at work would help him get his thoughts off of Emma and back in order.

Emma closed her laptop after charting her last patient of the day—a two-year-old whose mother suspected an ear infection. It turned out to be molars.

"Hey, Em?" Katie knocked as she walked in. "We've got a walk-in if you have time. Older lady...fell in her garden and feels a little dizzy."

"Of course I have time. It is a little warm out today. Let's make sure she isn't overheated. Room two?"

"I'll grab her chart and get her settled."

It was almost as if her uncle—who she still struggled to think of as an *uncle*—knew she'd be coming and converted all of their charting to an electronic system before she arrived. It was a system that she and Katie were familiar with, which made the transition a little easier.

Right on cue, a new appointment popped up on her schedule. Emma clicked to open the chart and read about a seventy-four-year-old in nearly perfect health. She grabbed a cold bottle of water from her mini fridge and made her way to room two, hoping all the woman needed was a chance to cool down.

Emma knocked and stepped into the room.

"Good afternoon, Mrs. Keller. I'm Dr. Cunningham. I hear you feel a little faint after some yard work today. How are you feeling now?"

"Hello, Dr. Cunningham. You know, I'm feeling a bit better after sitting here in the cool air."

"Can you tell me what happened?" Emma reached for her stethoscope to take a quick listen to her heart and lungs.

"Well, I was pruning my begonias—they are just lovely this spring already—and I was feeling a bit warm, but then I guess I felt a bit woozy. So I called my neighbor and asked her to drive me over, and here I am."

"Alright. Well, I'd like to do a basic exam, just to check your vitals. Is that okay with you?"

"Whatever you think is best, dear." Mrs. Keller settled onto the exam table as Emma listened to her heart, checked her blood pressure and pulse, and took a quick read of her temperature. Just like the chart had indicated, Mrs. Edna Keller was in perfect health for a woman of her age, and even for one much younger.

"Mrs. Keller, I think you might have just gotten a bit overheated—possibly a little dehydrated. I'm happy to order additional tests if you'd like, but I think you might just need some water and some rest."

"Oh, no dear, that won't be needed." She took a sip from the water Emma offered. "I'm sure you're right. It was probably just the heat. This water will do the trick. I'm glad I got the chance to meet you, though."

"I'm glad I had the chance to meet you as well, Mrs. Keller. Although I'd have liked to meet you under better circumstances, of course." Everyone in town seemed to want the details. So she offered them without needing to be asked. "I'm here to fill in for Doctor Oliver for a little while. He's just got some personal business to handle. Everyone's been shocked to see me. I suppose that will stop pretty soon, though."

"Oh? Why is that?" Edna's ears perked up, putting a smile on Emma's face. Old ladies always knew what was going on in town.

"Well, I've been invited to a fundraiser. I'm told I'll meet just about everyone while I'm there."

"Oh, so you'll be at the auction?" Mrs. Keller seemed as excited as a child who learned they wouldn't need a shot.

"An auction? I didn't realize that was part of the fundraiser."

"Oh, of course. There's always an auction of some sort here in Boone Heights." Emma barely caught the change of subject. "Did you know I used to be the head librarian? This fundraiser has such a special place in my heart. I'm so glad you'll be there. You'll have to bid on something. Maybe I can pick that something out for you."

Emma had a funny feeling about Mrs. Keller's intentions but didn't dare to contest her. "Of course. I'd love to bid on something. And, while we've just met, I trust your judgment. Go ahead and pick something out for me. But then I want you to sit back and take it easy. Drink plenty of water today, okay?" If Edna managed to choose something outlandish and expensive, maybe it would earn Emma a bit of favor with the town. She had enough money in savings to handle just about anything the scheming patient might throw her way. She helped Mrs. Keller off the exam table—not that she needed the help. She moved with the agility of someone half her age. Mrs. Keller gave Emma a hug and then reached to pat her cheeks as a grandmother would have.

"Well, I look forward to seeing you at the fundraiser, Dr. Cunningham. It will be a wonderful evening, one to remember, I'm sure." Emma watched her patient leave and replayed the conversation in her mind. She couldn't help but second guess what she might have gotten herself into.

CHAPTER FIVE

"I'm still curious to know why you're so excited for a small town fundraiser," Emma said as Katie stood in her closet in a bra and underwear, tossing dresses left and right. The event was in a few hours, and Katie had practically begged Emma to get ready together the way they used to for events in school. Emma agreed begrudgingly, wishing instead that she was curled up on her back deck in the chaise lounge she'd grown to love, reading the new romance novel she'd picked up at *A Novel Idea* on Main Street in town. She was halfway through *The Estate* and was desperate to see how a sunshine soul like Ruby Dixon would mend the heart of the Ervin Estate's new ranch hand, Hobie Logan—a retired U.S. Marine and possibly the loneliest and grumpiest man she'd ever met.

Emma wasn't usually one for romance novels but had to purchase *something* from the bookstore to hide the fact that she'd gone inside in hopes of learning more about Nick Ewing. That was the real reason she went to visit Mr. Higgins on Friday afternoon—not that he needed to know that. Hence, the book purchase. If she was really going to be honest with herself, she might have chosen that particular book because the poster on the wall displayed a character that looked a lot like someone she used to know. A pillow whacked Emma across the face and snapped her attention back to Katie.

"What was that for?"

"Because you clearly weren't listening to me or looking at my dress." Katie twirled in a one-shoulder body-hugging dress with an off-centered thigh-vent. She looked incredible, and there was no denying it. The deep emerald color was a perfect compliment to her fair skin, and the tie at the waist put her hourglass figure on full display.

"Are we trying to get to know the residents in town or the fire department? That dress is actual *fire* on you."

Katie beamed. "Flattery doesn't make up for the fact that you weren't listening to me, but it helps." Digging through the pile on her bed, Katie held up two others for Emma to choose from. The strapless black dress was an automatic no, so she grabbed the second option in hopes that it was slightly less form-fitting and slipped it on.

Emma reached up to fasten the three small buttons at the nape of her neck and stepped back to look in the mirror just as Katie peeked out of the closet. Whatever her best friend was going to say died on her lips as her eyes grew wide.

"Emma," she gasped, "you look stunning. That *has* to be what you wear tonight."

Staring into the full-length easel mirror, her own reflection shocked her a bit as she took in the rose-colored a-line dress that hit just a few inches above her knees. The delicate lace neckline and capped sleeves gave it a touch of a Victorian look, but the real allure of the dress was the back—or the lack thereof. She turned to find the scalloped edges of the lace form a deep open diamond shape that went all the way to the small of her back. It was the embodiment of classy meets sexy—provocative, yet professional.

"These. Put these on." Katie practically threw a pair of nude peep-toe heels at her that seemed to perfectly complete the outfit. Emma hadn't felt this confident in an outfit in a very long time.

"You are just...breathtaking. It's like that dress was made for you. I don't even know why I had it in my closet. Just take it home with you—I'll never be able to wear it now." Katie flung an arm to her forehead for the dramatic flair she was well known for.

"Let's just finish getting ready so we're not late," Emma smiled. "We can discuss custody of the dress after tonight."

"There's nothing left to discuss—you didn't choose that dress, Ems. The dress chose you." Katie flounced into the bathroom to finish her hair and makeup.

Boone Heights, Maryland was no New York City, but they pulled out all stops for town events—which was endearing and annoying at the same time. It was just a small town library fundraiser, but each of the bachelors donned their best formal wear—most on loan from Max Miles, a Boone Heights native turned big-time fashion editor in Manhattan. These days, Max spent most of his time funding fashion startups from his office in Los Angeles.

While he was more of a jeans-and-a-polo kind of guy, Nick pulled off the well-tailored, midnight blue suit very well. A few weeks before the auction, Max—their designer friend—had arranged a suit for Nick to wear on stage. He thought Max was joking when he first brought out the suit and vest a few weeks before, but he trusted that his friend knew top fashion, and politely accepted. He'd opted for a simple white button-up underneath the vest and managed to convince the designer to forgo the tie, instead leaving the first two buttons of the shirt undone. The gray shoes from Max's personal wardrobe were the perfect final touch, leaving Nick thankful that he and his former lacrosse teammate still wore the same size shoe.

"You look dapper." Tyler stood next to Nick backstage at the auction.

"Thanks, Ty. If you tell Nate I said this, I'll kick your ass, but I'm actually kind of excited for tonight. Knowing that all I have to do after this is fix Mrs. Keller's fence makes this a lot less stressful for me."

"You may have spoken too soon." Tyler nodded toward the petite woman heading their way with a very determined look in her eye.

"Mom!" Nick said, extending his arms out in hopes of a hug. The familiar look in her eyes told him a hug was not what she was after. He'd done something she did not approve of.

"Nicholas Francis Ewing, don't you *Mom* me. Did I hear correctly that you've already promised yourself and a new fence to Edna Keller?" Nell Ewing stood before her two youngest sons with her hands firmly on her hips.

Nick glared at Tyler, whose face reddened as he tried to suppress his laughter, and turned back to his mother with an innocent smile. "Mom, you know she needs a new fence, and this was a great chance for me to do it. Plus the library will be getting a sizable donation from me, which I'm sure is what the board had in mind when they planned this whole shindig." Nick laid the drama on thick, knowing full well that his mother planned the event with the intention of getting her son—or sons—paired off on a date. It was no secret that she thought her boys had been single for far too long. Nell would never admit to her motivation for the bachelor auction, but everyone knew why she chose it instead of the second option—an art walk.

"I'm sure your donation was generous," she replied. "and of course, I'm glad you're fixing the fence. That woman refuses to ask for help. I'm proud of you—even if you used her fence for your own benefit." Nick smiled at Tyler, highlighting what he'd gotten away with.

"Well, mom, I should probably go and figure out what the heck I'm supposed to do on stage."

"Yes, and I need to go mingle and make sure everyone's wallets are full and open. Would you like to join me Tyler? Your father is running late and I'd love an escort around the room."

"Yeah, Tyler. Go with mom. Unless you'd like to throw on a tux and join the auction block..." Tyler didn't waste a second before taking his mother's arm and using his chance to escape.

"Let's go, Mom. I could use a drink anyway." Nick watched them walk away before joining the rest of the bachelors backstage.

The ballroom of the boutique hotel was elegantly decorated. Emma and Katie looked around to soak it all in as they made their way to their assigned tables. Soft white lights hung across the ceiling and down the walls, creating a shimmering curtain. The pale-pink linens and white floral centerpieces filled the tables with soft color. It was all so much more than Emma was expecting—not that anything of the last six months had been what she would have expected.

"Wow," Katie whispered, almost under her breath. "This is beautiful. I don't know exactly what I was expecting, but it wasn't this. Maybe something a bit more...small-town."

"What exactly does small-town look like?" Emma laughed.

"I'm not sure...but not this. I kind of expected more of a...backyard barbeque type of thing. That's why I didn't understand the request for formal wear. Of course, now I do."

"I've wondered what this hotel looked like on the inside. It almost seems out of place in Boone Heights. It's just so much more exquisite than I pictured."

"Oh, look. Table three—right there by the stage." Table numbers stood out from the flower arrangements. "Let's put our things down and go find a cocktail. The tickets said there's dessert later, too." Katie clasped her hands together in excitement.

Emma looked around and noticed a bar area near the back of the room and wait staff walking around with trays full of appetizers. As she set her clutch on a seat, a familiarly attractive man approached them.

"Hello there," he said. "I was wondering who my mother had found to fill the last two seats at our table. Mystery solved!" He extended a hand to Katie first and then Emma. "I'm Nathan Ewing. My mother, Nell, is the mastermind behind this whole thing."

The pieces all fell together in Emma's mind. Nathan looked strikingly similar to the man who'd occupied her every thought for days now.

"Oh, Mr. Ewing. It's so nice to meet you in person. I'm Emma Cunningham—we spoke on the phone the other day about Teddy.

This is my friend, Katie. She's my nurse at the clinic, and she helped me patch Teddy up."

"Ah, of course! It's a pleasure to meet you both. I can't thank you enough. You've got a new fan, you know. Teddy was quite taken with you."

"He's so sweet," Katie said, "and he was very brave about the whole thing. I think his uncle was a little more shaken up by it all than he was. Isn't that right, Emma?" Katie jabbed her elbow into Emma's ribcage.

"Your brother loves your son very much. He reacted as any family member would have." Emma silently plotted ways to retaliate for the way Katie forced her into the conversation; stealing her signed and framed Jonas Brothers poster from high school was the first idea that came to mind.

"I'm sure," Nathan said, sharing a conspiratorial glance with Katie.

"We were just off to find a drink," Emma said, hoping to change the subject. "Would you like to join us? I'd be happy to answer any questions you might have about Teddy's hand."

"I was actually going to run backstage and make sure everything was set for the auction first. My father is the auctioneer and I promised I'd stop by when I got here." Emma assumed she would be bidding on baskets of local goods, or maybe a spa gift certificate or movie tickets. The way the stage was set up, paired with Nathan's comments about an auctioneer, she was starting to think there was a lot more to it.

"We won't keep you then. I hope to hear a few stories about Teddy at the table later, though." Emma smiled.

"As long as my mother doesn't jump in with stories of me when I was a kid...I think I can do that." Nathan nodded with a smile and walked off in search of his father—the *auctioneer*.

"Damn," Katie stared at Nathan as he walked away. "That family hit the genetic jackpot."

"Come on. You need a cool drink to calm yourself down and I need to meet some more people from town." The girls each ordered a glass of Pinot Grigio from the college-aged boy behind the bar and were just about to walk away when someone got their attention.

"Dr. Cunningham! Katie, I'm so glad you made it."

"Hello again," Emma said with a smile, greeting the woman from the coffee shop who had invited them.

"You both look marvelous this evening," the woman gasped, moving her hand to her heart in dramatic surprise.

"You know, I don't think I caught your name the other day and I feel horrible for not asking," Emma said.

"Well, I don't suppose I even offered it—how unwelcoming of me. You actually stitched up my grandson the other day—Teddy. I'm Nell Ewing." The rest of the puzzle pieces fell into place and Emma realized they would be spending the evening with the entire Ewing family. She wondered if Nick had mentioned her to his family. Surely he mentioned the doctor they saw, but she had no reason to assume that he'd said anything more than that. Why would he? Unless of course, he *wanted* to tell them about her. Her thoughts raced again, spiraling just like they had when she first met Nick in the office. Something about that man, and apparently his entire family, had complete control over her.

Katie jumped in as if she knew her best friend needed a save. "We just loved your grandson, Mrs. Ewing. Teddy is precious."

"He was quite proud of his stitches. Apparently, his Uncle Tyler, my youngest son, told him scars are cool. He's hoping for a big one," Nell laughed.

"And here I was hoping I'd stitched him up well enough to not leave a scar at all," Emma laughed. "I'm sure he doesn't need any help being cool." She took a sip of her wine, hoping that she'd managed to keep the conversation on medicine. "We should let you go. I'm sure you're busy with the event, Mrs. Ewing."

"Dr. Cunningham, please call me Nell."

"Only if you'll call me Emma."

"Done," Nell agreed.

"Nell, before you head off...maybe you could introduce us to some of your friends later tonight. You can help us wear off the shock everyone seems to have when they meet us."

"I would love to, but first I need to check on the bach-uh...the auction. I'll need to check on the auction items." She waved to a few people across the room. "My husband is the auctioneer, and I just need to make sure he has everything settled with the audio system. He's a loud man, but I have a feeling he will need a microphone to be heard at some point."

Emma sensed someone approaching behind her. "Have you met Mrs. Keller? I know she would love to introduce you to her friends. She's our favorite retired librarian, and knows everyone here."

"Dr. Cunningham!" Edna Keller joined the trio. "I am so happy to see you, and pleased to report that I've been feeling fit as a fiddle, thanks to you." She pulled Emma into another hug.

"You look great! I'm sure you remember my nurse, Katie, from the office."

"Hi, Mrs. Keller. I'm so glad to see you're feeling better," Edna wrapped Katie into a hug as well.

Small town medicine. Patients hug you at fundraisers. Grandmothers persuade you to buy tickets. Brothers and fathers sit with you at said fundraisers.

Emma was starting to feel that it was going to be a long few months in Boone Heights.

"Edna," Nell said, bringing Emma back to the group. "Would you be a dear and introduce Emma to some of your friends? It seems that Milton neglected to let the town know he was going to be away for a spell. I thought this would be the perfect place for Emma to introduce herself, and quickly."

"Of course," Edna agreed, "and we have a few other things to discuss, don't we dear?" Recent events had admittedly made Emma a bit more suspicious, but now she was certain something was going on—she just didn't know what it was. She tried to push her worries aside to enjoy the event while meeting their new community. Nell was right—it was a wonderful plan. Apparently, most of the people at the fundraiser owned small businesses in town and would be helpful in spreading the word about her temporary place at the clinic.

After another glass of wine and brief chatter with Katie, Mrs. Keller, and Mrs. Keller's friends—which seemed to be everyone—the lights dimmed and a gentleman who looked like an older version of Nick and Nathan Ewing stepped onto the stage.

"Welcome friends," he began. "For those who may not know me, I'm Ross Ewing. I'm your host for the evening and the ever grateful husband of the wonderful woman who coordinated this evening's festivities. We're going to start the auction in ten minutes so if you'll please make your way to your tables—and get your wallets open, ladies!"

That's when Emma's concern became overwhelming. Looking around the room, she noticed that most of the crowd was women of a certain age—her age. In fact, several of the tables around the event hall seemed to have a girls-night-out aura about them. Like a lightbulb went off—or maybe a grenade—Emma realized exactly what she'd been tricked into: Mrs. Keller was going to have carte blanche over the "local item" Emma would be placing a winning bid on.

CHAPTER SIX

The din of the crowd in front of the stage grew quiet. If he wasn't so humble or trying to avoid being eye candy at a bachelor auction, he would have outright admitted that he was going to bring in a donation that challenged the rest. Nick knew what women wanted, and he had a lot to offer.

He owned his own business and his own home. He had a dog. He wasn't half bad to look at. And he knew how to please a woman in bed. All of which were top on the list of why he feared who might bid on him in the auction—until he made his pact with Mrs. Keller.

There was a small part of him that was looking forward to the night, excited to be supporting a good cause. Plus, he scored one over on Nate with his plan. As the middle sibling, the victory was satisfying.

Nick wasn't the first bachelor to be auctioned off so he sat and finished the beer Tyler had brought him earlier to kill some time. As they had so often recently, his thoughts drifted to Emma. Her number was still sitting on the nightstand by his bed, but he'd yet to do anything about it. He wasn't one to shy away from pursuing a woman he was interested in; then again, he'd never been so interested in a woman so instantly.

He either needed to put the number to use—even if it was intended for his brother—or find a way to stop spending every waking moment thinking about her. Although he hated to admit it, he'd been driving past the clinic more over the past few days, even when it was out of his way. Nick Ewing was many things, but he didn't dare to add stalker to the list.

"Mr. Ewing, you're up next." The fair warning came from Kelly, the college freshman who spent most of her time volunteering for the library. Nick's mother had recruited Kelly to manage the bachelors backstage.

"Great, thank you. Do you have somewhere I can recycle this?" He gestured to his empty beer bottle.

"Sure, I'll take it for you," Kelly said. "Oh, and heads up—the bids are getting outrageous. Mr. Hyde just went for over five hundred dollars." Mr. Hyde had been the high school principal since Nick was a Wolverine. He got a little nervous, hoping he had given Mrs. Keller enough money.

"All the better for the library, right Kelly?" The young woman's face turned a little red at the fact that Nick seemed to know her name. It gave him a burst of bravado as he made his way to the side of the stage where he was supposed to make his entrance. "Here goes nothing," he muttered as he watched his father hush the crowd ahead of his introduction.

As he walked out onto the stage, he was instantly drawn to the woman at the front table with his family and Mrs. Keller. Every bit of breath in his lungs disappeared. Emma Cunningham was seated with the rest of his family, right next to Mrs. Keller who was set to bid on him.

Emma's butterscotch curls framed her face. They'd been clipped back when they met in the office. Her lips were stained a soft rose color that matched the lace of the dress at her neck. He watched as her slate gray eyes widened at the sight of him, paired with a surprised o-shape to her lips. Mrs. Keller inched her chair a bit closer to Emma and leaned in to whisper something that seemed to surprise Emma. He nearly melted as her eyes filled with heat.

This auction was about to take a turn for Nick. The only question that remained was if he was still going to need to build a fence.

Arriving at the fundraiser, Emma was curious to see what local items would be on the auction block. Emma recalled childhood memories of visiting auction houses with her parents in Boston and feeling enamored with the art, historical items, and even furniture her parents would often bid on. She knew the items at this auction would be different, but she hadn't realized how different until the first *item* took the stage.

As the first bachelor walked out, Mrs. Keller reminded Emma that she had to bid on *anything* she wanted. Katie was practically giddy at the idea of a bachelor auction but was significantly less surprised than Emma was—which made her wonder if Katie knew about the type of auction all along.

Emma's heart rate settled as the first two men were auctioned off—a very married Boone Heights Mayor (whose wife shut down all the other women immediately) and the slightly aged high school principal who both surpassed a five hundred dollar bid. When the applause for Ken Hyde quieted, Ross Ewing prepared to introduce the next bachelor.

"Alright ladies, our next bachelor is a special one indeed—and I say that with only slight bias, since I'm his father." Gasps and cheers and even high fives filled the room.

Emma's settled heartbeat returned to chaos, so much so that she could have presented with a heart attack. Two Ewing sons were sitting at the table with her, and by process of elimination—unless there was a fourth Ewing son—Emma suspected that she was about to watch a room full of women bid on Nick.

The very idea of it left her feeling like she'd been punched in the gut. Watching Nick Ewing walk onstage looking criminally handsome in a deep blue suit with an unbuttoned jacket that showed off his matching vest underneath was enough to make her just about die. The top buttons of his white shirt were undone and Emma started to envision opening the rest of them. The scruff that drew her in when they'd first met looked even better tonight, if that was possible.

Edna Keller leaned in to remind Emma that she was bidding on whatever—or rather, *who*ever—she wanted.

"Well dear, I think that this bachelor looks like the perfect lad for you. I know he's going to be a hot one so you just let me know if you need me to open my pocketbook. I came prepared. Nicky is sure to go for a pretty penny." Emma felt a flare of jealousy build up. She wasn't sure if she wanted to bid on Nick Ewing, but she was certain that she didn't want anyone else in the room to win him either.

"Oh, I didn't miss Nicky!" A woman collapsed into the chair next to Nathan and pulled out her phone to begin filming.

"Sarah Elizabeth Ewing," Nell whisper-yelled. "Put that phone away right now. We are here to support the library, not to build your collection of brother blackmail."

Sarah, who had the same chocolate brown eyes as her brother, stuck her tongue out at her mother and followed orders, sliding her phone back into the pocket of her long boho styled dress that seemed like it was just made for her.

"Alright ladies, what do you say we open the bidding at one hundred dollars," Ross suggested. His introduction proved to be unnecessary as a flurry of hands went up.

"One hundred dollars!" A handful of women placed starting bids at the same time.

"Get ready," Mrs. Keller advised. "These women can get wild. But this one—he's yours!" Edna looked prepared for battle, and Emma wasn't sure if she was happy—or terrified— to have Edna Keller on her side.

How had Emma even found out about this auction? From the little Nick had learned, she hadn't been in town very long. And Edna Keller had managed to snag a seat at the same table as his family...and Emma. The coincidences were starting to be less and less of a shock. The bids being hollered from all directions brought Nick back into the moment. He hadn't planned on selling himself and working for a bid, but considering who Mrs. Keller's table buddy turned out to be, he changed his mind.

"Well, that sure is a lot of starting bids," Ross Ewing answered. "Let's take it to two hundred and fifty then?"

"Two fifty!" Nick couldn't quite make out where that bid had come from.

"Do I have three hundred fifty?"

"Four hundred," Shelly Kirkland, the younger sister of one of Tyler's friends, stood in earnest.

"Five hundred!" Jenna Ory had tried valiantly for years to get Nick to take her on a date, all the while marrying and divorcing three different men.

"Five hundred fifty dollars," Shelly countered.

"Six hundred fifty dollars," Jenna shot back, standing up.

Come on Edna, we had a deal. When he looked at Mrs. Keller, he found her in a staring contest with Emma.

"Seven hundred dollars," Shelly bid again and Ross beamed at the success his son brought to the auction.

"Nine hundred dollars," Jenna yelled, shooting daggered eyes at Shelly who shrunk under the glare.

Panic built in Nick's chest. A date with Shelly wouldn't be unbearable; they could probably go to Baltimore for an Orioles game and a few beers before calling it a night. But Jenna? He had no interest in getting locked into a date with her, regardless of the good cause.

Nick's plan had seemed foolproof until now, as he watched it unravel in front of him. He knew that something had to change, and he shot a pleading glance to his brothers, both of whom seemed to be enjoying the bidding war too much to notice.

If he ended up on a date with Jenna Ory—who, by the way, dated Nathan in high school until she cheated on him with the quarterback from their rival high school—Nick would never hear the end of it. Then again, that would be one woman his mother would not pester him about marrying.

What is Mrs. Keller waiting for?

"One thousand dollars!" Jenna shouted before Shelly slumped into her chair in defeat. The friends around her table quickly dove into their purses, likely scrounging for money.

"One thousand dollars is the bid right now, ladies," Ross repeated. "Surely this handsome, strapping, man—who happens to look just like I did at his age—is worth more than that." A beat of silence played out in slow motion before his father continued.

"Alright then. Going once." He paused again, and Nick looked to Mrs. Keller in desperate frustration, only to find her in an intense conversation with Emma while waving her cash envelope toward her. "Going twice." Another pause. And then, as if in slow motion, Emma picked up the envelope and stood.

"Four thousand dollars! I bid four thousands dollars."

Mouths fell open wide as everyone gasped and stared at Emma. She was certain that her face looked nearly the same.

What just happened? She'd gone from politely arguing with a patient about bidding on the man to standing up and bidding four times the current offer.

Yes, she had promised to bid on whatever local item Edna Keller suggested, but she had no idea that the item would turn out to be a human being—the very human being she couldn't stop thinking of. Now here she was, in a room full of people, bidding four thousand dollars for Nick Ewing. Perhaps she could claim temporary insanity with just a touch of jealousy. Watching women bid on him with predatory eyes was like a tipping point for her. Now, all eyes—including the woman in the entirely too tight and too short black dress, with excessive makeup and enough hairspray to bring the eighties back—were on her.

Ross Ewing didn't miss a beat. "We've got a bid of four thousand dollars from the beautiful woman sitting with my family, who I assume I'll get to meet later—going once. Going twice. Sold!" The crowd stayed silent until Katie jumped from her seat and cheered, inciting everyone to join her.

Emma reached for her now warm glass of wine and finished it in one large gulp. She couldn't bring herself to look at Nick quite yet. Instead, she took a quick look around the table, finding smiles from everyone—especially Nell Ewing.

"That was impressive, dear. I don't think anyone has ever stopped Jenna Ory in her tracks quite so well. Impressive indeed." Mrs. Keller smiled, satisfied that her plan had worked so well.

Emma wasn't concerned about the money, and it was for a good cause, but four thousand dollars? When Edna offered two grand for her to bid on Nick, she was shocked. After the women in the crowd started a bidding war over him, Emma knew she had to do something. It was almost as if she sensed desperation from him all the way on the stage. She didn't hesitate for a single second after Edna Keller offered up that money. She just snapped and doubled it.

"Well, that was exciting, wasn't it?" Ross Ewing asked from the stage. "And to the beautiful woman who has no doubt made my son's head grow even larger with such a generous bid, just remember to stop by the front table before the end of the night to make your donation."

Emma finally turned to Katie who was now sitting silently next to her. “Don’t you say a word. Not here,” she warned as she used her hand to mimic zippering her lips shut. Katie simply smiled and then turned to the stage to watch the next eligible bachelor take the stage. It was Luke Brewer—their favorite coffee shop owner.

The crowd began to cheer again, not as loud as they had for Nick, but it seemed that Luke would still bring in a sizable donation. Katie seemed to be cheering the loudest, and Emma realized she’d missed the fact that her best friend had developed a major crush on the man who made their maple lattes.

Maybe I won’t be the only one placing a winning bid on a ‘local item’ tonight.

CHAPTER SEVEN

Walking off the stage in a fog and sweating through his tux, Nick took a cold bottle of water from Kelly. He felt as if a herd of elephants had gathered on his chest. His plan had gone entirely wrong in the most incredible way.

Edna Keller had managed to rope Emma into his plan. Nevermind the fact that both ladies seemed to have found themselves at the family table, or the fact that Emma even heard about this fundraiser in the first place.

He recalled the look of disdain on Jenna's face after the winning bid. That woman had talons longer than any bird of prey in existence. The sweet doctor could probably use a fair warning about that one, and Nick intended to deliver it.

"Way to go, Nick. That was impressive." Ken Hyde reached to shake his hand, complete with a congratulatory slap on the back. Nick choked on his water before he answered.

"Thank you, sir. You did well yourself."

"Let's not kid ourselves, young man," his former principal laughed. "You are the clear winner tonight. In more ways than one, if you know what I mean," he said with a wink. "Your date doesn't look familiar, and I know most—if not all—residents of the town."

"Ah, yeah," Nick said, "The new doctor at the clinic. She's filling in for Dr. Oliver for a bit while he deals with some personal business. Teddy and I met her earlier this week. We had a little accident at one of our job sites."

"Ah, so you do know her. I feel a bit better, then. Four thousand dollars is a lot to bid on a bachelor—even one as eligible as yourself." Nick waved off the compliment.

"It's all for a good cause. Maybe she just wanted to make a good impression with a large donation to the library."

"If that's your story, I'll stick to it."

Why had she bid so much on him? Nick wasn't sure what it meant. Emma didn't seem like the type of girl to participate in some prank with his brothers—not that he'd put a prank past any of his siblings—but what else could have caused her to bid such an astronomical amount so dramatically? She'd clearly used Mrs. Keller's cash—err, *his* cash—but why? What was Edna up to? Would he still need to build her a fence?

In all fairness, if Edna Keller was the reason he had a date with Emma Cunningham, Nick would happily build her a fence that would rival all fences from now until eternity.

A date with Emma Cunningham. The night was turning out better than Nick expected.

"I don't know about you," Katie said, "but I could certainly go for some chocolate right about now." Emma wasn't shocked that her best friend was so giddy—she'd bid on Luke and won, edging out the same woman who fought so hard for Nick. That woman looked like she wanted their entire table to explode after Katie bid eleven hundred dollars to win Luke Brewer. If nothing else, everyone would know there was a new doctor and nurse in town after tonight's auction.

"Did someone say chocolate?" Tyler arrived at the table, presenting the goodies he'd rounded up for the girls.

"That would have been me," Katie said. "Apparently spending over a thousand dollars on a date with a man makes me crave sweets."

"It makes me crave something else," Emma said, under her breath and not intended for anyone else to hear.

"Consider me your Special Sweets Delivery man then," Tyler said proudly as he sat down next to Katie.

"The two of you have started quite a bit of chatter tonight," Nell said, seemingly pleased. "I think the days of surprising patients are behind you. Everyone knows who you are now."

"Well, tonight didn't exactly go the way I thought it would," Emma said, reaching for a mini fruit tart. The spread Tyler created seemed to have a little bit of everything, and it all looked divine.

"I'm not sure what I like better—the fact that you bid an insane amount on my brother, or that the two of you both managed to edge out Jenna Ory. Nick and Luke will both want to thank you for that."

"You're the second one to say something about Jenna—your sister mentioned her earlier. Who is she?" Katie reached for another cheesecake bite.

"Let's just say—in high school she seemed to forget that she was dating Nathan while she went out with someone else. She's also been through a few husbands in recent years. That and, between each husband, she's gone after Nick, too." The thought of someone pursuing Nick, especially outside of the bachelor auction, left a funny feeling in Emma's stomach.

"Speaking of wins," Emma said, using a napkin to delicately touch her lips and wipe her hands, "we should go and claim our prizes, Katie. I also need a word with Mrs. Keller before we leave. She seems to have taken off somewhere. She's quite agile for a woman who struggled to plant flowers just the other day."

A belly laugh came from Tyler. "Edna Keller could outdo me in just about any physical activity, and everyone in town knows it. It would take more than a little gardening to get that woman down." Tyler stole the last dessert from the plate and stood. "I should go find Nick." He turned to Emma "Or, maybe you should. He is yours after all."

"He is certainly not mine. I was simply supporting a patient by making a donation to the library. Nick just happened to go along with that." Although the idea of Nick being *hers* made her insides twist. Katie did say the ball was in her court. Maybe this was a sort of blessing in disguise.

"Alright Ems, let's go pay for our men," Katie said as she took her credit card from the tiny purse she used.

"We're not buying men, Katie. We're just making donations to the library."

"The lady doth protest too much," Katie joked. Emma couldn't be sure, but she thought she'd heard Tyler laugh as they walked away. She spotted Mrs. Keller talking with a group of older ladies. "Detour, Katie. I need to speak with a patient about something medically urgent—and it can't wait."

"Urgent? Here?" Katie clearly didn't understand.

"Well, depending on what this patient has to say it could become very urgent. I have a suspicion that Edna Keller set me up tonight, and she hurried away from the table before I could ask for an explanation."

Katie tried her best to keep up, but Emma had longer legs and shorter heels. She was a woman on a mission, and didn't slow down until she approached Edna Keller. Emma was acting out of character and Katie wasn't sure what to do with it. Edna looked up and smiled at the girls, causing Emma to stop abruptly, and Katie to stumble into her.

"What was that about, Emma?" Katie righted herself and fixed the single strap of her dress that had fallen from her shoulder.

"I feel like I was set up. I've got a suspicious feeling that Edna Keller only came to the clinic to start her work on getting me to bid on Nick."

"What? How?"

"I'm not sure, but I do want to find out. Maybe now isn't the best time, though." Emma returned a smile to Edna Keller before finding Nick's sister to make her donation.

ǂǂǂǂǂ

"So how do we claim our winners?" Luke asked Nick as they stood backstage.

"That's an interesting way to think of it, Mr. Brewer." Ken Hyde spoke with a tone that rivaled George Feeny. Though most of his students were grown, he still spoke to each of them the very same way he did when they were kids. “I do think we’re supposed to go set up our dates, though. I can’t wait to hear exactly how much money was raised tonight. Thanks to the two of you, I think we might have far exceeded our goal.”

Nick didn’t want to seem overly eager, but he’d been desperate to get to Emma since his father announced her winning bid. Instead, he stood with a group of bachelors that didn’t know what to do next. *Wasn’t that Kelly’s job?*

“I guess we can head out front now. I know that some of you know your winning bidder—” Nick said, casting a glance at the mayor— “but I need to catch up with my date, and I bet some others do too.” The boys made their way to the main room, quickly running into Tyler.

“There you are,” he said dramatically. “Luke,” he said, fist bumping his friend. “You both killed it up there. I think the ladies deserve a thank you for out-bidding Jenna.” Tyler nodded toward the front of the room.

“Why was Dr. Cunningham seated with our family?” Nick asked.

“Beats me. I just do what mom says. I will say, after seeing those two bid on you jokers,” he paused to nod toward Emma and Katie, “I’m a little bummed that I avoided the auction in the first place. A date with one of them wouldn’t be so bad. Then again, even Shelly seemed to be getting in on the action,” he finished with a hint of desire sparking in his eyes.

“Can it, kid,” Nick said. “You wouldn’t have gotten even half of what I did and you know it.”

"I'm the younger brother with a hell of a lot more stamina. Maybe I should go and see if the fine doctor would change her bid to a different Ewing. Maybe I can get another grand for the library."

"I said, can it," Nick hissed with a bite in his voice that he knew his brother could hear.

"Territorial already, I like it."

"I said to stop it Tyler, and I mean it. Since when do you talk about women that way, anyway?" Nick felt himself getting overly agitated with his younger brother.

"Since I knew talking about that woman would get you all worked up." Tyler spoke with the bratty tone he'd mastered over the years. Nick didn't care that he was wearing a tux that cost more than the entire fundraiser had made. He pulled his brother into a headlock and started to noogie his head until he heard his mother's voice.

"Nicholas Francis Ewing! You stop that right now," Nell approached her sons and their friend.

Nick let go, adjusted his clothes, and straightened up before faking his most innocent smile. "Of course, Mom." He cleared his throat. "Luke and I were just heading up to the collections table to make sure we square everything away with the auction winners...and Tyler needed some help with his hair. Just being a good big brother."

Nell raised five children, and knew what fighting brothers looked like. "Of course, Nicholas. Go on, then; you wouldn't want to keep them waiting, would you?"

"Yes, Ma'am. I mean no ma'am," Luke answered.

"I can't believe you're still afraid of my mother," Nick said quietly as they walked away.

"One time, dude. She caught me in Sarah's room one time. We were studying. I was helping her out—as a friend." Luke shook his head. "But yes, she still scares me. I don't think I've been back to your house since that night actually."

"I remember, Sarah wasn't happy about that—with Mom or with you."

"Speaking of your sister. She seems to be chatting it up with our dates."

Nick felt a stirring in his pants—and elsewhere—when he saw Emma. Away from her seat for the first time that evening, Nick was able to get a better look at her. She was beyond gorgeous. The lace at the neck of her dress matched her plump and kissable lips, and carried around to the back where it ended in a deep diamond shape—leaving most of the skin on her back exposed to him. The dress ended in a flare above her knees, a perfectly respectable length that still managed to give him a clear view of the toned legs he'd been imagining wrapped around his hips, and even his head in some of his dirtier thoughts. The idea of stripping her out of that dress and leaving it in a pool on the floor with her panties to follow would never leave his mind.

A shy smile crossed her lips, adding an intriguing layer to the confident doctor he'd met in her office. He longed to taste her lips, to delve his tongue into her mouth as he pulled her tight against him. He wanted to run his hands down her exposed back as he explored her curves.

"Hello, ladies," Luke said as they approached the table.

"Hi, Luke," Katie said, reaching out to give him a hug. "It seems strange to not have a coffee counter between us," she laughed.

"Ems and I were just about to settle up with our donations. How does this work now though? Do I plan the date or do you?"

"Believe it or not, I've never actually participated in a bachelor auction, so I don't know. I'm more of a traditionalist, though, so why don't I take the lead?" Sarah scoffed under her breath. "Any requests?"

"Just a—" Katie didn't get any farther before Luke interrupted.

"Besides a maple latte..."

They both laughed and Emma shook her head. Nick tucked that little nugget about Emma's friend away for a rainy day.

"I'm easy," Katie said with a flirty wink.

"I'll keep that in mind," Luke added to their banter. "What about you, Dr. Cunningham? Are you easy too?"

Nick felt himself holding his breath, and wanting to tackle Luke for asking. He also really wanted to know the answer.

Emma seemed to blush before replying, "Since my date didn't ask, I think I'll pass on answering that, Luke."

"Before either of you have a date you need to settle up your donations." Sarah seemed uncharacteristically annoyed, watching it all unfold from behind the collections table. Nick noticed the extra attention from his sister and wondered how many times Luke and Sarah had run into each other since she'd moved back to Boone Heights a few months ago.

"Of course," Emma said, handing an envelope of cash to Sarah before adding her credit card to the stack. "I didn't realize the bid would get so high, or I'd have made sure to bring extra cash with me."

"Same here," Katie said as she handed over her own card.

As Sarah charged their cards, Nick felt like he needed to break the silence.

"It's a nice surprise to see you here tonight, Dr. Cunningham. I didn't realize you had already plugged yourself into local events."

"First," she started, "you should probably call me Emma. I just donated enough money to rent a villa on the Italian countryside for a month. And second, we only learned about the fundraiser when we met your mother at The Roasted Bean. She said this would be a great place to get to know people in town. Hopefully a four thousand dollar bid got my name out there."

"All for the good of the clinic then?" Nick tried not to sound as disappointed as he felt.

"Something like that."

"Alright ladies, you're all set here," Sarah said as she returned the girls' credit cards. "We'll mail your receipts. Your donations are tax deductible, so hang on to them." A line of other women—and a few men—formed to finalize their winning bids, so the foursome moved out of the way.

"I don't know about any of you," Luke said, "but I could sure use a drink."

"Same here," Katie replied. "Why don't we head over to the bar. Nick, Emma, would you like anything?"

"I'd love another glass of wine," Emma said. Nick couldn't quite decipher her smile.

"I'll have a beer."

"Wine and beer coming up," Luke said, as he extended his arm to Katie. "Lead the way Katie—my datie." Alone with Emma for the first time, Nick felt at a loss for words.

Emma watched Katie walk away with Luke and hoped they'd return quickly. Standing next to Nick—who looked so incredibly handsome—made it hard to concentrate. Since the auction, he'd loosened another button on his shirt, and an ache grew in her as she imagined what he might look like with *every* button undone. When a waiter bumped into her from behind, Emma stumbled forward before catching her balance just a few inches from Nick. She blushed as she noticed the perfect combination of a woodsy pine scent on a handsome man.

Nick reached out to stop her fall and seemed to lose his breath as he grabbed her arm. She couldn't help getting lost in the heat that rose up in his eyes and the veins that bulged in his neck.

"I'm so sorry." Emma stepped back, trying to regain her balance.

"Don't worry about it," Nick said, staring intently. "You aren't hurt, are you?"

"Nick," Emma rolled her eyes. "I just lost my footing. I'm fine, but thank you for catching me. I'm just glad I wasn't holding a glass of wine. We'd both have ended up a little wet." She smiled until she saw his eyes heat up even more. Maybe she was playing with fire, but she enjoyed getting a rise out of him—whether it was from touching her, or an accidental *that's what she said* joke.

"I should probably take you on that date first," he said.

Emma felt her whole body blush. This was not how she expected their conversation to go, and she desperately wanted to gain control over herself—and the situation.

"Yes, a date. So, are you a traditionalist like Luke? Want to plan everything yourself? Or, as the winning bidder, are the details left up to me?"

"How much of Boone Heights have you seen?"

"Well, I've gotten pretty familiar with Main Street...at least with the route from my house to the clinic. Obviously Katie and I have been to The Roasted Bean more than a few times."

"I've lived here my entire life. Maybe I should be the one to plan our date and show you the real magic of Boone Heights."

"That sounds lovely," Emma said smiling. "I've been so busy trying to get a grip on the practice, I haven't really ventured out to explore the town."

"What are you doing on Saturday?" Nick asked as Katie and Luke returned with their drinks.

"You know, I had a date planned with One Tree Hill reruns and catching up on patient charts," Emma joked, "but I think I'll be able to fit you in."

"It's a date," Nick said.

"It's a date."

Somehow, Emma felt as if she was agreeing to so much more than a date won at an auction.

CHAPTER EIGHT

Three days after the auction, Nick could hardly control his thoughts. The way she looked in that dress, the way she'd bid on him so passionately and expensively, and most importantly, the way she acted after the auction. She was such a professional when they met at the clinic, and by the end of the auction on Sunday night she'd managed to show him just a hint more.

It was clear that she had some sort of feelings about him—even if it was just curiosity—which only fueled his desires more. He'd been completely distracted by thinking about her at work, which probably wasn't safe. Since Teddy's accident, Nick had worked to make sure that every single Ewing Brothers Construction site was fully stocked with emergency supplies and every truck packed with a first aid kit, just in case. They even had new safety protocols that were being strictly enforced.

Nathan laughed at his younger brother when he was presented with a ten page single-spaced document. Teddy's accident was minor, but he knew that Nick was only trying to prevent something worse.

Between working on the new safety protocols, and planning his date with Emma, Nich hadn't hammered a single nail. But what was the point in being your own boss if you couldn't choose how to spend your time?

At home that night and fresh out of a shower, he sat on the back deck in only a pair of red athletic shorts while he nursed a glass of Jameson on the rocks and toyed with the now dog-eared note that held Emma's phone number. It wasn't until they had parted ways after the auction that Nick realized he hadn't officially gotten Emma's phone number, and he obviously wasn't about to confess to hanging onto her note for himself. He was torn on how to reach out to her to finalize their plans for Saturday: leaving a message for her at the clinic seemed like a bit much. Then again, so did admitting to holding onto her phone number when it was meant for Nathan.

Nick looked down at his watch. *Nine thirty.* He picked up his phone, added her to his contacts, and opened a blank text message. Staring at the flashing cursor, he began to type. He was no rookie when it came to women, but things with Emma seemed different. He didn't want to come on too strong, which alone was a feeling he'd never even considered with anyone else.

Nick: How many picnic baskets could you buy for $4000?

The three bubbling dots on his screen caused a sigh of relief and a touch of excitement. He could have sworn they hovered there for hours until her reply came through.

Emma: I'd ask who this is, but I think I have a good idea. To answer your question...far too many to carry.

Nick smiled. *Bullseye*. Emma Cunningham was a clever woman. Nick slipped the note back into the back pocket of his shorts—still unwilling to part with the memento.

Nick: I'm very strong. I build houses for a living, remember?

Emma: Maybe, but carrying $4000 worth of picnic baskets would defy laws of physics. Should I assume that our plans for Saturday involve a picnic?

Nick: Don't let anyone ever question your detective skills, Dr. Cunningham.

Emma: Ha. Well, you made it pretty easy. And I thought we'd agreed you'd call me Emma. Four grand is a lot of money to spend on someone to keep such formal titles.

Nick: Alright, Emma. Does a picnic lunch sound like a good start? I have a favorite spot, a little off the beaten path, that I'd love to show you. It's a bit of a walk, but I saw your legs in that dress. I think you can handle it.

He immediately worried that the comment was too much, and hoped that he'd read her well. The hovering dots returned for a moment, but disappeared. He held his breath until they popped up again.

Emma: I'd say you judged my legs appropriately. I think they can handle a bit of walking. Perhaps I'll have the opportunity to judge yours on Saturday.

Nick: For four thousand dollars, I suppose you earned it. Good night, Emma. I'll give you more details tomorrow.

Emma: Good night, Nick. Sleep well.

Emma set her phone face-down beside her and cast the book she'd barely read onto the coffee table. Technically, she'd given him her number. Although, technically, it was meant for Nathan in case anything came up with Teddy. *Did he save my number for himself before the auction?* The thought sent a smile across her face and butterflies through her stomach.

Maybe he was more affected by their first meeting than she'd realized. She was out of practice when it came to men, but she could still tell when a man was flirting—and Nick was definitely flirting with her. That and he'd clearly noticed her legs. She'd never been so thankful for high school cross country, which taught her that running made for a great escape from the pressures of life, and an excellent way to tone her legs.

She tucked those legs beneath her and reached for her favorite gray throw on the back of the couch. Reaching for her phone, she reread the conversation she'd just had with Nick. She couldn't remember the last time she'd been on a picnic, or if she'd ever even been on a picnic. Kyle never would have put that kind of effort into a date.

She always credited his lack of intent to being busy with school and residency and then running a practice, but something in her always knew that she was just making excuses for a lackluster relationship.

In some ways, she was thankful that Kyle eventually became so careless and showed his true colors before things got too serious. She still couldn't believe how he had the nerve to try to get her involved with fraud. When she really thought about it all, she honestly wasn't too sad that the relationship had ended.

Of course, she missed the companionship. Coming home to someone after a long day was comforting and she'd been grateful to have a partner who understood the demands of medicine. No one ever complained about being busy, or about work interfering with their time together. Then again, that might have been part of the problem. Even when Kyle opened up a family clinic with fairly traditional hours, he didn't mind at all that Emma maintained her eighty hour work week. Somehow, even after joining him at the clinic, they never managed to spend much of their free time together. All of those things should have been red flags—not for Kyle's panache for fraud, but for the fact that they probably had no business spending the rest of their lives together. Maybe if Emma had accepted those red flags from the get go, she wouldn't have nearly lost her medical license.

It was her mother's unwavering faith that carried her through the stress of the legal process, and asserted confidence that Emma was never involved in Kyle's fraudulent activities. Her mother played a key part in her ability to move on with an unblemished career.

Thinking about what could have been sent a chill through Emma. Kyle could have ruined everything she'd ever worked for, and she would never forgive him for that. Pulling the blanket around her just a bit tighter, she tried to chase away those thoughts. She looked down at her phone one more time and reread her conversation with Nick.

The banter she shared with Nick Ewing was flirty, but she still didn't feel like an expert. If she was being honest, she was what most would see a novice. She considered sending Katie a screenshot of the conversation to get her take on it all, but she knew that her best friend's reaction would be over the top—they almost always were.

Emma never was a social butterfly, and had rarely come to regret it. She had acquaintances from medical school and work over the years who texted now and then to check in or share fascinating articles or new advice, but aside from Katie there was no one else she could discuss her troubles with— certainly not *boy* troubles.

She picked up her book again in hopes of finding enough concentration to focus on the words on the pages, resolving to show Katie the text messages at work the next morning. Maybe in the clinic, Katie would be able to keep a reasonably professional composure.

Nick woke up with Emma on his mind and a smile plastered across his face. He was briefly tempted to send Emma a 'good morning' text message, but didn't want to push his luck. Emma was different from the girls he'd dated before, and he hesitated in hopes of handling himself differently as well.

Emma seemed to enjoy their brief time together, but remained reserved and a bit hard to read. Through their text messages, it almost felt as if she was able to loosen up a bit and joke around. Nick felt more for Emma in the little bit of time that he'd known her than any of the women from his past. A loud pounding on his door interrupted his train of thought. He stepped into a pair of shorts on the way to the door and opened it to find his brothers on the other side—standing tall with grins like the Cheshire cat.

"Did I miss a run this morning?" He asked as they pushed past him and into the living area of his house.

"No, but you've been avoiding us since the auction and we want details." Tyler crashed into the couch, ready for a story.

"Avoiding you? I've seen Nate every day at work."

"You've *seen* me, yes. But you've had your head buried in your computer and bailed on lunch every day," Nate argued. The boys tried to meet for lunch a few times a week, enjoying the opportunity to talk about business away from the rest of their crew.

"It's nothing personal, I've just been busy. I wanted to lock down the safety procedures so we can make sure each crew has them. What happened to Teddy will never happen again."

"You've basically disappeared from our group chat, too. Even when Nat was talking about some new guy at work. What gives, Nick?" Tyler wasn't going to let up.

"Just because I didn't razz our sister for mentioning a man means something has to give?" Nick began to understand the reasoning for the early morning visit, and could only assume that his mother and sisters had conspired to arrange the recon mission.

"Doesn't it?" Nate asked confidently.

Have I really been avoiding them? He couldn't exactly deny it, but it was okay to need space. Of course, needing space was actually code for planning four-thousand-dollar-bid level picnics, which had oddly enough not been brought up once by his family. Truthfully, just as he should have given his sister some heckling over a new man in her life, someone in his family should have been knee deep in heckling of their own about his winning bid—or the lovely lady responsible for it.

"Maybe Natalie doesn't need us all up in her business—something the two of you could try to learn." His tone came out a bit more defensive than he'd intended, and the boys only laughed in response.

"You're the nosiest out of all of us, dude," Nate scoffed.

"A quality you got from Mom, for sure," Tyler added. "And the student becomes the teacher."

Nick picked up one of the gunmetal gray throw pillows from his sofa and launched it at his brothers, missing as they both ducked out of the way.

"So I've been a little preoccupied the past few days. Is that what you wanted to hear? Has your brotherly concern been assuaged?"

As they all settled back into the leather couch, Tyler raised his hands in defeat. "Alright, alright. So what has you so preoccupied? Perhaps I—the smartest in the family—can help you figure things out."

Nathan threw another pillow from the recliner, whacking Tyler in the face. "I haven't offered any help, Tyler," he said.

"Morons," Nick groaned as he walked into the kitchen to start a pot of coffee. If his brothers planned on staying, he was going to need caffeine. As Nathan and Tyler discussed who was smarter, Nick began to regret the open concept first floor he'd created when he renovated his home years ago.

Have at it, boys. Nick knew he was going to have to own up to everything with Emma sooner or later. At least their fighting had him off the hook—for now.

"Oh, coffee." Tyler broke up their fight and moved into the kitchen. "You didn't need to provide refreshments, but I'll gladly take a cup—and breakfast if you've got it."

"I'm not cooking for you, dipshit. Mom will make you whatever you want. Open menu at the Blue House."

"Teddy spent the night last night so I'm sure she's up and cooking a breakfast fit for a king. Since the king is a picky five year old," Nathan reached into the refrigerator for creamer. The entire family treated every house as their own.

Pretending to whisper, Tyler got back to the topic at hand. "You know I can't show up there without information. We have a mission here, Nate."

"Well, at least the real reason for your early morning visit has been cleared up." Nick returned to his recliner with a steaming cup of coffee he'd poured before the pot even finished brewing.

"What? You wouldn't have believed that we just wanted to spend time with you this morning?" Nate asked.

"Not at..." Nick looked down to his watch. "...six thirty in the morning."

"Fair," said Tyler, "but seriously, Nick, are we going to talk about the fact that a woman—a gorgeous woman, a doctor—dropped four G's on you at that bachelor auction?"

"Subtle Ty, real subtle," said Nathan.

"What? He knows we aren't here to discuss the weather. Who are we kidding, Nate, he's probably the smartest of us all anyway."

Nick's knucklehead brothers drove him crazy, but they were without a doubt his favorite knuckleheads, and he knew he was lucky to have them. Maybe they could help him plan the second half of his date with Emma,

Nick sighed, and regained their attention. “Clearly the auction didn’t go exactly as I had planned, but I can’t say I’m upset with the outcome. I still don’t understand why Emma made such a large bid, although I’m sure it has something to do with the fact that she was sitting at a table with Mrs. Keller and mom.”

“I was shocked to see her at our table,” Nathan said. “It was nice to meet her in person, though.”

“I’ll get to the bottom of that mystery at some point but right now I’m still trying to decide on the second half of our date.”

“You’ve already got the date set?” Tyler asked. “You wasted no time, man.”

“He didn’t want her getting snapped up by another, more handsome, Ewing man, “ Nate added with wagging eyebrows.

“You two are relentless. Yes, we are going out on Saturday. So far I’ve planned a hike near the river and a picnic lunch, but if that goes well, I’ll need some sort of plan for the evening.”

“Heading into the night. I approve,” said Tyler, nodding his head with a cocky smirk on his lips.

If he hadn’t been holding hot coffee, Nick would have hit him with another pillow. Tyler was as far from a player as someone could be, yet he always made comments that would make you believe otherwise. It drove Nick crazy, because he knew that no one treated women with more respect than Ty.

“Don’t be an ass,” Nathan said before Nick had the chance.

"Honestly, I don't want to just take her out to dinner, but I don't know if she'd be interested in something like Level Five. I can't tell if that's a scene she'd be comfortable with."

Level Five was a nightclub owned by Jason Teller—a friend of Natalie's who served in the military before moving back to Boone Heights.

"Why don't you just play it by ear?" Nate offered. "Maybe try and gauge what she'd be into during your hike and then come up with a plan after lunch."

"Does that make it seem like I'm just winging it though? I want her to know I put some thought into it all."

"So just go with a few ideas in mind and pick one. When you know, you know. How do you even know she'd want to go for a hike?" Tyler asked.

"She said she would be up for it." Nick regretted his words immediately, realizing that they proved he'd already talked to her about it.

"You've talked to her?" Nate stared at Nick, jaw-dropped.

"I sent her a text last night to make sure she'd be okay with an outdoor start to our date."

"So you used the number then? Or did she give it to you...again?"

"Yes, Nate. I kept the number she gave me for you. You told me to keep it. She bid on me. It was fair game."

"My big brother is smitten. I'm so proud." Tyler's sarcasm was painful as he blotted fake tears from his eyes.

"You are making me regret talking to you. Although I do appreciate the advice."

Tyler straightened up into a serious stare. “I’m sorry, Nick. I know you felt something for her when you met, and I think it’s awesome she bid on you. Although anyone would have been better than Jenna Ory.” At the mention of Jenna’s name all three brother’s groaned and the conversation turned to her time with Nathan in high school.

Nick glanced at his watch again. Maybe by the time his brothers finally left it would be an okay time to send a “good morning” text. He had an overwhelming desire to talk to his four thousand dollar date again.

\#####

Emma began to tell her best friend about the text messages and immediately regretted it. Katie’s excitement actually made Emma nervous. She was already overwhelmed with the idea of a potential love life, and her friend joining in on the swooning wasn’t as helpful as she’d hoped. Then again, Kyle had never done anything worth swooning over.

“A picnic. How adorably small town is that? And romantic.” Katie had the same dreamy look in her eyes as she did when they watched rom-coms on the Hallmark Channel.

“A picnic in Boone Heights will be nothing like one in Boston.” Emma sat up, suddenly second guessing herself. “When he mentioned my legs, he was flirting, right?” Emma didn’t trust her gut when it came to men.

“Clearly!” Katie grabbed Emma’s phone from the desk, and raised a finger in the air as she quoted from the recent text messages. “...but I did get a glimpse of your legs in that dress and I feel like you should be able to handle it." Smirking, she added, "I bet there is a lot of Nick Ewing you want to handle."

"Katie! Stop it!" Though she had to admit her friend wasn't wrong. She'd found herself thinking about Nick more and more often, and even had a dream the night before that he'd kissed her. It was a perfect kiss. His lips were warm and inviting and he tasted just a little bitter, like her favorite dark chocolate. She'd woken up before the dream could go any further but that didn't stop her from imagining what might have happened next while she showered later that morning. After a few minutes, she turned the water ice-cold in an effort to focus on her day and not be late to work.

"Emma." Katie turned uncharacteristically serious. "I know what happened with Kyle hurt you, and scared you, and made you doubt yourself. We don't have to talk about it if you don't want to, but...just remember that we can." Emma's heart softened more for Katie, a girl who'd always stood by her side and just *got her*. "And I want...no, I *need* you to know that what Kyle did to you says everything about him and nothing about you. He was a horrible person. He wasn't right for you. Nick is not Kyle, so just...don't hold him responsible for Kyle's mistakes."

"You always know the right thing to say when I need to hear it, Katie. You're right. I guess second guessing Nick's flirting is probably more like second guessing my own judgment in general." Emma was relieved to feel a bit more centered on it all, and more certain of her attraction to Nick Ewing. "And it's not like we're going to run off and get married and start a family after one picnic. Maybe he's just a serial flirter."

"You would make cute babies though." The dreamy look returned to Katie's eyes. Emma tossed a stack of napkins at her friend as she dove into her takeout salad. Noticing the time, she stood to wrap up their lunch break. Afternoon patients would be arriving soon.

The women froze when a chime sounded from Emma's phone. They stared at the phone, and then each other, before Emma reached for it.

Nick: I hope your day is going well, Emma. I was going to check in this morning but my brothers paid me an unannounced visit before seven and overstayed their welcome.

Katie catapulted from her chair to read the text over Emma's shoulder and squealed. "Aw, he was going to send you a good morning text!"

"Why is that so special? And how do you know that?" Emma was again grateful for Katie but a little annoyed she had to ask her friend about typical dating etiquette.

"You know, like a quick message to say good morning. Just because he's interested in you." She must have seen the mild confusion on Emma's face because she continued to explain. "It means he's thinking of you early in the morning. It's sweet."

"It's like I need a manual on dating."

"Right here." Katie bowed and spun around. "I'm an expert, and I've got your back."

Emma was book smart with an education and a list of achievements a mile long. Plus, she'd spent nearly a quarter of her life with Kyle. So it wasn't her fault; she'd been otherwise occupied all these years and was just out of practice.

"Alright, coach. We need to get back to our real lives and our jobs."

Katie looked dumbfounded. "But aren't you going to reply?"

"I am, and you're going to go and see if our next patient is here and start their intake."

"But I'm invested now," Katie argued. "I need to know what you're going to say." Her dismay at getting kicked out of the conversation was entertaining.

"I'll give you an update tonight. You bring the wine this time."

"Fine," Katie said, dragging herself from Emma's office. Emma knew she only had a few minutes until Katie would have the next patient ready, so she typed out a reply as quickly as she could.

Emma: Ouch, that's early! Although...I was probably on the second mile of my run at that point. I'm in training, you know. I want to be ready for the walk to our picnic this weekend.

And my day has been lovely. I hope yours is, too.

Nick: We should go running together one morning. As long as you think I can keep up with you.

Emma: I'm sure your legs would be able to keep up with mine just fine. I'd like that.

She couldn't be certain, but it was almost as if Nick was planning more time together before they'd even had their first date. Emma smiled, blushing.

Nick: Oh, so you have *checked out my legs! Strictly in a medical capacity, I'm sure.*

Emma: Is it more professional to lie to you and tell you it was completely with regard to my role as a physician or to correct you?

Nick: Ha. Correct me. Just because I'd like to hear it.

Emma: Or read it?

Nick: Or both?

Emma: What were we talking about again?

Emma's confidence increased with each message, and her cheeks strained from smiling.

Nick: Does the medical board know that you have a hard time remembering recent conversations? I'd hate to be the one to tell them.

Emma laughed out loud. He'd added a winking emoji, and it felt flirty.

Emma: I can self report right now if that would make you happy. Wait...what am I self-reporting again?

Emma couldn't get over how fun it was to talk with Nick. She waited, watching the three dots bounce on her screen.

Nick: Should I call 911? Is this a true medical emergency? You won't forget about our date, will you?

Emma: How could I forget?

Nick: Well, you did pay $4,000 for it.

It sort of bothered Emma to be reminded of the amount. Unsure of how he felt about it, she worried that it might change how he felt about their time together. When Mrs. Keller offered the money—in the midst of Emma's sudden emotional duress—she was overwhelmed with the idea of doubling it. So, she did.

But almost as if he could read her mind, Nick sent another message.

Nick: Which, by the way, I'm flattered. You're incredibly generous, and the library will thrive with that gift.

Just like that, Emma relaxed. It was like he'd read her mind. An alert popped up on the computer that her next patient was ready.

Emma: Thank you. I actually have to go. My next patient is ready. Have a good afternoon, Nick.

Nick: Talk soon, Emma.

Emma slid her phone into the pocket of her white coat, grabbed her stethoscope, and left her office with a smile she'd been missing and butterflies in her stomach.

CHAPTER NINE

"He's going to be here soon, Katie." The girls spoke over a FaceTime call as Emma got ready for her date.

"And you're basically ready. All you need is lip gloss. Something neutral."

They'd been on the call at least forty-five minutes now. Katie had insisted on helping Emma get ready. If she'd really had her way, she would have been there in person, but Emma knew better than to let that kind of uncontrolled enthusiasm into her cottage.

She'd spent the evening before trying on multiple outfits in search of something casual but attractive. She finally settled on a pair of army green linen joggers and a fitted tank top. Spring in Maryland was still chilly, so she tossed an open cardigan over top. She finished off the outfit with a pair of white sneakers, her hair loose over her shoulders, and two hair ties in her pocket—just in case.

Emma wasn't one to go overboard with makeup, but Katie's suggestion for a neutral lip-gloss was the perfect final touch. After smoothing the shimmery nude color on her lips, she added just a hint of light bronze eyeshadow and a few layers of mascara. She knew she'd put together the perfect look for their date, and the newfound confidence felt like a relief. She always worked to look so professional, and over the years had perfected a very curated style—mostly thanks to her mother. It wasn't often that she dressed for a date, rather than a day at the office.

"Prop the phone up on your dresser so I can see the whole look." Katie was demanding when it came to fashion. Emma rarely asked for her help, so when she had the chance she practically exploded with excitement. This was the second time in less than a week that she'd gotten to play fashion consultant.

Emma did as she was told, complete with an annoyed eye roll and a shrug of the shoulders.

"And the verdict is?"

"Eleven out of ten! Nick Ewing is going to have to wipe up the drool when he sees you."

"Which is going to be soon." Emma checked her watch. Nick would be there at eleven. She thought back on their conversation; flirty but easy. It wasn't hard to feel comfortable with Nick, at least when it came to text messages. He'd asked about her favorite foods and anything she wouldn't eat. When she said she was easy to please, he replied with another one of those winking emojis. Her heart had skipped a beat and sent a rush of heat to her core.

They'd briefly talked about family. Emma shared that she was the only child of a lawyer mother and doctor father. Nick mapped out his entire family, explaining that his younger sister Sara was an animal lover who worked for the local veterinarian and that his brother Nathan was co-owner of their almost ten year old construction company. He didn't say much about the business, but from what she could gather, they were relatively successful.

Nick continued to send a good morning text message each day through the rest of the week. The morning of their date, he included a selfie of him packing their picnic lunch. His hair looked slightly disheveled and he had more scruff on his face than Emma had seen before. She enjoyed the view of him in the morning, and it seemed to give her more of a jolt than her morning coffee offered.

"Earth to Emma," Katie hollered. "Where did you go?"

"What? Nowhere." Emma blushed. She wasn't quite ready to admit that her thoughts of Nick were becoming less and less innocent, and more and more distracting.

"Well, assuming Nick is punctual—which I am— you've got about five minutes. And as much as I want to keep chatting, I think maybe you should go try to relax." Katie always knew what Emma was feeling, and she was thankful to have a friend who understood her so well.

"Remind me to grab a bottle of the good champagne for our next girls night," Emma winked. "I love you. Thank you for getting ready with me." Emma blew a kiss and ended the call just before a knock on the door announced her date's arrival.

After one last look in the mirror at the entryway and a deep breath to settle her nerves, Emma opened the door to find Nick casually leaning against the porch railing with a cup from The Roasted Bean in each hand. The man looked better dressed for hiking than he had in an expensive and perfectly tailored suit. His khaki pants fit like they'd been sewed just for him and his plaid shirt was the perfect combination of dark blue and maroon, which was apparently the exact color match for his tanned olive skin. Complete with a green linen jacket, Nick Ewing could have been on the cover of the next Land's End catalog.

His hair was a bit more tamed than it was in the photo he sent, but still looked effortlessly casual. She had to will herself not to reach out and run her fingers through it. To top it all off, he hadn't taken a razor to the scruff on his chin—which sent a familiar wave of heat through her body. The feeling was becoming a natural response every time she thought of Nick and was even stronger when he was close enough to touch.

"Maple latte—Luke told me they were your favorite." Electricity shot through her when her hand touched his to take the drink.

A heavy warmth seeped through his body when her fingers touched his. He wondered if she felt it too, and hoped that her deer in headlights look was a good indication. Emma looked incredible—casual but classy, a trait that Nick had quickly grown to love about her. Until he met Emma, he'd never noticed the same characteristics missing from the women of his past.

"Thank you," Emma said after her first sip. "Katie and I have developed a serious addiction to these." When Emma smiled, Nick felt like everything in his world had fallen into place; the noise quieted and his breath reached deeper into his lungs. Standing in front of him, smiling and dressed for a hike to one of his favorite places in the world, Emma seemed to unlock a part of him he didn't realize could be opened.

"Come on in while I grab my things, I just need a minute." Nick followed her inside, taking the time while her back was toward him to center himself and settle his emotions.

"Take your time. We're not in any hurry—at least I'm not."

"I'm not either; I've blocked off my whole day for you." Emma turned her head and winked at him over her shoulder before she walked down the hall to what he assumed was her bedroom. For a moment, it felt like there was a hole in the room where she'd just been standing.

She lived in one of the small cottages just off the main street of town. Most of the homes were built in the 1950's and many, including Emma's, had been updated in the years since. Her living room was warm and inviting but had a touch of elegance that only the generations could offer. From the bone white sofa and matching chair to the pale blue pillows and gray throws, and the photos that sat atop the console under her mounted television, Nick could see small touches of Emma everywhere.

The bookshelf in the corner by the large side window held medical textbooks next to more photos, a small vase with fresh flowers, and a few succulents. In the other corner was a large basket that overflowed with more throw blankets underneath a tropical plant strung from the ceiling.

Nick noticed another plant and wondered if nurturing living things was embedded somewhere in the strands of Emma's DNA. He found it endearing. Moving past the coffee table, he noticed an open book faced down to mark her page and a stack of recent medical journals. Next to the television, framed photographs caught his eye.

One showed a younger looking Emma and Katie in caps and gowns. Another showed Emma standing between who he assumed were her parents. In her hands was a newly framed medical license, and on every face a proud smile. A few candid photos of her with friends and a few more candid shots showed Katie and a few others in scrubs outside of a hospital.

He picked up the photo of Emma holding her license.

"Those are my parents. That was an amazing day."

"They look proud." He set the photo down and turned to face her. Her expression changed and a wistful look crossed her face.

"They are proud. I know that. I worked my whole life to be a doctor. It was really nice to spend a day celebrating that accomplishment."

At the bench by her front door, she slid a lip gloss and her phone into her bag and reached for her keys.

"Ready?"

"I've been ready all morning, Emma." Maple lattes in hand, they stepped out the door toward his Suburban. Nick beat her to the passenger side door and opened it for her, putting a smile on her face. When he offered a hand, she rested her palm in his—the first time they'd touched...intentionally. The heat he'd felt when she took her coffee felt like a winter storm compared to the blaze that took over his body as he held her hand. It took every ounce of restraint he possessed to resist pulling her against him to capture her lips in a kiss.

Emma seemed to hesitate, stopping to look him in the eyes and smile before she stepped into her seat. He shut the door and walked around to his side slowly, trying to get a grip on his suddenly increased libido before he scared her off. She was making it nearly impossible without doing much at all.

He couldn't wait to taste her lips and feel her curves mold against him. He'd never been one to plan out a first kiss—those sort of things tended to just happen naturally for him—but he'd already imagined the first time he connected with Emma. In fact, he'd played the scene so many times in his mind, he was already convinced that the moment it happened would be pure magic.

⧻

They drove in an easy silence other than the few times they both piped up to sing along with the radio. They seemed to share a love for 80's pop music. After about fifteen minutes and one lively rendition of *Don't Stop Believin'*, they pulled off onto a dirt road.

"This could be the start of an awful horror movie." Emma shot him an accusing glare. "Unsuspecting woman in a car with a man she doesn't know very well...pulling off onto a dirt road in the middle of nowhere."

"It does seem like a good plot twist," he laughed. "So, what can I do to assure you that you're safe with me?"

"Isn't that what a killer would say?"

"Fair enough," he agreed with a laugh. "You could always share your location with Katie."

"You know, as much as she would like that, I think I'll just trust you." Emma was thankful that the same easy banter from their text messages had translated to their in person conversation. She hadn't worried too much about it, but was still thankful that it was all so easy with him.

Nick pulled off into a makeshift parking spot and shifted into park. "You're safe with me Emma, I promise." The sincerity in his voice was so genuine that Emma knew trusting him would be easy, too.

"I know." She couldn't take her eyes off of him, and he seemed to be having the same problem. His eyes were warm and his lips were inviting. She began to imagine how the scruff on his jaw would feel against her skin and leaned into him as if a magnet was pulling them closer. She saw his pupils grow larger and his jaw clench tight, as if he was trying to gain self-control—a feeling Emma could relate to.

As if intentionally trying to break them apart, a giant hawk flew right past the windshield, cawing at something in the distance. They separated quickly, startled by the bird.

"Well, we're here." Nick cleared his throat and brushed his hands over his thighs. "Are you up for that walk? It's worth it, I promise."

"I'm looking forward to it," Emma said, noticing that her heart rate was slowly returning to normal.

At the back hatch, Nick opened the trunk and reached in to grab a yellow and white striped picnic bag. It was large enough that Emma wondered how he planned to carry it, until he slid the straps over his shoulders like a backpack.

"That's clever," she said.

"You'd be surprised what you can find online these days with expedited shipping." It sounded as if he'd bought the bag specifically for their date—and the idea of him searching the internet for the perfect picnic basket filled her with happiness. She'd never known a man to pay so much attention to her, and follow through with such sweet gestures.

"Should we head out? I'm excited to see this special spot you've talked about."

"I'm excited to show you."

"Why don't you lead the way." They took off on the narrow path, and Emma naturally fell in line behind him.

"There's room," he said. "Walk next to me." They followed a well-worn trail into a deep grove of trees. Less than two weeks since they met, under rather stressful circumstances, to say the least—it felt more like they'd known eachother forever.

"Do you come here often?"

"Honestly? There was a time I'd come here every afternoon. Right before Nathan and I started our business...I was having a hard time...had some decisions to make. I stumbled upon this trail—which, at the time, was far more overgrown—and the walk really helped me clear my head. Then I got up there, and the view...well, it's slightly addicting."

"I can't wait to see it."

"All in good time Skipper, all in good time."

Emma laughed as they kept walking. Soon, the trail narrowed and as they adjusted the distance between them, the backs of their hands brushed together. They looked at each other in perfect sync, and without a single hesitation, Nick took Emma's hand in his. At the contact Emma felt herself stumble nervously, and Nick tightened his grip.

The feel of his hand holding hers was perfect. His hands were rough from work; so different than the smooth hands of a physician. She could only imagine how they would feel touching her breasts, and other sensitive places. She couldn't tell if her warmth was due to a good sweater, or the man walking next to her. If she'd been a betting woman, she would have put her money on the latter.

"So how are you liking Boone Heights so far? Was it a big adjustment from life in Boston?" It was almost as if he knew she could use a distraction, and she was thankful for the small talk.

"It's been a bit of an adjustment, I guess. But so far, I love it."

"I've wanted to ask about how you ended up here in the first place, but you were pretty vague at the clinic. I wasn't sure if you wanted to share." She knew the question was coming. In fact, she was shocked it took him so long to ask.

"It's a little complicated and...well, I'd prefer if it stayed between us for now." She didn't know Milton well enough to spread his business all over town.

"Scouts honor." Nick raised two fingers from his free hand in a salute.

"The fact that you were a boy scout is one of the least surprising things I've ever heard," Emma laughed. A man who put this much thought into a date—who had been so resourceful with his nephew—must have been a scout.

She took a deep breath and willed herself to open up with Nick. "So, a few months ago, I got a package from Milton Oliver. I'd never heard of him before but it turns out...he's my uncle, from my mother's side of the family. Somehow, he knew about me and knew that I was a doctor. I guess he'd also learned that I was...well, I was looking for a change. He said he had some personal business to take care of and asked if I could run the clinic while he was gone."

She could feel Nick's surprise, and turned to see his jaw had dropped while he waited for more. "He'd included a contract...my lawyer reviewed it and I called to talk to the office manager. We decided it sounded legit, so I agreed. My parents still don't know that I know about him. They think I was just looking for a change and moved here." Other than his shock, Nick's face was hard to read as she continued. "I've never spoken to Milton Oliver myself. I've never met him. The whole town seems to love him though, which makes me happy. Honestly, I don't even know how long I'm going to be here at this point. The contract was open ended."

They walked in silence as Nick seemed to process what she'd said. Emma was thankful that he hadn't let go of her hand as she went through her crazy story. In fact, he'd given her hand a reassuring squeeze several times as she talked.

"You know, that wasn't exactly the story I was expecting. But, it makes sense that you're related to Doc. There's a calming thing about you. He has that, too." She enjoyed learning little bits about the uncle she had never known.

"In fact," Nick continued, "now that you mention it, the way you were with Teddy reminds me of how Doc handled me when I was four. Nate dared me to climb this huge tree, and I fell out and broke my arm."

Emma felt conflicted. She didn't want to admit that she came to Boone Heights to find out why her mother had this secret brother. She'd never mentioned a falling out of any kind with anyone in her family. Rather than a castaway, Milton Oliver was more like nonexistent. On the other hand, everything the residents of Boone Heights had to say made him sound like a great man. It all left her feeling confused. Her parents weren't known to be the warmest people on the planet, but they were good people—kind and fair. She felt desperate to understand what could have happened that led to an uncle she never knew existed.

"Thank you. It's kind of like I've been getting to know him through everyone here. Maybe one day I'll have stories of my own." After one last reassuring squeeze, Nick let go of her hand and jogged a few hundred feet ahead. Emma was surprised when he took off, but didn't mind watching him run from behind.

He turned back toward her with a huge grin. "I was nervous there might be other people here, but it seems that my spot is still a secret." Emma caught up to him and gasped as she took in the view in front of her. It seemed like all of the trees had grown together in such a way that they formed a shelter. There was an opening directly in front of them and Nick pulled out a flashlight as they stepped further in. It wasn't dark by any means but Emma appreciated the fact that he'd thought to light the way. Nick set down the picnic backpack and gestured around them. "Well, what do you think?"

Emma was taken aback. The spot, nearly a mile and a half from the road, was magical.

"It's incredible," she said breathlessly.

⧻⧻⧻

The look on Emma's face was priceless, and certainly worth the express shipping he paid to get the picnic backpack in time for their date. Her reaction was exactly what he'd been hoping for when he imagined bringing her to his "Secret Tunnel"—a nickname he'd given the place when he first found it. He remembered the wonder he felt stepping through the opening in the trees that seemed to be intertwining as they grew. He was awestruck at the vast clearing underneath a massive canopy of Live Oak trees that has all grown together.

Over time, it became a sort of oasis from life. One time, it had even protected him as clouds rolled in unexpectedly fast, and the sky opened up around him. He'd sat among these trees too many times to count; thinking, listening to music, and even falling asleep. Until now, he'd never shared the space with anyone—like he was waiting for someone he knew would appreciate it as much as he did. Emma was the one, and her reaction confirmed it.

"Welcome to The Secret Tunnel. It isn't really a tunnel but that's how I thought of it the first time I was here so...the nickname kind of just stuck."

"I can't believe this is real." Emma looked above and all around. "I've never seen anything like it."

Nick pulled a thick blanket from the bag and spread it out on the ground. He sat down and reached up to invite Emma to join him.

"I felt the exact same way. Mother Nature is incredible." He turned to grab two chilled bottles of water, handing one to Emma. He noticed a bit of worry in her eyes, and wondered what had caused it and how he could make it go away.

"And thank you." He nudged her with his shoulder. "Thank you for sharing that story with me. I know it's personal, for both you and Doc, but your story is safe with me. And...if you ever want to talk about it...I'd be honored to listen." The worry vanished from her eyes and the blue around her irises seemed to sparkle a little brighter.

"So, what did you pack in the bag, besides water?" She changed the subject, clasping her hands together in excitement. Nick was glad he'd lightened the mood.

"Wait, I was bringing the food?" He could hardly keep a straight face. "I distinctly remember you saying you'd handle lunch—I even skipped breakfast because I wanted to make sure I enjoyed your cooking."

Nick watched as a wave of panic flushed over Emma's face until realizing that he was, in fact, joking, and suddenly she let out the most beautiful sounding belly laugh. Nick couldn't help but join her.

"You totally had me," she cried as she laughed and wiped away the tears from her eyes. "Until I realized you wouldn't be carrying the largest picnic basket of all times on your back with just a blanket and water in it."

"Who says doctors aren't smart?'

"No one." She paused and shrugged her shoulders. "Well, maybe some people."

Nick loved how easy it was to talk to her. He reached back into the bag and pulled out a small champagne bottle and two glasses.

"Are we having a liquid lunch?"

"You really are impatient, Skipper."

"Skipper?"

"I know you like to be at the wheel, but I'm steering the ship today."

He pulled out the salad he'd prepared with spinach, bacon, apples, and pecans and a separate container of his mothers famous Dijon dressing. Next was the fried chicken he'd picked up from Southern Blues, one of his favorite restaurants in the next town over. He and his brother had done several renovations to the owner's home a few years before, and they always hooked him up with an obscene amount of food. Last was the potato salad—also from Southern

Blues—and the fruit he'd cut up earlier that morning. Dessert would have to wait.

"Oh my gosh, Nick! This all looks amazing. Thank you for putting so much effort into all of this."

"Well, I can't take credit for the chicken and potato salad. I picked that up last night." Nick was suddenly feeling shy at her praise, which wasn't like him at all.

"Nick." He looked up to find Emma staring at him with a fierceness in her eyes. "Do not downplay how much you put into this date. This is one of the nicest things anyone has ever done for me."

His chest filled with pride at the realization that he'd impressed her so much, and an annoyance that no one else ever had. She deserved the world, and he was getting more and more certain that he was going to be the one to give it to her.

He pulled white plates, yellow cloth napkins and utensils with yellow and white striped handles out of the backpack.

"Well then, let's not have my effort go to waste. Dig in." The cork popping from the bottle of champagne sounded of celebration, and that's exactly how it felt.

CHAPTER TEN

Laying back onto the blanket, Emma put a hand over her stomach.

"I cannot possibly eat another bite. That was so good. I'm going to need more of that fried chicken, too. I'm not sure how I've survived thirty-one years without it."

"Only one strawberry left—don't let it go to waste."

Nick had outdone himself with a large plate of the juiciest chocolate-covered strawberries that were just imperfect enough that Emma knew he'd made them himself. As if she needed another sign of all the effort he'd put forth.

"You have to eat it. I couldn't possibly." Suddenly, Nick hovered the last strawberry over her mouth and swayed it back and forth, tempting her to take a bite.

"Just one bite, Emma. Don't let this poor strawberry think you don't want it." He pouted his lips in dramatic sadness. Emma hadn't realized a man like this existed. Nick had been so playful and even more considerate. He even packed an extra sweatshirt in case Emma was cold. She was fine in her sweater but she thought about lying just so she could see if the sweatshirt smelled like him. She would have given anything to be wrapped up in his scent.

"Playing dirty, Ewing. You're playing dirty." Against her intentions, she found herself opening her mouth while Nick lowered the strawberry closer, and took a bite as the chocolate-covered fruit made its way to her lips. Her appreciative moan made a flame flicker in Nick's eyes.

He laid down beside her with his head in his hands and his eyes shut. His scent floated around Emma and the familiar tingle tossed around her stomach. There was something about laying under the cover of majestic trees next to a man who had fed you the most magnificent meal that had Emma struggling to resist her urge to reach out and latch onto him—and maybe never let go.

Instead, she straightened herself and brought her hands to her sides like a soldier standing—or lying—at attention. Without missing a beat, Nick lowered his arm along Emma's, lightly holding her hand while tracing circles on her palm with his thumb.

Emma felt boneless—her worries melted away while her senses heightened. Nick continued the slow rhythmic circles in her palm as her pulse raced. She turned to face him, finding his eyes closed, but tension on his face. His expression told of some battle inside while his touch remained calm and gentle. She sat up next to him, the movement causing Nick to open his eyes and sit up to face her. They sat frozen for what seemed like forever. She wasn't sure who moved first, and she wasn't sure how she'd ever be the same again, but she was one hundred percent certain that kissing Nick Ewing was something she never wanted to quit.

His lips were soft but firm and met hers tentatively at first, gently gliding over each other like they were each learning the curves and ridges of the other. The soft moan that escaped her lips seemed to encourage Nick, who threaded his hand into her curly hair, angled her head, and deepened his kiss. His tongue teased the seam of her lips as if he was desperate to taste her but patient enough to ask permission. She softened and his tongue slipped inside to meet hers. The groan in his chest made her move closer to him. When she couldn't get any closer, the hand that had been so wound into her curls released them and joined the other at her hips, gripping them and pulling her onto his lap.

She'd never experienced anything like this in her life, and she knew she never would again. She settled onto him as his grip returned to hair and her hands found his biceps—holding on for dear life while his tongue delved deeper into her mouth, seeking every nook and cranny and driving her crazy. She shifted on his lap and he groaned, gripping her hips even tighter—as if he was afraid she might escape. She felt herself spiraling and leaned into Nick, pressing her breasts against his chest and pulling tighter on his arms to anchor herself to him.

They stayed right there on that yellow and white striped blanket underneath the cover of trees and explored each other's mouths, tongues, and teeth until their lips finally parted, leaving her breathless and dazed. The feeling was quickly replaced by a burning desire for more when she saw the penetrating and lustful way Nick looked back at her.

It took every ounce of control Nick could muster up to remove his lips from Emma's. She tasted even better than he had imagined, and the way she responded to his exploration of her mouth had reached down deep into his soul and ignited an inferno. The feel of her tight ass pressing into his lap had nearly done him in. As his hands closed around her hips, he had to resist the desperate urge to press his arousal into her. But when her chest met his and her breasts crushed against him, he nearly abandoned all ideas of civility and took her right there under his favorite trees.

Emma's lips were swollen and her eyes glazed. Her chest rose and fell quickly and she made no attempt to tame the hair his hands had mussed up. Just in case she was thinking about removing herself from his lap, Nick tightened his grip on her hips—a subtle order to stay right where she was.

The kiss had robbed Nick of any ability to form a coherent sentence, and while he struggled with what to say, Emma broke their silence.

"I feel like I should say something about how I'm usually not that forward—and I'm not—but I don't really want to make an excuse. I've been told that I need to get better at taking what I want—I don't regret doing that."

Relief washed through him, followed by pride and a possessiveness of her that he'd just recently come to understand. He wouldn't have known what to say or do if Emma felt regret after that kiss, but he had to admit that his male ego was stroked when she admitted that she wanted him.

"Regret is not a word I'd use to describe the way I feel right now either." With Emma still straddling his lap, Nick raised his hips just slightly to let Emma feel the effect she had on him. She lowered her head with a shy smile and blushed cheeks, but Nick gently placed a finger under her chin and lifted it until her eyes met his again. He leaned forward and placed a gentle kiss on her forehead until he felt her sigh and lean into him even more.

He could have easily become addicted to the feel of Emma's skin on his lips. The scent of fresh orange blossoms and coconut rose from her hair, transporting Nick's mind to the beach. Whatever shampoo she used, he wanted to buy it in bulk so that he would never forget this moment.

A loud clap of thunder entirely too close for comfort snapped Nick from his daydream. "That sounds close," she said, jumping from his lap before he reached to gather the remnants of their lunch. They each picked up a side of the picnic blanket and began to fold it the same way Nick and his siblings folded sheets together when they were kids.

He stuffed the blanket into the bag and tossed the bag over his shoulders while Emma picked up the trash bag he'd tied off.

"We should probably make a run for it. I don't like the idea of being under all of these trees if lightning is close by."

"I can keep up," Emma said. "You lead the way and I'll follow." As they left The Secret Tunnel, another clap of thunder sounded and suddenly the clouds opened up and it began to pour.

"Go!" Emma hollered with a laugh as they both took off in a sprint. She kept up with ease, impressing a long-legged man who prided himself in his athletic ability. With over a mile back to the car, Nick could have kicked himself for not thinking to bring an umbrella. Not that the weather had called for any rain—he checked.

As they closed in on the Suburban, Nick reached into his pocket to grab his keys. Just as easily as the rain had started, it lightened up until it stopped completely. They locked eyes and burst into laughter. It was one of the best moments Nick had ever experienced, and he stared at her in an attempt to soak it all in. Tears streamed down her cheeks.

"What just happened?" She said through laughter, looking up to the sky as the sun reappeared. "How can the sun shine like that and we stand here looking like this?" She gestured between the two of them, sopping wet and catching their breath.

Nick couldn't help but stare at the white tank top that stuck to her skin, giving him a tantalizing peek at the outline of the lace trim on her bra. He felt himself harden, which was uncomfortable given how tightly his rain-soaked pants clung to him. He knew that he had no hope of hiding the outline of his—now throbbing—manhood; and he didn't even try.

"I wish I knew. That was wild." He dropped his backpack on the ground and opened the tailgate, reaching into his gym bag for a towel.

"Another item from that gym bag of yours is saving the day." He watched as she towel dried her hair, sending a bolt of lightning to his heart as he realized what she meant. He'd used a shirt from the same bag to wrap Teddy's hand after the accident.

She started to dry off her clothes and laughed, "this is pointless. I should probably just wring out my sweater and call it a day."

"I'm so sorry, Emma." Nick was starting to shiver and realized Emma must be cold too. "Why don't we just get you home. I'll get the heat on in the truck."

"Why are you sorry? It's not like you caused a random thunderstorm. So we got a little wet. It was actually kind of fun." Nick threw a soggy backpack into the trunk and Emma tossed the towel on top.

Of course she isn't upset. Emma was like no other woman he'd ever met. He watched as she peeled off her sweater and twisted it into a tight knot to drain the water. If her wet tank top had him at half-mast, seeing it cling to every curve of her hourglass shape had him hard as a rock.

A shiver coursed through Emma as she worked to get as much water out of her cardigan as possible—an effort that seemed to have been in vain. Except, of course, for the way it seemed to affect Nick, who struggled to hide the eight or more inches of man trapped in his rain-soaked pants.

"This doesn't seem to be doing much, does it?" Emma didn't want to put the wet wool back against her skin but she was desperate to stop the chills.

"Don't put that back on." Nick reached into the backseat and grabbed a blue hoodie with a logo on the back that matched the one on the side of his truck. "This isn't fresh and clean, but it also isn't really dirty. I only wore it to meet a client the other day."

Emma took the sweatshirt he offered and pulled it over her head, inhaling deeply to gather as much of his scent as she could. It seemed to surround her like a warm hug. As her head emerged from the hoodie, she noticed the heat had returned to Nick's eyes as he watched her dress. She rolled up the sleeves that were entirely too long, but there wasn't a single thing she could do about the hem that ran almost to her knees.

She gave a little spin. "Well, if it isn't the season's newest fashion trend."

Nick let out the most wholesome and heartwarming laugh. "It should be."

Emma nodded down at the sweatshirt now covering her body and keeping her body heat close. "Thank you for this. I'll make sure it's washed and dried before I return it."

"I'm not concerned about it, Skipper. Not even a little bit."

The two of them stood there with the tailgate still open, just staring at each other. It could have been ten seconds or ten hours. Just as she felt Nick stepping closer, a loud caw came from right above them and a hawk circled several feet above them. Emma was sure it had to be the same fowl from earlier and was wondering what this bird had against her.

"Should we get in the car? We can turn on the heat and the seat warmers and maybe we can both stop shivering."

Looking closer Emma noticed Nick's teeth were almost chattering from the cold, his clothes still dripping wet.

"You must be freezing. A seat warmer sounds lovely."

Emma hurried around to the passenger side and got in before Nick had the tailgate shut. He joined her in the car and turned over the engine before adjusting the heat and fans to full blast, before adjusting a heated seat as well. Her bottom quickly warmed to a tolerable toasty temperature and she sighed in contentment.

Nick rubbed his hands together and blew on them before holding them up to the hot air coming out of the vents. "That's so much better. I can't believe I didn't think to bring an umbrella."

"If it makes you feel any better, that rainstorm was so heavy, I don't think an umbrella would have done much." She paused, and smiled before adding, "Besides, this is a much better story for how my $4,000 date ended."

Nick turned to face her quickly. "Ended? You're ready to go home?" Disappointment seeped from his eyes which sent another shiver through her—one that she knew had nothing to do with the rain.

"I assume you want to change into something a little less soggy. I know I do."

"Oh, right—dry clothes." Nick paused to think for a moment. "But, then I was hoping we could continue our date after that. Maybe dinner and drinks, or even some dancing? If you're not feeling up to it though, I totally understand." He sounded desperate to keep their date going, and Emma loved the admission. She felt giddy again and wondered if this was how Katie felt all the time.

"Dinner, drinks, dancing. It all sounds fun," Emma laughed, "although I should probably warn you...I'm not the best dancer. At least that's what I've been told." Self-doubt crept in as she remembered the time in college that Kyle took her out dancing. He said he didn't think she could keep up with him, that they didn't seem to fit on the dance floor. They'd only been together a few weeks at that point, and looking back, it was another red flag that had gone ignored.

"I'm sure you're an excellent dancer. I bet Katie thinks you're the next Madonna."

"Katie is known to dance," she laughed. "Our bedroom dance parties are legendary."

"I'd like to see one of those." The wink he added was so clearly exaggerated that Emma knew he was flirting—and she wanted to play along.

"Well, it takes a lot to be invited to a bedroom dance party. I'll have to see what kind of moves you've got yourself first."

"Challenge accepted, Skipper. Challenge accepted." Nick put the truck in gear, made a u-turn, and started back toward town. Emma sat quietly next to him, smiling wider than she ever had before.

CHAPTER ELEVEN

Nick dropped Emma at her cottage to dry off, change, and get ready for dinner. Then he went back to his house and jumped into a hot shower, quickly turning it cold. He couldn't stop thinking about the kiss they'd shared—one she had, at least partly, initiated. The images of her soaking wet and laughing in the rain seemed to be permanently etched into his mind. He took matters into his own hands in an attempt to release the pressure—just to make it through their evening without embarrassing himself. Afterward, he still had to let the cold water beat down on him for a few minutes before he was calm enough to leave.

He returned to find Emma waiting for him on the front porch swing. She looked stunning in a strapless black romper with a slight dip at her breasts that showed off her amazing cleavage. She had also straightened her hair. Nick loved how unruly her curly hair seemed at times, but seeing it sleek and straight, falling over her bare shoulders was so sexy it stopped him halfway up her porch steps. The cold shower was suddenly useless.

They enjoyed a wonderful dinner at Mama Carmen's, where Emma didn't even flinch as Nick speared an arugula and parmesan ravioli from her plate. She retaliated by stealing a forkful of his creamy bacon tortellini a few minutes later. He couldn't quite explain it, but everything about being with Emma felt familiar—as if they'd known each other for years, not days.

Later, he watched her ass sway back and forth as she led him onto the dark dance floor of Level 5. His mind raced with desperation to get to know her even better. As the music changed from an upbeat hit to a slower soulful song, her confidence became uncertain; her eyes turned downward. Nick didn't know who had put such doubt in her mind about dancing but he could only assume it was a man—and Nick wasn't about to let thoughts of any other man enter her mind while she was in his arms.

He took her chin between his thumb and index finger, lifting her eyes up to meet his. A small smile settled on her lips, and Nick took it as a green light. He pulled her into his arms, her body landing flush against his. With his left hand on the small of her back and his right on her hip, his fingertips grazed over the silk fabric, which felt cool to the touch.

After the smallest of gasps, Emma looped her arms around his neck. Nick rolled his hips, guiding hers with his hands until they fell into the rhythm of the music that pulsed through the club.

Their bodies were a perfect fit. Her high heels raised the top of her head to just underneath his chin. As they moved to the music, she lifted her eyes to find Nick. Whether it was the look in his eyes or the arousal pressing against her belly, the confidence returned to her face and she began to move to the music on her own.

The rest of the room seemed to fade away as Nick's mind flooded with thoughts of the girl in his arms. His body seemed to react to each subtle roll of her pelvis into his. When she glanced at him the mixture of coyness and seduction in her eyes nearly sent him into orbit.

She may have paid four thousand dollars for this date, but he was certain that he would have paid any amount of money to stay like this, right here with her, forever. A hand—much larger than Emma's—landed on his shoulder, pulling him from his thoughts.

"What's up, Bro? I didn't know you were coming out tonight." Tyler came into view with three women close behind him. As if noticing Emma was an afterthought, Tyler added, "Hey Emma! I certainly hope this guy is giving you your money's worth tonight."

"Ty," Nick's tone was firm and he hoped that his little brother would get the hint and move on. Nick held on firmly to Emma's hips, even as she loosened her hold around his neck and attempted to put some distance between their bodies.

"Hi, Tyler. It's nice to see you again." Damn, Emma had that professional tone to her voice she'd had the first time they'd met and even at the auction after she'd bid on him. Nick was going to destroy his brother the next time he had a chance.

"We were just heading to the bar for a refreshment." Tyler gestured to the three women behind him, all of whom had dressed to impress for the evening in short skirts, bra tops, and heels. "Want to join us?"

Nick was about to decline when Emma dropped her arms from him completely and turned toward the bar. "That sounds great," she said. "Lead the way." Nick quickly took her hand in his, giving a small squeeze and relaxing just a bit as soon as she squeezed back.

The group maneuvered through the crowd on the dance floor to reach the bar, but Tyler stopped at a table instead, opting for table service instead of waiting for his drinks at the bar. Tyler let the girls slide into the booth he'd clearly reserved for the evening before scooting in behind them. Out of nowhere, Brett Caulder—Tyler's business partner and best friend—appeared with his younger brother Sammy.

"Sorry we're late ladies, I got hung up in the shop," Brett said as the brothers joined them.

Sammy reached across the table for a fistbump to Tyler and nodded at the rest of the table. "Ladies," he said with a tone full of intentions.

Nick had had enough of it all. Normally he loved spending time with his brother and their friends, even at clubs where entertaining members of the opposite sex was involved, but he had no patience for it tonight.

Just as he was about to get up and pull Emma back onto the dance floor or out of the club entirely, a petite redheaded waitress stopped by the table with a bottle of top-shelf vodka, several mixers, a bucket of ice, and a dozen glasses.

"Kylie, sweetie," Brett exclaimed, "it's so good to see you again!" The waitress acted excited that Brett remembered her name as she smiled wide, batted her eyes, and puffed her chest up even more.

"Hey cutie, it's been too long." Kylie began setting the items on their table without taking her eyes off of Brett. As she finished up she threw a wink at Brett and told him to not be a stranger before sauntering off.

Tyler poured drinks and Sammy turned his attention to Emma, extending a hand and kissing hers. Nick felt his blood boil. The sound of his own pulse in his ears was so loud he could barely make out the conversation between Sammy and Emma but he heard Emma introduce herself, letting Sammy know she was the temporary doctor in town. The term *temporary* stung a bit.

Nick tried to cool off. He'd never been bothered by a guy's attention to a girl, even one he was currently out with. He never wanted to be like the stereotypical men who seemed possessive, claiming women as their own. He wasn't even sure if what he felt was possessiveness, jealousy, or just an overwhelming need to keep Emma to himself.

"Hey man," Tyler said, snapping Nick back to the table. His brother offered him a drink and had already given Emma one of the same. Nick downed the drink in one gulp, almost hissing as the vodka burned its way down his throat. Tyler stared quizzically, and then—as if a light bulb went off in his head—Nick saw the moment Tyler realized the problem. Nick wanted to spend his evening with Emma and preferred not to be surrounded by his brother and their friends.

Emma had turned quiet and sipped her drink while taking in everything happening around her. Either she'd shut down Sammy's advances without Nick realizing or Sammy had decided she wasn't interesting enough to pursue. Even that thought had Nick heated. He didn't want Sammy hitting on Emma, but he knew damn well that she was a catch and that a man should have done everything in his power to get her attention.

Nick could feel himself start to twitch, feeling crowded—as if the booth was suddenly getting smaller. He set down his now empty glass and stood, reaching a hand down to Emma who joined him with a smile.

"I think we've still got some dancing left in us before we call it at night. You all enjoy yourselves." Nick nodded at his brother and added, "See you tomorrow at the Blue House for dinner," and took Emma back to the dance floor.

ǂǂǂǂǂǂ

Emma had quickly become overwhelmed by the attention at the table and sighed in relief when he led her back to the dance floor, thankful to be alone with him again. She followed as Nick took her to the far corner of the room, away from the crowd.

Her pulse picked up as Nick slowed and guided her into a small private nook and turned her to face him. Heat flooded her body and her heart raced. The look in Nick's eyes could have scared her, but instead it made her feel safe; uncomfortable in the most comfortable way.

He stepped forward, nearly pinning her against the wall. As if he needed permission, the aggression in his eyes turned into a pause. Emma reached for him without a second thought—a move so bold, so unlike her—and a growl ripped from Nick's throat as he claimed her lips in a punishing kiss. Her arms flew to his chest and her fingers clung to his shirt, holding on tight to keep herself from floating away.

As Nick deepened the kiss, Emma felt her lips part. Encouraged by her invitation, Nick slid his hands down her sides and gripped her ass, hauling her even tighter against him. As his arousal pressed into her stomach, the heat Emma had been feeling throughout her body seemed to pool at her center. She let out a moan that Nick matched with another throaty growl of his own. The music drowned them out entirely. Time seemed to stand still, and Emma felt as if her soul was floating from her body. There was no telling how long they stayed there in the corner, lips fused, exploring each other with tongues and teeth.

Thoughts intruded and distracted her. *How long can a person survive without oxygen?* A giggle bubbled up inside of her and interrupted their kiss. The man had lowered all of her inhibitions, and there was nothing she could do to stop it. Nick pulled away from her, just far enough to show his amusement.

"What's so funny, Skipper?" Still close enough to feel his chest rising and falling as he tried to suck in all the air they had been missing, Emma smiled shyly and shook her head, unable to believe she was about to admit the ridiculous thought she'd had while engaged in the most earth-shattering kiss of her life.

Taking a big gulp of air she looked up at him through hooded eyes. "Honestly, I was wondering how long a person could survive without oxygen...because I wasn't ready for that kiss to end, maybe not ever."

The fierceness returned to his eyes, just before letting his head fall backward as a hearty laugh poured from him. The sound was perfect, a sweet relief. When his eyes returned to hers, an inferno took over. Nick leaned in and nibbled at her bottom lip, sparking another one of those purr-like moans to come out of her. Emma had to stop herself from trying to jump the man in a dark corner of a club, which should have concerned her, or at least shocked her back to reality. Instead, it only fueled her desire.

"Oh, Skipper," his voice had deepened. "My guess is that you and I could survive forever." His lips met hers again, but only for a few seconds—not nearly enough to leave her satisfied.

He seemed to look so far into her eyes that he could have found the very core of her soul. "You're incredible, Dr. Emma Cunningham," he whispered. It was that moment that she felt a piece of herself attach to him in a way she'd never experienced before.

"Can we maybe go somewhere else?" she asked. For the first time, Emma struggled to read Nick's face—an ability she was coming to cherish. Afraid he'd take her question the wrong way, she pushed forward as a blush took over her cheeks. "I just meant, maybe we could go and get a cup of coffee, and hang out a little more. Or maybe, something to eat. Or maybe, just...you know, go somewhere that your brother and his friends are not."

"Emma, I'm sorry. I didn't even think about Tyler and his friends being here." Nick began to run his hand through his hair, almost obsessively, as he continued, "All I was thinking about was you and me. I mean that's not an excuse, at all though."

He was spiraling out in front of her. She pulled him toward her and pressed her lips against his. "Nick, you're thinking more about this than I am. We're both adults. Adults are allowed to kiss—even in public. Besides, no one can see us tucked back here." She just wanted him to relax. "I wasn't implying we should go somewhere more private in a cliché way. I just meant that it would be nice to be somewhere we could talk more, like we did this afternoon. And honestly, I could probably go for a sweet treat right now," she said, almost embarrassed. "Apparently dancing and kissing burn more calories than I've consumed today."

Calm seemed to wash over Nick and started to look more like the man she'd been with under the trees that afternoon and not the man she'd first met when his nephew was bleeding in her office.

"Well," he said, "If sweetness is what the lady wants, then sweetness is what the lady is going to get." They walked hand in hand through the crowd and to the door. A man she'd bid on at a date auction—at the forcible persuasion of an elderly patient—had nearly changed her entire world in less than twenty-four hours. And she was desperate for more.

CHAPTER TWELVE

Nick drove them about fifteen miles out of Boone Heights to find a tiny diner that served what he promised to be the best milkshakes she'd ever had—and he was right.

Over two mint cookies and cream shakes—because neither of them could decide between mint chip or cookies n cream—they talked about their families and what life was like growing up.

Nick couldn't imagine what it was like to grow up without siblings, while Emma felt overwhelmed at the stories of birthdays and holidays in the Blue House. Emma was a bit shocked that he hadn't asked for more information about her move to Boone Heights, but he seemed to navigate around the topic anytime it even came close to coming up—like when he was sharing how his Uncle Kevin and Aunt Kerri also had five kids that lived in Virginia...so extended family gatherings were even crazier. Emma went on to explain her lack of siblings, cousins, and anyone else to share her life with.

At the end of the night, exhausted but desperate to extend their time together, Emma wondered when she'd be with him again. As if he could read her mind, he asked if she would be up for helping him with a project the next day. She quickly agreed and had no desire to backpedal when he let her know there would be a fair amount of manual labor and dirt involved. He seemed to strategically avoid sharing the details, but she didn't need them. Time with Nick was what she wanted, even if it involved tools and dirt.

When they pulled into her driveway that night, Emma realized she'd forgotten to leave the porch light on. She opened the small clutch she'd brought and pulled out her keys so that she wouldn't need to fumble with them in the dark.

Nick parked the car, cut the ignition, and met her at her door to open it for her before walking her to the door like the gentleman he was.

"I'll see you tomorrow morning around nine if that's not too early." Nick shoved his hands into the front pockets of his pants and then pulled them out as if trying to decide what to do with them. "I'll text you when I'm on the way."

Emma smiled. "That sounds perfect. I'll make sure I wear something I don't mind getting dirty." Nick stared at her with frozen hands. This was where she was supposed to tell him that she had a lovely time and that it was the best four thousand dollar date in the history of dates—but she couldn't do it. She couldn't put her key in the lock and turn the deadbolt just yet. Nick didn't seem to be in a hurry to leave her porch yet either.

Nick said her name through a sigh and reached for her, kissing her soft and slow. His touch at the club had caused fireworks, but the sweetness of this kiss seemed to tether them together. Her hands landed on the back of his neck, reaching up into his dark hair while his circled her waist and settled on the small of her back. The scruff on his face rubbed against her, and she wondered again how it might feel on her breasts, or even on her thighs. Nick seemed to sense the change in her mindset and moved into her for an intense moment before separating.

"I should get going." He caught his breath and his voice became shy and husky. "We have a busy day tomorrow and I need you to be well-rested."

She knew that he was only referring to the supposed manual labor, but his words caused her to flush. He smiled and kissed her forehead.

"Sweet dreams, Skipper," he said before taking the key from her hand and unlocking the door. She stepped inside and shut the door, turning to look through the peephole at the man who stood still until he heard her turn the deadbolt.

As she slid into bed, the coolness of her sheets fought to bring her body temperature back to normal. Emma closed her eyes and drifted off to sleep with a smile on her lips and images of Nick Ewing dancing through her mind.

Nick barely got a few hours of sleep that night. When he made it home, he let Bo outside and joined his dog on the deck with a few fingers of bourbon—needing a stiff drink to calm him after his date with Emma.

Spending time with Doctor Emma Cunningham felt bigger somehow. And kissing her? Kissing her was more incredible than Nick had imagined, and he'd imagined it quite a bit. There was something so polished about her but also so raw—she seemed so unsure of herself sometimes, as if she didn't see what she did to him.

Nick woke before his alarm the next morning. He'd made a list of supplies he needed and knew that most would be in the warehouse at his office. He still needed to make a quick stop at the hardware store and didn't want to keep Emma waiting. Downstairs, he let Bo outside and started the coffee pot. No time for a run, he pushed through a few ab and arm exercises on the deck while his coffee brewed.

With a cup of hot coffee in hand, he stepped into the shower. Normally he would have shaved, but when he remembered the way Emma touched his beard the night before, he decided to keep it.

He dried off and grabbed some of his nicer job site clothes. He popped a bagel in the toaster and shot Nate a quick text to let him know he'd be going to take some supplies from the shed. They co-owned the company, and the materials, but they both worked to keep meticulously detailed books—something their father had instilled in them as children.

Ross Ewing owned a landscaping company before retiring a few years prior at their mother's request. When the kids were younger, Ross had a business partner that made a few shady business deals—nearly costing them the entire company. The partner ended up with a few months of jail time, and Ross bought him out to salvage the company, which he renamed Blue House Landscaping.

Nick had a distinct memory of coming downstairs one morning to find his mother with tears in her eyes as she sat holding a newborn Sarah in her arms—terrified that the business partner had cost them everything. He never wanted to feel that way and didn't want to be the reason anyone else did. He'd been financially straight and narrow from the beginning—as had Nathan.

As he was walking out the door with his breakfast in hand, a message from Nathan sounded on his phone; thanking him for the heads up and instructions to work safely.

He'd just finished his bagel when he pulled into the warehouse parking lot, backed up to one of the small trailers they had on site, and hopped out of the suburban to attach it to the hitch before pulling it around to the loading area of the warehouse.

Unlocking the padlock and pulling up the garage-style door Nick quickly entered the code into the security system keypad beeping on his left. Their warehouse was small but stocked with basics and super organized. He grabbed a lumber cart and walked over to the stack of fence panels and posts he wanted for Mrs. Keller's property. He added a few buckets and bags of cement and took it all outside to load into the trailer. Last on the list were nails and screws, and an extra pair of work gloves for Emma—a pair much smaller than his own.

He returned the cart to the warehouse and set their alarm as he left. It was only eight, so he went over to the hardware store for the last few things on his list: a new gate and latch system. He used the few minutes he had to spare to call Mrs. Keller and let her know he'd have an extra pair of hands for the day.

The woman followed through for him and kept Jenna Ory away from him. She had been rather dodgy earlier in the week when he'd run into her at the grocery store. He would have bet his prized baseball collection that he saw the older woman smirk as he moved to ask her how it was that Emma had ended up at a table with his elderly co-conspirator that night, let alone in possession of his envelope full of cash. Instead, she'd claimed she had to get her ice cream home and into the freezer before it melted and scurried away before he could get his answer. There had to be a story there, and he was hoping to hear about it.

When the brothers first started their company, they knew it would have been financially smartest to buy their supplies from national retailers, but they were both determined to keep business as local as possible. Earl Kell, the third generation owner of the hardware store, had done his very best to remain their supplier of choice, routinely selling their materials at near wholesale prices.

The familiar chime sounded as Nick walked through the door. Josh, Earl's seventeen-year-old grandson, sat behind the counter with a book. "Pap's in the back...in gardening. Spring rush will be here soon!" The boy knew Nick well and didn't budge other than to smile and wave.

"Thanks, buddy. Enjoy your book." Nick grabbed a flat cart and made his way to gardening to find Earl. The squeaky wheels announced his approach, and Earl turned around before Nick could even say hello.

"Nick! Great to see you, son. On a weekend...what's the occasion? Does Nell have you boys tinkering on something at the Blue House today?"

Nick took Earl's extended hand in a man's handshake—firm, but friendly. "Not today, Earl. I'm actually here for the fence gate Leanne ordered for me the other day. And a few more things I'll need to build it."

The new gloves in Earl's hands were leather at the palm with the smallest floral pattern in shades of blue on the opposite side. "Do you think the leather on those would be thick enough to protect against a rogue splinter or calluses from hammering?"

"It's a nice, thick leather so I'd say that would be a safe bet. They might be a little small for your hands though," Earl chuckled.

Nick suddenly felt a little off balance. He wanted to scream from the rooftops that they were for Emma, but he also wanted to hold his time with her close, and not let anyone else in quite yet. Judging from the glint in Earl's eye, he knew exactly who the gloves were for.

"Dr. Cunningham is helping me with Mrs. Keller's fence today. I have an extra pair for her, but I think these would fit her much better. Plus they seem a bit more suited for her than the ones we usually wear."

"I heard about some excitement at the fundraiser last weekend. Leanne said the bidding for you got a bit tense—and expensive."

Nick realized that there must have been some talk around town since the fundraiser. He'd been so consumed with planning their date and working on the safety manuals and kits at work that he hadn't had time to think about anything else. His own family hadn't even mentioned it, which he found strange.

"It was an interesting experience without a doubt." Nick checked his watch. "I hate to cut this short, Earl, but I do need to get moving. Any chance you can bring out the panel I ordered while I grab the rest of the things I need?"

"Of course, son. I'll meet you at the front of the store with those in a few minutes."

A few minutes later, Josh rang up the purchase. "Should I put this on the account?" He asked. Nick pulled the credit card from his wallet. "Nah, use this one. This isn't a work project."

One more stop and he'd be with her. He couldn't believe how much he was looking forward to seeing Emma again after less than twelve hours away. His need for her was strong. Before her, the feeling would have stressed him out. Nothing in his history would have suggested he would be doing anything but that right now.

Nick smiled as he pulled into the empty spot behind Luke's truck. On top of wanting to get her a maple latte and a pastry, he couldn't stand the idea of going any longer without seeing her.

Relieved to find an empty cafe, he stepped up to the counter with a bit of pep not usually found in his step.

A five o'clock alarm, a five-mile run, and even some yoga hadn't been enough to release the restless energy Emma felt knowing she was going to see Nick soon. As if that wasn't difficult enough, she knew that things would heat up between the two of them. At the very least, they were doing some sort of physical work today. She assumed it would have something to do with construction, and the thought of seeing Nick in the work environment he seemed to love so much sparked an unusual excitement in her.

She hated when her thoughts would return to Kyle, but the idea of him at the hospital or clinic had never made her feel that way—even in the beginning when his residency was so new and exciting.

"Hey Alexa, play my study playlist," she called out. She'd cultivated a list of songs into a strong study playlist years ago in college and hoped the music might bring her back to center—but even that wasn't helping.

She didn't dislike the feeling. In some ways, it was invigorating. She was finally beginning to understand the "butterflies" all the rom-com heroines talked about. She was tempted to call Katie, but as much as she wanted to share the excitement with her best friend, she also wanted to sit with these feelings herself for a bit.

Noticing her watch at five to nine, her stomach rumbled—a reminder that she'd forgotten to eat. Just as she reached the refrigerator to grab a yogurt, a knock at the door interrupted her. She practically ran to open the door, abandoning all thoughts of yogurt for the delicious-looking man she knew was standing at the other side.

Nick leaned casually against one of the beams on her front porch. The hands she'd been dreaming of rested on his hips as he stood to face the street. On the porch railing sat two hot cups from The Roasted Bean, and a to-go bag. The man was spoiling her, and she loved it.

As he heard the door open, Nick turned to face her. The scene felt like slow motion as Emma took in how perfect the moment could have been in one of the romance movies she and Katie loved to watch. He was dressed far more casually today in what Emma assumed was his typical work attire: worn jeans, a long-sleeved thermal, and work boots that had seen more than their fair share of a hard day's work. But it was the smile across his kissable lips that had Emma leaping into his arms.

Nick greeted her with a kiss that said more than hello. He was slow and soulful, wrapping his arms around her waist and pulling her closer. They must have bumped into the porch railing, and the to-go bag fell to the ground. Feeling the surge of confidence that Nick Ewing seemed to fill her with, Emma parted her lips and leaned into his, needing him to feel what he did to her. She darted her tongue out and along the line between his lips.

A quiet sound of satisfaction escaped him and he let her in. Emma took his bottom lip between her teeth and tugged—something she'd never done before but felt so right. The move unleashed a hunger in Nick, and suddenly the pair stumbled backward into her house, making a full circle as he spun her inside. Nick slammed the door shut just before her back crashed into it, pinning her arms above her head with one hand while the other still held on firmly at the small of her back.

A quick glance—almost as if he was making sure she was alright—and his hand began to move up her spine, sending tingles shooting throughout her body. Emma closed her eyes and felt her head lull to the side and suddenly Nick's lips were there, exploring the curve from her shoulder up to her ear with his mouth, tongue, and teeth. As his teeth caught the tendon near her shoulder, the tingling sensation was replaced with a burning heat.

At that moment, she needed this man more than she'd needed anything in her life. Sounds escaped her lips that felt bare without his, and her ears rang along with the pulsing sound of the blood rushing through her body.

Her hips began to grind against Nick, yearning for more connection, which seemed to fuel his assault on the sensitive skin on the left side of her neck before leaving to continue on the other.

With her hands above her head, Emma felt helpless in the most amazing way—more turned on than she'd ever felt before. She resisted the urge to break free and use her hands to explore Nick's body.

As his lips slammed back into hers, he let go of her arms. Her fingers found their way to his hair and down his face, feeling the coarseness of his beard that had just marked the skin along her jaw.

He wrapped his fingers over her hips and slowly worked his hands underneath the dark-blue long-sleeved tee that served only as an annoying barrier between them. Feeling his hands on her bare skin was magical; the roughness of his palms slid up her sides and her breasts began to ache for his touch—a desperate desire for the same roughness to cross her nipples.

Her back arched away from the door as Nick pulled himself away from her lips to fall to his knees in front of her. She hadn't realized how high he'd lifted her shirt until she felt his tongue making circles around her belly button. The noise that came from somewhere deep inside her could only be described as sinful.

Every cell in her body vibrated as the scratch of his beard, the wetness of his tongue, and the strength of his hands inched closer to taunt her nipples. Just before his fingers could reach her breasts—which were straining against the lacy cream- colored bra she'd just put on—the shrill sound of his phone pierced the air around them.

"Fuck," Nick muttered. As if it was the hardest thing he'd ever done, Nick released his hands from her sides and took several steps back as he pulled his phone from his pocket.

Emma's mind was reeling over the sensation she'd just experienced. Was it normal to want someone so much? She straightened her shirt, smoothing it back down over the top of her jeans and fingering through her hair as she worked to regain a normal breathing pattern. Knowing it was a futile task, she instead pulled a tie from her back pocket and tossed it up into a messy knot at the top of her head. As if by instinct she touched her neck, hoping any type of beard burn wouldn't be visible.

She and Nick made eye contact then, which he sealed with a wink—like he knew she wanted it. He gave her a thumbs up and said, "Yes, Mrs. Keller. We are on the way. I got caught up for a few minutes, so we're just a bit behind, but we'll be there soon."

Mrs. Keller? The matchmaker patient? They were going to see her today?

Noticing the quizzical look on her face, Nick covered the phone with the hand she was missing so much. "I'll explain in a minute," he whispered, still listening to the old woman on the other end of the line. After a rushed goodbye, he returned his phone to his pocket.

"So...Good morning?" Nick joked with a grin. Emma laughed at the man who was proving to be too charming for his own good—not that it would get him out of explaining why they were heading to do physical labor at the home of the woman who forced her to bid on him at the auction.

"Oh, is it? It could go either way for me." Her faked nonchalance got a growl out of Nick as he playfully lunged for her, pressing a small peck to her forehead.

"Nope! We have to get going or we'll have a seventy-four-year-old lady hunting us down. And she's got plenty of time and energy. So we'd better get to it." With a quick tug on Emma's ponytail, Nick ushered her out the door. "Come on, Skipper. Our breakfast is out on the porch."

CHAPTER THIRTEEN

Nick laughed as they made their way to Edna Keller's house. "That woman is sneaky." He'd spent the first part of their drive explaining his brilliant idea to Emma—the way he got roped into taking Nate's spot in the auction, and the way he tried to make use of the misfortune.

When he mentioned the money he'd given to Mrs. Keller to ensure her winning bid, Emma gasped. No wonder Nick was so shocked to see her lay down all that money at the auction. He had to commend the old lady for her quick thinking. As the pieces of the story fell together, he learned that Edna Keller faked a reason to visit the clinic just hours after making their deal. He only wondered if his dear, sweet, innocent mother had been involved in the entire scheme. The whole thing had Nell Ewing's stamp all over it.

"And now we're headed to build the woman a new fence after she managed to trick us both," Emma shrieked.

"Honestly, Emma..." He looked at her with a face full of contentment. "I can't complain. I feel like I need to add her to my Christmas list. Top of it, actually." That still didn't seem like enough of a thank you for the gift he'd been blessed with over the past week.

Her smile had him weak at the knees—luckily seated. He still couldn't believe that his passenger seat was filled with the doctor who'd kept his mind racing since they met.

"You know," she paused, "I may have to go in on that gift with you." She reached her hand across the center console to rest on his thigh as they drove. He still wasn't used to her touch and wasn't sure that he ever would be. He laid his hand on top of hers and caught his breath. They rode like that in perfect silence until they arrived at the Keller house. He reluctantly pulled his hands from her to parallel park in the only available spot on the street. Emma kept her hand in place for a few extra seconds before returning it to her own lap—the loss leaving a cold sensation where her hand had been.

As he shut off the ignition, he could have sworn that he noticed a curtain fall shut in the front window as if someone had been watching. Nick rolled his eyes and laughed as he stepped out of the car and walked around to Emma's side. He would have a conversation with the retired librarian later on. Edna was taking on quite a few of his mother's traits recently; frustrating, but not unhelpful.

When he reached her door, he realized that she'd waited for him to open it, causing his insides to toss around. They'd spent so much time together over the past twenty-four hours that they seemed to be falling into a routine. Normally that would have scared the shit out of Nick, but it didn't—not even a little bit.

Mrs. Keller appeared on the front porch and waved.

"Well, good morning, Dr. Cunningham," she shouted as they walked up to the porch. "What a sweet surprise to see you this morning. Nicky, sweetheart," she grabbed his hands and leaned up to kiss his cheek, "always a joy to see you too." Edna donned an apron covered in handprints from the local kindergarten class, and for a moment, Nick forgot he'd been so irritated with her.

"It's wonderful to see you again Mrs. Keller," Emma said. "I hope you've been taking it easy as we discussed." The knowing look she shot to Edna Keller seemed to make clear that the pair had figured out her entire scheme.

"Oh, of course, Dr. Cunningham. I've felt excellent ever since our visit." *That woman takes it as well as she dishes it out.*

"And you, young man. I didn't know you were bringing someone with you today. Had I known, I would have prepared more than your sweet tea." The scolding was all in good fun. He was well aware that Edna would have made a huge fuss if she'd known Emma would be joining him—and he didn't want any drama. He knew Emma wouldn't have liked it either.

"Why don't I let you catch up with your patient while I get our supplies from the trailer. I'll only be a minute." Nick left the ladies on the porch. He'd had some of his crew stop by to rip out the old fence on Friday afternoon. Demolition was usually his favorite part of the job—taking out the old to make room for the new—but it was more than a one-man job. Until recently, he didn't know he'd have help.

At the trailer, Nick looked up to the porch to find the ladies chatting away. He felt himself go stiff when he saw that Emma was watching him, rather than checking in on her patient. From across the yard, he could see the desire in her eyes, and it took all of his self-control to get back to the task at hand instead of running to the porch, throwing her over his shoulder, and going back to her cottage to finish what they'd started.

Something came over him that morning, and his desires to taste her—to devour her—had completely taken over. Her breasts had practically been spilling out of the cream-colored lace covering them and he felt absolutely powerless to stop his hands from reaching for her. He wanted to take the dark nipple he'd seen through the lace between his thumb and index finger and tug until she moaned—and he was certain that he'd get back to that at some point soon.

He wanted to taste her sweetness on his tongue as she moaned, giving in to the pleasure he filled her with. She seemed to enjoy the way his beard felt on her neck. He could only imagine how she'd react when it brushed against her most sensitive area while her legs wrapped around his head. He knew that he would bring her to a peak with his tongue and the picture in his mind almost caused him to drop the fifteen- pound bag of concrete in his arms.

Maybe, if they got their work done quickly, he could turn that vision into a reality. His watch read nine-thirty, and he knew it would be a painfully long day—hopeful that the physical labor would keep his dick in check, and make the time fly by.

Emma was still in shock after learning the lengths Edna Keller had gone to to see that the auction ended the way she planned. The small town scheming was more impressive than she'd first realized, and she wondered if there was a therapist in town to offer the residents some sort of intervention.

On the other hand, Nick's original plan was pretty solid. He quickly mentioned that it was all in an attempt to avoid the women of Boone Heights—but she caught the words and wondered why he had such a goal, and if it changed anything about the past twenty four hours they'd spent together. He was clearly an experienced man—so where did he meet women?

For as many answers as she'd been given recently, she felt like she'd only been filled with more questions. That, and she really wished she'd had a chance to change into a fresh pair of panties before they left. It was hard to listen to Mrs. Keller go on about her prized begonia when the dampness distracted her.

"Oh yes, they really are beautiful," Emma managed to reply.

"But not nearly as eye-catching as some other things in my yard at the moment...right, dear?" Mrs. Keller gave Emma a knowing nod toward Nick with a wink before pretending to fan herself with her hand.

Emma was almost too stunned to answer. The lady was more feisty in her seventies than Emma was in her thirties. Maybe there was something to be said for getting older and experiencing more of life.

As if she didn't expect Emma to answer, Edna continued. "Have you had enough coffee this morning? I can put on a fresh pot if you'd like."

Almost thankful for the change of subject, Emma politely declined. Her heart was already racing and she wouldn't need caffeine to make it through the day.

Nick seemed to have finished unloading the trailer of large wooden beams, bags of concrete, and several buckets of tools to the middle of the yard and counted the orange cones that had been set up where posts ought to go.

"Alright, Skipper, " Nick called from the yard, "Ready to earn your tool belt?"

She could feel Edna's eyes burn into the back of her head, probably seeing straight into her soul.

"About time," Edna Keller said under her breath. Louder, she continued. "Since I was told my services aren't needed today, I'm going to go inside and bake some of Nicky's favorite cranberry chocolate chip cookies for lunch. Holler if you need anything."

Emma stepped down the side stairs of the porch and into the yard. She noticed Edna's garden, and how it looked nearly ready for spring. It was filled with custom pots that looked to be homemade. Other posts held lights from the back of the house to the garden and green plants lined the walkway. It was clear that Edna Keller spent much of her time in the garden.

When she reached Nick in the yard, she noticed a brown paper bag in his hands and a look of uncertainty on his face.

"Reporting for duty, Boss Man," she said in her most manly voice, attempting to lighten the mood. Nick laughed.

"Well, you seem to be missing a crucial part of your uniform." He handed her the bag and she took a quick peek inside, gasping lightly when she realized what he'd brought. "I figured you'd need something to protect your hands today—we can't have the only doctor in town needing stitches."

Emma pulled the gloves from the bag and smiled as she looked over the leather-wrapped palms and the lady-like fabric that was starkly different from the worn canvas of his own. She wasn't sure she'd ever received a more thoughtful gift. Her parents never skimped in the gift department—she got a pony when she turned eight, for goodness' sake—but something about the simplicity of this gift felt even bigger and almost life-changing.

"Nick," she started softly, "thank you. These are beautiful—and so thoughtful." It was then she realized there was something else in the bag. She handed the gloves to Nick before reaching back into the bag. She pulled out a Ewing Brothers' Construction hat and she felt her smile widen. The idea of wearing a hat with Nick's name on it had her a bit smitten, a feeling she'd need to add to the list of things she planned to catch Katie up on.

She adjusted the hat on her head and tucked her ponytail through the back before looking to Nick for approval.

His eyes were hungry—like he needed her more than he needed his next breath. The butterflies danced in her stomach again, and electricity crossed her scalp.

Without breaking eye contact, he reached up and fixed the brim of her hat with his free hand, adding a wink for good measure.

Emma felt as if he'd branded her—a mark she never wanted to have removed. Suddenly she remembered that they were standing in a wide-open backyard, where her elderly patient—or anyone else for that matter—could see them standing so close.

Unsure of it all, she got back to business. "Is my uniform presentable now, Boss?"

"Put these on and you'll look perfect." Nick handed her back the gloves. "They're almost too pretty to wear," Emma said as she slid her fingers into them. Nick pulled a worn pair of his own gloves from his back pocket.

"Well, I can always get you a new pair of gloves. But I can't replace those hands."

"Well, I'm no surgeon," she threw back. "My hands aren't exactly the money makers."

He looked over his shoulder and answered. "I wouldn't bet on that Skipper. I think your hands have some magic in them." He reached for the water hose on the side of the house. "Let's get to it, Cunningham. This fence isn't going to build itself."

As much as he wanted to turn back to her and see her reaction to his joke, he continued to work. He had no idea how he would make it through an entire day of building a fence with the woman, and he was thankful that Edna Keller's yard wasn't all that big. He had plenty of motivation to move fast.

Seeing Emma in the Ewing Brothers' hat nearly did him in; it wasn't often that a woman—other than his mother and sisters—wore something with his name on it, and the idea had never made him feel any sort of way—until now. All he could think when he saw her in his hat was what she'd look like standing in front of him wearing nothing but the lace bra he'd seen earlier with matching panties—and that hat.

Shit. He was going to need to spray himself down with that hose. A few kisses with her had him feeling like a horny teenager with a crush. But he was a man, and the crush was more like red-hot lust with a touch of something more. He tried desperately to focus on adding water to the buckets he brought to mix cement.

He carried one to the first cone which was set where a post used to be. He made a mental note to thank Eddie—one of his foremen—and his son for doing such a great job on the old fence. They'd even prepared the post holes to be the right size, shape, and distance apart—and filled them with a few inches of gravel in preparation.

"Nick," Emma said as she approached cautiously. "You do know that I've never done anything like this before, right? I have no clue how to help you."

"You mean you don't moonlight as a fence builder after a full day of treating patients? Color me shocked, Emma. Shocked, I tell you."

She took a playful swing at him and Nick caught her hand. He pulled the glove down a bit to expose a small patch of skin on her forearm and kissed it. His lips seemed to be drawn to every part of her body.

"I'm going to grab one of those posts and set it in the ground. You can help me hold it straight while I fill the hole with concrete. I'll add some temporary support to hold it while it sets, and then we'll move on to the next post. I have full confidence in you."

Emma practically skipped over to the pile of posts, with more enthusiasm than any member of his crew had ever shown.

"Well, what are you waiting for? I've got a tool belt to earn, remember?" Nick matched her enthusiasm and they set their first fence post in record time. By the time they got to the tenth or eleventh post, Emma was trying to pour and level the concrete herself.

She's amazing. Emma was throwing herself into work that wasn't at all glamorous and did so with ease. He'd never brought a woman to a job site, but none of the women he'd known before would have even considered carrying a post or pouring concrete—let alone calling it a date.

By the time they got to the last post, Emma was even setting the support beams by herself. At this point, there was nothing she could do that would shock Nick.

“Do I need to worry about my job?” he joked. “You’re not going to decide medicine isn’t for you, start your own construction company and drive me out of business, right?”

She tossed a towel at Nick and laughed. “I think your life’s work is safe. Although, to be honest, this is a lot more fun than I thought it would be. Maybe my hands are money makers after all.”

There was his dick again, just begging to say hello. He’d made it nearly two hours in her presence without the intrusion, but one quick mention of her hands had him straining against his jeans again.

Just in time for a save, Mrs. Keller appeared at the back door and stepped outside.

“You two have made so much progress,” she exclaimed. “A dream team!” Nick could tell by the tone of her voice that her matchmaking skills were far from retired. He began to wonder if she’d been on the phone with his mother all morning, updating her on their every move. Nell Ewing would love nothing more than a play-by-play of her son on a date.

“Now is actually a great time to take a break if you’re hungry, Emma. I had promised Mrs. Keller lunch from the deli. I can place a quick delivery order.” Nick looked to Mrs. Keller for a response.

As if they’d rehearsed it, she said “Oh sweetheart, you don’t need to buy me lunch. I did change up the deal on you a bit.” She added a guilty pout to her act.

“I think it turned out okay, Mrs. Keller,” Emma answered. “I’d love it if you joined us for lunch. I would really like to hear about this garden if you’re up for it. I can tell it means a lot to you.”

She'd really been pushing the matchmaking, but Edna Keller couldn't resist an opportunity to talk about her garden. It was the only thing that seemed to stand a chance at rivaling her library.

"I would love that," she said as she turned to Nick. "As long as Nicky won't be too bored. He's only heard about it his entire life."

"You know I love hearing your stories." He smiled and pulled his phone from his pocket. "Why don't you ladies go wash up and I'll place an order." He turned to Emma. "Mrs. Keller and I have a usual order at the deli. What would you like, Emma? They have amazing sandwiches, and Jeremy went to culinary school before coming home to take over the deli after his father passed away. The daily special will never let you down."

"I'm not too picky. Whatever the special is sounds fine with me," Emma said with ease.

"Come inside, dear. You can wash up in the powder room while I put those cookies on a plate. Then I can start to tell you all about my garden."

Emma followed Mrs. Keller into the house, turning quickly to smile at Nick behind her. He felt like the luckiest man alive. As he called the deli, he couldn't help but wonder how it had all happened so fast.

Emma was shocked at how much they'd accomplished in one day. She stepped back to admire their work as Nick put one last nail in the panel they'd been working on. Nick was right about the deli. The daily special was a chicken salad on a freshly baked roll—and it was perfect. After lunch and a few of those cookies, Mrs. Keller promised to deliver another batch to the clinic that week.

Her original thoughts of Edna Keller as the town busybody were being replaced with thoughts of endearment. Edna Keller was an accomplished woman. She'd shared stories of her time in college and how she'd met her husband Harry when she was only twenty-two. They'd been married for fifty years before he passed away after a heart attack. He spent his free time woodworking—and had been the one behind the garden posts she'd admired earlier that morning. They were an anniversary gift, and another year he built a walkway from the house to the garden.

The stories of the love they shared seemed to unleash something in Emma that she didn't realize she had buried. She listened to the stories and looked at Nick, often finding him looking back at her. They continued to sneak glances at each other as they built the fence panels, attaching them to the posts after the concrete had set. When Nick stepped behind her to show her how to use the nail gun, she could have sworn he was aroused.

Nick watched closely as she wiped the sweat from the back of her neck. After a long day in the sun, she was eager to have a little fun at his expense. Mrs. Keller took off to run to the store and now that the fence panels were up, they were mostly blocked from anyone's view.

At the cooler, she grabbed a piece of ice and—without so much as a pause to see if Nick was watching—she began to rub it around the back of her neck, just below her curls. The ice felt incredible on her sunkissed skin, and a shudder raced through her at the sensation.

She sensed his presence before he even touched her, and suddenly the ice cube was gone and replaced with Nick's warm lips.

"Dangerous move," he whispered into her ear, his voice deep but soft. Quickly, he brought the ice back to her neck before dragging it down and around to her collar bone. His lips followed the trail.

The mixture of cool and warm drove Emma insane, each change in temperature sending a shock to her system. With the ice she craved the warmth of his kiss, and as soon as his lips found her skin, she burned and longed for the icy sensation.

His free hand gripped her hip from behind, anchoring her body to his. Her hips began to move with a mind of their own and she felt his hard cock press into her back as she ground her ass into him. If she could have escaped Mrs. Keller's backyard, she would have circled into orbit.

"I'm not sure I've got much self-control left, Emma," he said in a strained whisper. She turned within his grip to face him.

"Well that makes two of us," she said before fusing her mouth to his.

This kiss was unlike anything she'd ever experienced before, even the kisses they'd already shared. It was raw and fueled simply by lust and desire. Nick moved as if he couldn't get close enough, pressing his lips into her with a force like he was fighting for control in a fury. His hands smothered her body like a man looking for lost treasure.

Emma saw stars when his hands reached her breasts and pinched her nipples through her shirt. The sensation overwhelmed her senses and poured through her hands as they clawed at any part of him she could reach, and from her throat as sounds of pleasure crept up and out. Noises of his own answered hers like a language of their own that seemed to imprint on her soul.

"I need more, Emma. I need to see you...and taste you."

"More, yes more," she said in syllables as Nick pulled her shirt over her head. His mouth found the peak of her left breast while his hand gave equal attention to her right nipple.

"More...please..." was all she could manage. When Nick's teeth scraped across her nipple and tugged toward him, her world exploded. In a matter of seconds, Nick had taken her nearly to the top and then tumbling over without even grazing her center.

Slowly, and testing her legs to make sure they were still holding her upright, Emma returned to her body. Almost as intensely as the orgasm she'd just experienced, shock and embarrassment flooded her as she searched frantically for her shirt. A man had just given her an orgasm in an old lady's backyard without so much as removing her pants. She shuttered at the thought of what Nick might think of her, barely hearing him as he said her name. As she reached to the grass below for her shirt, his firm hand wrapped around her wrist and pulled her upright.

"Emma," Nick said forcefully. "Talk to me, please. What's going on?" The lust that continued to seep from him was marred by concern on his brow. Emma straightened with her shirt gripped tightly in the hand that Nick was holding. She looked down at it and back up at him, adding to his concern.

A timidness took over as she felt the last few tremors pace through her body, and she could barely bring herself to look at the man who had just sent her to the moon and back.

Gently, Nick repeated himself. "Emma, please? I'm sorry."

"What are you sorry for?" She shrugged. "This?"

"What is this?" He asked.

"Letting this happen here—allowing myself to do that." Emma wanted to dunk her head in the cooler of water. She was a doctor for crying out loud, and she couldn't even say the word orgasm to the man who'd just made her explode.

Realization hit Nick like a ton of bricks. "You're apologizing for *that?* Seriously?" He laughed. "Oh, Emma," he said as his pupils enlarged and his view settled down to her breasts, still covered only in the lace of her bra. He reached underneath her chin and lifted until she was forced to look into his eyes. "Emma, that—the way you react to me touching you—that was the hottest thing I've ever experienced in my whole life. Knowing that I do that to you..." He stopped long enough to take a deep breath, searching for composure. "Let's just say...there are so many ideas in my head right now. If I shared even the tamest, I'd probably scare you away."

Emma started to speak, with a mind to make excuses. *I've never done that before.* He silenced her with a finger on her lips before she could say it out loud.

"Nope, not another word out of you. I'm as hard as that wood post over there, and we have a job to finish. That, and we need to clean up and get out of here before Mrs. Keller catches us in a...compromising position."

A pinkness tinted Emma's cheeks but she stopped protesting or trying to apologize. With her shirt still in her hand, Nick couldn't help but notice that her chest was rising and falling just as fast as his own.

"Lead the way, Boss Man." Emma pulled her shirt over her head. "Let's finish up."

She managed to get back to work, but all she could think of was everything else she wanted to do. Judging from the way he looked at her the rest of the afternoon, he was thinking of the same thing.

CHAPTER FOURTEEN

Riding down Main Street in the passenger seat of his brother's truck, Nick couldn't help but appreciate how much better this ride was than the similar path he'd taken just a few weeks before. Instead of holding a shirt around his bleeding hand, Teddy was playing with the stuffed dog that Sarah had given him at dinner the night before. She was hoping that a stuffed animal to hold on to might make getting his stitches removed a bit easier.

As usual, Nick's thoughts drifted back to Emma. Building a fence with her the day before was something he would never forget. He wasn't sure how Emma would feel about construction for a date, but she'd thrown herself into it with such enthusiasm. There was nothing about her that he didn't like, and so many things that were quickly threatening to turn his lust into so much more.

And good God, the lust. Remembering the way she looked in her lacey cream bra as he took her over the edge filled his dreams the night before, waking him up rock solid that morning. He'd taken care of himself in the shower that night after taking Emma home and again after dinner with his family. He was surprised that a morning tent was even possible.

He was desperate to continue what they started, but after finishing the fence, she mentioned a busy Monday ahead of her more than once on the drive home. He respected Emma and the dedication she had for her work and her patients just as much as he craved her touch, so he settled for a chaste kiss in the car that evening. He stayed in the car and watched her walk to the door, admitting that if he followed her to the door, he'd have been a no-show at family dinner night.

"Uncle Nick? Hello! I asked you a question," Teddy said from the backseat.

"Sorry, buddy. I wasn't listening, was I? What was it you were asking?" He heard his brother scoff but chose instead to focus on his nephew.

"I just wanted to know if you thought Miss Emma would be gentle when she took out my stitches. I mean, I'm not scared or anything," he added quickly, "I was just wondering."

"Dr. Cunningham will be as gentle as she can, buddy. But remember what she said about being brave? It's okay to be scared, and it's okay to tell her if you feel that way. That doesn't mean you aren't brave."

"A wise woman, that doctor is," Nathan said with a smirk.

"Not sure what you're getting at." Nick was already a little annoyed with his brother since he'd announced in the group chat that Nick would be accompanying them to the appointment. His phone blew up with messages about Emma after that and hadn't stopped. Apparently Tyler had also opened his mouth about seeing them together at the club on Saturday night. As if on cue, another alert sounded from his phone with a message from Natalie—sent only to him.

NATALIE: Don't tell anyone I said this because I'll deny it but...I'm happy for you Nick. Honestly. I know it's only been a few dates but something seems different about you now. Don't overthink it though. Love you.

Nick smiled as he read the message. Natalie always seemed to understand him in a way the others couldn't. And he knew that he wasn't overthinking anything. He was just looking forward to seeing Emma again.

Nate swung his truck into the only empty parking spot at the clinic. "They are busier than I expected," he said. "Maybe mom's plan worked a bit too well."

Nick was shocked to see how packed the clinic was, almost wondering if there was some viral outbreak he wasn't aware of. The chaos explained why she hadn't answered his text message earlier that morning.

Nick jumped out of the car before Nathan had even put it in park and was headed across the parking lot before his brother and Teddy had a chance to get out of the truck, the anticipation of seeing Emma fueling him forward without a backward glance.

In the waiting room, he was surprised—and relieved—to find it filled with the older residents of Boone Heights. Mayor Fran Masso's wife, Claire and Janet Ellingsworth—the owner of A Dress for You, a local boutique, sat together. They all seemed to be in perfect health, catching up with each other and milling about. Nick was thoroughly

confused and caught off guard when everyone turned to look at him as he stepped inside. Nathan and Teddy walked in right behind him, distracting everyone from staring at Nick.
They moved toward the reception desk where Annie Garrett sat on the phone, looking a bit frantic. She smiled and raised a finger, letting them know she would only be a moment.

"What is going on here?" Nate seemed to share in his brother's confusion. "When I had to reschedule the appointment last Wednesday Dr. Cunningham told me her Monday afternoon was wide open. Clearly no one here looks overwhelmingly sick."

"I have no clue. She did mention a busy Monday but I didn't expect...*this*."

"Oh? She mentioned a busy Monday?" Nate had a familiar shit-eating grin on his face. Nick just shook his head.

"I like her, man. We talk. You've got to let it go."

"I'm sorry about that," Annie said. "The phone has been ringing off the hook for days now. Seems like suddenly everyone in town wants to schedule a visit."

"We see that," Nathan answered. "We're actually just here to get Teddy's stitches out. Is Dr. Cunningham running behind today?"

Annie laughed. "Oh don't worry, Teddy is next. Everyone here is just waiting for an opening. Janet has been here since ten."

"Is there some epidemic we don't know about?" Nick asked.

"Yep. It's called...Boone Heights got a beautiful new doctor who placed an irrationally large bid on the town's most eligible bachelor'-itis." The three of them laughed, and Teddy looked up at them, confused.

Nick felt terrible. Emma was slammed at work because of a town full of nosey people. Katie opened the door and waved, leading the entire clan to the back.

"Hey Teddy," Katie said as she lifted him onto the exam table. "How is your hand? Are you ready to get these stitches out?"

"I'm feeling a little scared, but I'm going to be brave," Teddy said. "And I have my new puppy. This is Snowball. Aunt Sarah got him for me." Teddy lifted the dog for Katie to see. She met him with the perfect amount of excitement, in a way that seemed to ease Teddy's nerves.

A tray sat in the corner that seemed to hold everything Emma would need to take out the stitches. The door opened then and it felt as if the air was sucked from the room as Emma walked in. She didn't seem shocked to find Nick there, and instead met him with a smile—the sexiest smile, followed by a wink.

"Three Ewing men in my exam room today," she started. "My lucky day, isn't it?" Nick couldn't pull his eyes from her as she walked over to the sink and washed her hands. Her black pants were professional but managed to hug her curves in all the right ways.

Emma noticed Teddy's stuffed dog and stopped to ask about it. Teddy beamed as he told her all about Snowball, and didn't even notice Katie stepping closer with their supplies.

Those two are a dynamic duo.

After a minute or two of cooing over Snowball, Emma was ready to remove his stitches. She explained the procedure to Teddy and asked if he wanted his dad to stand with him. Nate went and held the hand that wasn't resting on the tray Katie had rolled over. Nick almost felt out of place, suddenly worried that he shouldn't have come.

"What about Uncle Nicky?" Emma asked. "Should we have him come over too?"

"Oh yeah. Come on, Uncle Nicky. It won't be scary, I promise." Nick joined him with a pat on the back. Emma smiled at him briefly before returning her attention to Teddy.

"Okay buddy, here we go," she said as she slid on a pair of exam gloves and picked up the small pair of scissors and forceps from the tray.

ǂǂǂǂǂ

Emma was so proud of Teddy. He admitted that he felt scared, but knew the stitches had to come out. As he reached to give his dad, uncle, and even Katie a high five, Emma pulled out the bag she'd snuck into the room with her.

"I know you've got Snowball to keep you company today, but I thought you might enjoy a little building with these blocks later," she said as she handed Teddy the bag. He pulled out the container of blocks that she'd picked up from A Novel Idea. Eugene knew just the thing when she stopped by to look for a gift for Teddy.

Watching Teddy's face light up was all the thanks she needed, but the appreciative and hungry glance Nick threw her was like icing on top.

"Alright, Teddy. Dad—why don't we go and get you all checked out up front with Annie. I'm pretty sure she's got a stash of cookies on her desk she'd be willing to share." Katie winked at Teddy who leaped from the table and practically pulled Nathan out of the room.

"Miss Annie always has the best cookies, Dad! Let's go before Mrs. Ellingsworth gets them all."

"Nick, would you mind meeting me in my office for a moment? I have a few questions for you to finish up my paperwork from the accident."

Nathan stopped at the door and looked back at them with a knowing nod. "Oh, take your time. We wouldn't want there to be any missing information in your paperwork." Nathan was on to them, and Emma didn't even care.

"Lead the way, Doc." Nick said, far too professionally for anyone to take him seriously.

"Follow me, please," Emma said, attempting to match his tone, and leading Nick out of the exam room and down the hall to her office. She'd barely shut the door before Nick had one hand in her hair and the other gripped tightly around her hip. He kissed her quickly as if he didn't think he'd ever get to kiss her again. He tugged lightly on the handful of curls, forcing a sinful moan of pleasure from her lips.

"Your ass looks incredible in those pants, Skipper. I could barely focus on anything else after you walked into the room." He began to work his lips down the side of her neck and then back up—the way he knew she liked—before his teeth grazed her earlobe. Her head lulled to the side, unable to do anything but allow the pleasure to radiate through her bones.

"Your skin is so soft, Emma. So soft and so sweet." Emma could barely comprehend his words as he continued his attack on the sensitive skin down her neck and underneath her ear. The longer they continued, the louder Emma became as she strained to get her body closer to him.

"Nick, yes. Yes, please." Her hands reached to pull his navy polo from the waist of his jeans and up over his head. As she started to fumble with his belt, he took her wrists in one hand and pinned them above her head the way he'd done before—the way he knew would make her nearly crumble in his arms.

"Keep those there," he ordered, as he slid her blouse up over her head, leaving her in another lacy bra—pale pink in color and matching her sweater.

"Does this door lock?" Nick asked.

"Lock?" she replied.

"Yes Emma, lock. I don't want anyone walking in on what I plan on doing to you right now." Her core exploded as he looked back into her eyes. She quickly lowered her right hand to press the lock on the doorknob and returned it above her head, just as he'd demanded.

"Done," was all she managed to say before Nick's strong hands pulled her breasts from her bra. His face dove into the middle of her chest, kissing a trail before lavishing one nipple with his tongue, and then the other.

"So sweet. So hot. All mine," he huffed between tugs and pulls with his teeth and lips.

"I need to touch you, Nick. I need to feel your skin on mine." Nick understood and pulled her bare chest straight into the thick hair on his own. It tickled her nipples, making them even harder than they already were. Noises escaped them both, and a light hiss crossed her lips.

They slowed for a brief moment as Nick started to make small circles on her back with his thumbs. The sensation started a slow burn down her skin.

In the back of her mind was the long list of patients she had to see—even if they were more like social visits than actual medical exams. She didn't care. She wanted to live in this moment forever.

After a few quiet beats, Nick spun her around and her palms laid flat against the door, bracing herself for him. His mouth landed on the nape of her neck and started on a slow trail down her spine—arousing her in ways she hadn't felt before. She flattened her palms against the door until they were above her head again, and Nick returned his exploration to her neck.

It was like Nick knew she couldn't wait any longer. Emma gasped when one of his hands found its way to her stomach, and began a descent down into the waist of her pants, flirting with the top of her panties before using his leg to spread hers wider and offer him the access he needed to finally reach the center of her world.

"Emma," he grunted in her ear. "You are so fucking wet. Did I do this to you? Are you this wet because of me?" Her mind and her world spiraled out of control, and the only answer she could muster was to nod her head.

"Say it out loud Emma. Tell me I made you this wet."

"You did. You made me so wet," she admitted through ragged breaths.

Nick let out a primal groan as he slipped a finger between her folds and inside of her. Emma dropped a hand over her mouth to keep from crying out in pleasure. Before she could experience the magic of his hands, the intercom on her desk buzzed and Katie's voice filled the room.

"Ems, I hate to do this, but we have a two-year-old on the way in with a head wound. Fell into the corner of a coffee table. I've got exam room one for you."

"Oh, crap," Emma shrieked as Nick disengaged himself from her and stepped back. "Crap, crap, crap," she kept repeating as she went over to her desk to answer Katie.

She hit the intercom button and answered. "Got it. Thanks, Katie. I'll be right there." She knew her best friend would hear her breathlessness in her voice and sent up a silent prayer that Katie didn't allow their conversation to fill the waiting room on a speaker.

She looked up to find Nick there with his shirt back on and holding her sweater out for her. As she slipped it on, he stepped over to the refrigerator in her office for a cold bottle of water.

"I'm so sorry," she started to say before he silenced her by shaking his head.

"Nope," he said, offering her the water. "Do not apologize for anything." The look he was giving her was so sincere. "You're at work, Emma. I got carried away. I just can't help myself around you." Emma's heart skipped a beat. "Now go help that baby. This..." He waved between the two of them. "We will continue this later. And we won't be interrupted."

She took a sip of the ice-cold water and felt herself begin to settle. In every situation, Nick seemed to know just what to say. In a matter of minutes, she was composed and ready to face the unknown in exam room one. Nick began to usher her to the door.

"Let's get you to your patient Dr. Cunningham." Just before he opened her office door, he set a quick kiss on her lips, leaving her with a grin she couldn't hide.

"I'll call you," Nick said before joining his brother and nephew in the waiting room.

ǂǂǂǂǂ

A few hours later, Nick sent a text message and dropped his phone on his desk. He resisted the urge to bring his hand to his nose to see if he could still smell her on his fingers. He'd washed them more than once, but he was certain that any bit of her that lingered would be his kryptonite—or maybe the balm his soul so desperately needed.

Nate didn't give him too much shit on the way home for the amount of time he'd kept Emma in her office. Watching Bella Kennedy being carried into the office by her somber father, followed by her tearful mom, was enough of a gut punch that neither of them had much banter left.

Nick knew that the little girl would be fine and that Emma would take great care of her, but he couldn't help but think about Emma's heart after a day like that. They hadn't talked much about her residency but he was sure that working at a major urban hospital had brought her a few tough cases involving children. It bothered him, possibly more than it bothered her.

Katie: How'd you get my number? Your stalker skills are impressive. Emma should be wrapping up here and heading home in about thirty minutes. It's been a long day.

Nick laughed out loud. Even in a text message, Katie's personality shined through. He'd called Luke to get her number—not that Katie wasn't just as busy as Emma, but he needed some intel to pull off the surprise he had planned for her.

Nick: I've got my sources and they smell like a maple latte. Care to share her favorite wine?

Katie: Normally I'd charge for this information, but your intentions seem pure so consider this a freebie. After a day like today, she'll want something red—dry and bold. Maybe pounds of chocolate. Maybe both?

Nick: You're a solid best friend Katie! Thanks. I owe you.

Katie: Just do right by my girl Nick. That's all I ask. Have a great night.

Katie didn't need to worry about Emma when it came to Nick. In just a few short days, he'd realized his feelings for her went far beyond lust and some abstract fascination he'd originally had. Emma was special. She made him feel more than he ever had before.

Nick called Sarah and waited for his baby sister to pick up the phone. It had barely finished the first ring when an excited shriek filled his ear.

"Well? Did you find out her favorite wine? I have the cutest little basket put together. This is so perfect!"

He'd basically opened himself up to all of this when he willingly reached out to his sister earlier that day. He wanted to put something together for Emma after seeing her day take such a turn, and he knew that Sarah would jump at the chance to help. It didn't hurt that he'd given her unlimited access to his credit card, either.

"Something red and dry and bold. Think you can find the perfect wine?"

"Nick," she scoffed, "do you doubt me? That's probably a mistake."

"No doubt at all, sis. None. I promise." He knew better than to taunt her.

"I picked up the most amazing bath bombs, fuzzy socks, cozy pajamas, and the next book in the series she's reading—at least according to Mr. Higgins. Oh, also some decadent dark chocolate pieces. I'll swing by The Bottle Shoppe and grab that wine. Have you put in a food order yet?"

Nick knew Sarah was the perfect person to help him put together a care basket for Emma. He told her everything he was thinking of and sent her on her way. He'd have preferred to have gone shopping himself, but he had a meeting the next day with a potential client and he had to prepare. Sarah was the best substitute.

She'd even offered to drop everything off at Emma's doorstep, which was probably a good idea because tonight wasn't about anything more than comfort for the good doctor. Nick was fully aware that his self-control had its limitations, and after the past forty-eight hours, he didn't want to risk turning the night into anything but a night of relaxation for his girl. *His girl*. Yes, he was certainly starting to think of her that way now.

"I'm going to call the diner now and place an order. Can you pick it up in about an hour? That should give her time to get home and settled before you drop it off."

"Sounds perfect," she replied.

"I'll add an order of cheese fries and a burger for you too," he said with a smile.

"Payment in food? I'll take it." His sister certainly was easy to please. Although she was so excited, he wouldn't have been surprised if *she* brought *him* food as a thank you for being involved.

"Thanks again, Sarah," Nick said, full of sincerity. "I really do appreciate this. Just text me when you're almost there and I'll let Emma know a delivery is coming her way."

"Bye Nick," Sarah said before disconnecting.

Nick dialed the number for the diner from memory and quickly placed his order before packing up and heading home for the night. He knew he wouldn't get any more work done waiting for Emma to get her package.

It had been two days since the most heartfelt package arrived at her doorstep after a long day at work, and as Emma sat on her couch in soft pale pink socks with a piece of dark chocolate and a book, she was still in shock of what Nick had done for her.

Coming home after a long day during her residency had often felt lonely, even with Kyle there. The knock on her door Monday night came just after she'd arrived home and was debating eating cereal for dinner—or splurging for ice cream. The tomato soup and grilled cheese on her doorstep were the perfect comfort food, and the rest of the basket warmed her from the inside out.

She caught a glimpse of Nick's younger sister sprinting back to her car and knew he must have had a hand in the sweet surprise. A quick text to him confirmed her suspicions and was satisfied that a selfie in her new pajamas would serve as a sufficient thank you.

Nick insisted that they not text that night so that she could take a bath, sip her wine, and read her book. But he also insisted that if she needed to talk, she was welcome to call. The fact that he wanted to give her the alone time she desperately needed, but also offered to listen if she wanted to talk, meant the world to her. She was certain that there had to be some sort of explanation for the connection they shared—pheromones or hormones or some other "mones" that hadn't been discovered yet. It certainly was not the cheesy love-at-first-sight nonsense that she was reading about in the latest book.

Her phone pinged with a photo and a message from Nick.

Nick: Teddy seems to think Snowball is better at building houses than I am. So now I need to protect my business from a doctor turned fence builder AND a stuffed dog.

Emma: I'd be more concerned about Teddy's skills. That house he built is wonderful.

Nick: Well he's had a good teacher.

Emma couldn't pass up her chance at a jab.

Emma: Oh I'm sure Nathan has taught him well. Rumor has it he's the best builder in town.

She watched the three little dots appear and disappear several times and started to get a little nervous waiting for Nick to reply. Finally, a message came through.

Nick: I know what you're trying to do, but I'm too busy babysitting to come over there and remind you which Ewing brother is better at nailing things.

It had also been two long days since their incredible makeout session in her—or rather, her uncle's—office. She was definitely still on edge from it all, and the idea of Nick *nailing her* had her catching her breath. Before she could reply another message came through.

Nick: That may have backfired on me because I AM babysitting and CAN'T come over there. But we're still on for tomorrow night, right?

Emma smiled. Earlier in the week, they'd made plans to spend Thursday evening together, for dinner and a fire at his place. She was excited to spend more time with him but was also intrigued with the idea of finally getting to see where he lived. She wouldn't have turned that down if her life depended on it.

Emma: Of course! I picked up some things to make s'mores. I hope that's okay.

Nick: Perfect. But, now I'm being told my services are needed to read Snowball a story. Can't wait 'til tomorrow. Night, Emma.

Emma set her phone down and picked up her book again, craving him too much to pay any attention to what she was reading.

So much for just a few months. She still hadn't heard a word from her uncle about when he planned to return to the office. She assumed that the town would be talking more about his time away, but they weren't.

She made a quick note in her calendar to call the attorney who'd reviewed the contract to see if there was a firm timeline in place for her time in Boone Heights. She was going to need to make some sort of a plan soon.

Katie had brought it up just the day before on their drive to work. She admitted that she'd fallen in love with the town and all of its charm, and was starting to consider staying since the woman she replaced at the clinic had no plans to return.

It was harder for Emma to admit, but she'd grown to love the town as well, and practicing medicine in a small clinic in a tight-knit community seemed to be much better for Emma than she'd originally thought it could be.

Monday had proven that. When the Kennedys brought little Bella in, the whole waiting room sprang into action. Several of the older ladies took Brian, Bella's older brother, and entertained him while his parents took care of his sister. Others comforted Becky Kennedy while her husband, Ben, went back into the exam room with his daughter. Emma always hated asking one parent to stay in the waiting room, but she'd learned over time that one parent was usually able to remain calmer than the other.

Annie had, with the permission of the Kennedy's, served as the relayer of updates as Emma cleaned and sutured the small head wound the little girl had gotten from her fall. When all was said and done, the couple who'd shown up for their scheduled appointment offered to take Brian to the diner for dinner while the Kennedys got Bella home and settled.

Emma found herself putting down small roots in Boone Heights and the desire to stay in town was starting to sprout. What she felt for Nick Ewing only added to her desire. Before things went much further, she needed to decide what the future actually had in store.

CHAPTER FIFTEEN

Nick had been looking forward to his date with Emma on Thursday night, and the emergency trip out of town to a job site disrupted everything. He'd likely be gone for a couple of days.

He'd gotten the call that morning that the foreman on a huge project had fallen on a loose plank at the site, breaking his ankle. They were nearing the deadline on this project, so either he or Nate would have to get out there. Nick hated asking Nate to leave Teddy, so he volunteered instead. As he packed a bag, he called Emma to break the news. She answered immediately with excitement that made Nick's heart drop.

"Emma," he interrupted. She quieted instantly. "Emma, I'm so sorry to do this but I need to cancel tonight. And I don't think I'm going to be around for the next few days." He continued quickly to explain that it was work-related and not him wanting an excuse to cancel. "We had an emergency come up at a job site out of town and I need to head out there. Nate could go, but I hate him leaving Teddy for that long. Although I hate missing our date, too."

After a few seconds of silent disappointment, she answered. "Oh Nick, I totally understand. Nate and Teddy are so lucky to have you in their lives. And it's your business, Nick. Honestly, I'd be disappointed if you made Nate go...or didn't go at all...because of our date."

Nick felt relieved and grateful. He felt so lucky to have met a woman so gracious and understanding.

"I will make this up to you, I swear." Nick threw one last shirt into his duffle bag before zipping it closed, tossing it over his shoulder, and heading downstairs. "I really appreciate you being so understanding."

"Nick," the honesty in her voice came pouring through the phone. "I love that you're doing this so your brother doesn't have to leave his son. Besides, we have plenty of time to reschedule." With the flirty laughter that had become a consistent part of their banter, she added, "Besides, now you have a little extra time to plan something to impress me."

Nick stopped in the middle of the staircase. "Oh, I'll impress you, Skipper. I will certainly impress you."

At the front door, Nick motioned for Bo to follow him out to the truck. He was planning on dropping him off with Sarah before he headed out of town.

"I'm counting on it." Her voice was so seductive that Nick could have called Nate right then and there and made him go. He wanted nothing more than to drive straight over to her cottage and show her just how impressive he could be.

"Are you on your way now?" She must have heard the suburban turn over, and continued without waiting for him to answer. "Drive safe. I'll be around if you've got time to talk."

"I'm dropping Bo off with Sarah before I head into Baltimore. It's about a two-hour drive. We've got final checks, and a walk-through with the client all scheduled in the next two days."

Nick switched the call over to the bluetooth sound system in the truck before backing out of his driveway.

"Well, I'm about to head into the clinic for the day. It seems like the thrill of a new doctor has worn off. My schedule is starting to look manageable again."

"Have a great day, Emma. We'll talk soon, promise."

"Bye Nick."

He hated this even more now. Of course, Emma hadn't been mad at him—not that he'd expected that. The woman was perfect, and she always managed to surprise him.

On the way to his sister's place, he started to think through the ways he might make it up to her. He'd just had a gift delivered to her house, so that was out. But he had a few days to think on it—he'd think of something.

Emma sat at her desk, absentmindedly scrolling through hotels in Baltimore. She wasn't going to book one—that would have been over the top. Then again, she wasn't totally convinced that she *wasn't* going to click the large "Book Now" button on each option she looked through.

After a knock on the office door, Katie popped her head in. "Can I come in?"

"Of course. Since when do you ask anyway?" Katie had been letting herself into Emma's bedroom, dorm room, house, and office for as long as she could remember.

"Since you've got a new man in your life and I don't want to interrupt anything," she said without actually coming in.

Emma laughed. "Well, that's fair. But Nick's out of town right now so you're totally safe." She did blush a little, thinking about what had happened in her office just a few days before.

Katie burst in with a huge bouquet of flowers. "Oh I know, I'm assuming that's why he had these delivered for you." She stood across from Katie's desk, pushing the vase full of calla lilies, Gerber daisies, and greenery toward her.

"Oh wow," was all she could manage.

"Wait," she said, realizing that Katie knew Nick was out of town and was going to have to miss their date. "How did you know Nick was out of town? I didn't mention it."

Katie raised the vase just high enough to cover the guilt across her face. "There might be a note tucked in there. I might have looked at it."

"Katie," Emma admonished. "Is nothing private to you?"

"Honestly, I'm just not used to you not sharing everything with me, Ems. I mean, with Kyle you did, but I'm starting to think there just wasn't much to share. I'm just not used to you being such a closed book."

Katie sat Nick's grand gesture on the bookshelf behind Emma's desk and returned to sit in a chair across from her. She looked like a hurt puppy, but also one who had been caught trying to get into the treat jar. In all fairness, she was right. Emma had been holding back, but it wasn't intentional.

"Katie, I'm sorry," she sighed. "You know...it sort of feels like all of this is new to me too. I've been in one relationship before...and there aren't exactly a ton of similarities. I'm honestly not even sure what this is."

"I know that, but you were so quiet last night I thought you were mad at me or something. And then when I saw these show up I got worried maybe Nick had done something to hurt you. I don't know..." Katie's voice fell off.

Emma had been quiet about Nick the night before, but she didn't realize her friend had caught on or felt bad about it. She stood from her desk and walked around to sit next to her friend.

"Katie, you moved to a totally new city for me without even a second thought about it. You stood beside me through all Kyle put me through. You are my person...you always will be. I'm just-I'm...a little overwhelmed with my feelings toward Nick and what it all means. I guess I've just been keeping it all to myself."

When Katie looked up, Emma saw a tear fall—driving home just how much she'd let a man impact her relationship with her best friend over the course of a few days.

"We had plans for tonight but he had to go out of town for work unexpectedly. He called this morning to reschedule. I'm sorry I haven't shared more. I was a little afraid you'd say that this was a red flag or something—but it's not. I know it's not. He didn't want Nate to have to leave Teddy overnight for a few days. That's all."

She could tell by Katie's facial expression that Nick's gesture had the same impact on both of them.

"Honestly, I was sitting here looking at hotel rooms in Baltimore when you came in. That's where he's working. That's crazy, right? I can't go to Baltimore, can I?"

Katie's eyes widened as she looked at her best friend.

"Can I?" Emma asked again more urgently this time until the true Katie reacted showed with a concerning amount of excitement over the idea she was still processing.

"Well," she started, "you could, but that's like... rom-com cliché, isn't it? No, we need to do something else. Something less predictable." Katie stood up. "Grab your coat, Emma. We're going on a lunch mission. Nick Ewing doesn't know what he's in for."

Before Emma could catch her breath from her best friend's complete one-eighty, Katie was halfway out the door. She turned back only to holler, "Emma, we only have two hours until the next patient gets here and a lot to do—so let's get moving."

Emma took one last glance at the flowers on the bookshelf before following the blur of pink scrubs out the door, hoping she wasn't going to regret letting her in.

Nick had powered through the long list of things to finish before their final client walk-through, but knew he needed to oversee everything to prevent it all from falling apart. Their restoration of a one-hundred-year-old home into an office space for a small boutique law firm had the potential to lead to several more large-scale projects. This one, like all of their work, needed to be perfectly polished before calling it a wrap. He finally felt confident that everything was ready for the partners to take their final walk through the next day as he handed them the keys.

Nick walked through the door of his hotel room ready to collapse onto the fluffy king-size bed in the overly-luxurious room he'd booked. Of course, he'd booked the room with the idea that Emma might join him—not that he'd invited her—but the fantasy he conjured in his mind of her waiting for him on a huge bed wearing absolutely nothing when he got back from the site that day was enough to have him paying an absurd amount of money for the room.

He flipped on the light and closed the door behind him before noticing a basket on the bed filled with his favorite whiskey, boxers with hearts on them, bath bombs, his favorite snacks, and a card. He ripped open the envelope and pulled the card from inside.

Nick,

I know this isn't the most original surprise but it was either this or Katie was going to convince me to drive there and be waiting on your bed with a bow around myself. I hope everything went well today. When you're ready, room service is ready to cook a steak however you want it and deliver it to your room. Either tonight or tomorrow, whichever is best for you. See you soon.

–Emma.

Well fuck. Nick's brain flooded with the image of Emma on his bed in nothing but a bow. He'd thought he was too bone-tired for anything but a shower and collapsing into bed, but other parts of his body had new ideas. That, and his stomach rumbled at the idea of a steak.

She'd gotten so many of his favorite things—including Woodford Reserve whiskey—that he knew she must have reached out to one of his siblings. He was humbled, knowing that it must have been completely out of her comfort zone, but she'd done it anyway. He thought about how serious she must have been feeling about the two of them and felt like he was the luckiest son of a bitch that ever lived.

Flopping into the bed, he pulled his phone from his pocket to call his girl. She answered with a shy *hello*.

"Hello to you, too," he started. "I see the goodie basket was such a good idea that it bared repeating."

Her soft laugh made his senses peak, and he shut his eyes to the sensations flowing through him. "They do say that imitation is the truest form of flattery."

"Well, you can imitate me anytime, Skipper. Although I'd still like to explore that bow idea."

"Oh gosh. As soon as I got off the phone with the delivery service I realized I should have left that part out. I can't imagine how uncomfortable they must have been writing that." Her blush was almost audible, and Nick took the chance to have a little fun.

"It made some parts of me a little uncomfortable, too. So rock hard and uncomfortable." Her gasp egged him on. "I was imagining a red bow, but did you have something else in mind? I don't think there's a single color that would look bad against your skin. You're so smooth. So creamy."

He listened closely as her breath caught again, and noticed water sloshing in the background.

"Are you at the pool, Emma?" He prayed he was wrong.

"Pool? No." Her reply was breathless, as if she'd just run a six-minute mile. Nick smiled, hoping that she was right where he wanted her. "I heard water, Skipper. Where are you?"

The pause before she answered told him everything he needed to know.

"My house," she said softly.

"Where in your house, Emma?" He asked assertively. His heart went wild and the zipper could have burst from his jeans, but he needed to hear her say it.

"The bathtub," she said quickly as if she'd just finished a marathon. "The bath bombs you sent are just...heavenly."

If the idea of Emma waiting for him on his hotel bed hadn't been enough to work him up, the picture he had of her naked and in a bathtub did him in.

"Oh, fuck, Emma," he groaned. "Knowing that you're naked in that tub is just...if you could see what you're doing to me right now..."

"Me too," she said, a little more boldly than before.

"Are you wet, Emma? Wet for me, and not from the water?" He held his breath waiting for her answer.

"Yes," she panted. "I'm so wet."

"Are you touching yourself, Emma?" He wanted her to touch herself—just like he was picturing. Then again, he knew he wouldn't last if she admitted to it.

She did, though. Quickly and full of longing, she answered him. "Yes. Yes, I'm touching myself. And I'm imagining it's you, Nick."

The sound he made was inhuman, but he didn't care. "I need to see Emma. Please. Can I watch?"

Rather than answer, she sent a video request and he connected immediately. The image that filled his screen would live inside of him forever: her curls piled high on top of her head as she laid in the bathtub, water lapping against her bare breasts, taut nipples hard from the cool air rushing across them. She'd propped the phone against something near the foot of the tub, angled perfectly to allow him a clear view of her fingers rubbing her folds underneath the water.

"Fuck, Emma. I need to see more. Let me see more of you." Nick didn't know if he could even concentrate enough to unzip his pants and free his massive erection, but it was like Emma couldn't even hear him. He stared at the screen in awe, taking in every bit of her eyes closed and her head thrown back on the edge of the tub. The hand beneath the water moved faster while she pinched at her nipples with the other. Her chest rose and fell heavily until she began to moan his name. That finished him off, and there was nothing else he could do besides stare at the sight before him. Emma was coming undone, rubbing herself while thinking about him. As she cried his name out over and over, her body began to tremble and her orgasm took over. She peaked on a cry and then slowly caught her breath until she came back around. Still touching herself, she opened her eyes. Nick found contentment in them that he'd long for until he held her again.

She glanced at the phone and before she had the chance to second guess what she'd done, Nick spoke.

"That was incredible, Emma. I've never seen anything that hot in my entire life. I want you so bad right now. You have no idea." His words seemed to work because the blush never fully reached her cheeks as she sat up and took the phone into her hand and then laid back down.

"How hot, Nick? Hot enough that you need to do something about it?" The confident and seductive way she'd asked told Nick that he was up next. This woman was changing his life. He just hoped he could hang on for the ride.

ǂǂǂǂǂ

Emma felt boneless—sated in a way she didn't know was possible. And somehow, seeing the heat that burned in Nick's eyes, she still wanted more.

"Touch yourself. Now I get to watch," Emma said quietly, holding her phone in the trembling hand that had just brought her to release. Her heart was starting to race again, at the simple view of a naked man stroking himself on a cell phone screen.

The man who'd caused her to lose her mind the day they met in her office, who had her bidding thousands of dollars a few days later, and had her making out in Edna Keller's backyard still had the ability to scramble her senses.

"Emma," Nick said. She could sense his arousal as though he was right beside her. "Emma," he said again, taking himself in his hand. She'd completely missed that he'd removed his clothes and propped his phone up near the foot of the bed. As his eyes nearly rolled back in his head, Emma's mouth opened slightly, forming a small circle within her lips. She wanted to focus on his face—the desire in his eyes and the tightness in his clenched jaw, but instead, she was drawn to his hand stroking the most perfect cock she'd ever seen. Even on a small phone screen, she could tell that he was larger than average, in both length and girth. A rush poured through her as she imagined him inside of her—almost causing her to start touching herself again.

"Tell me what you're thinking about while you touch yourself, Nick."

"You," he answered without opening his eyes. "I'm thinking about you, Emma. I'm always thinking about you." He began to stroke himself faster. "I'm thinking about how sweet you'll taste when I finally get to lick you. I'm thinking about how—if I was there right now—I'd haul you out of that bathtub, set you on the counter and slide into your warm pussy. How I'd kiss your nipples until they were hard peaks. How you'd feel as you came around my hard cock." As he spoke, he seemed to grow even harder and bigger before Emma's eyes. He began calling out her name as release shot onto his bare chest in ribbons. His orgasm seemed to go on forever before he gave one last stroke and opened his eyes.

"Hey, give me a minute to clean up? Don't hang up, promise?"

Barely able to speak, all Emma could say was, "p-promise." Nick disappeared from the screen and Emma jumped from the tub, dried off, and slipped into the fluffy robe that hung waiting for her on the back of her door.

As she made her way to her bedroom and laid down on her bed, she couldn't help but think that she would be in a much better position right now if she'd listened to Katie and shown up at Nick's hotel room. Although, in some ways, what they'd just done felt even more intimate than had they been together. Emma had never done that before, yet she hadn't thought twice about connecting to a video call when Nick said he wanted to see her. She wanted him to see her, and she wanted to see him.

"Ah," he said, "I see you've changed venues."

"I was starting to turn a little pruney, and the water was getting a little too cold." Emma smiled when Nick let out a little laugh.

"Is 'pruney' a medical term, Dr. Cunningham?"

"It was in the Cunningham house when I was growing up. And my Dad is a doctor so it seemed legitimate when I was five."

"Well, then I'm sure we would also find it in the latest edition of Grey's Anatomy."

"I'll make sure to check when I get to the office tomorrow. If it's not there, I'll formally submit a paper on why it should be." Everything about the two of them felt so normal and easy. They'd gone from being naked together—though hundreds of miles apart—to joking about medical textbooks.

Emma was beginning to feel settled in a way she'd never expected. She hated the phrase 'everything happens for a reason," but she was beginning to see the validity in it.

"So besides copying my amazing gift delivery idea, how was the rest of your day?" Nick settled into the bed, resting his head on his hand on the pillow.

"Uneventful." Emma settled down a little deeper on her pillows and felt her eyes getting heavy. "Katie and I actually paid a visit to your brother to find out your favorite liquor and treats and where you were staying this week, but I swore him to secrecy."

"Ah, I wondered where you got your information," Nick laughed. "Which brother? And what did he earn for not telling me, because he didn't."

"It was Nathan. I bought him a bottle of his favorite liquor when I got yours. I'm delivering it tomorrow after work." Emma stifled a yawn. "He speaks very highly of you. I can tell it meant a lot to him that you went to Baltimore instead of him. He had no clue though that we had a date planned, so I'm sorry I spilled those beans." Another yawn escaped before Emma could stop it this time.

"He likes you. And he wouldn't have let me cancel our date—that's why I didn't tell him." Nick explained it all so nonchalantly, but Emma knew that he would do anything for his family, including rescheduling their date. She fought off another yawn and felt her eyes fighting to stay open. "Emma," Nick said softly.

"Yeah," she answered in a sleepy voice.

"I think it's time for you to get some sleep, Skipper."

"I don't want to get off the phone though," she said, fighting the fatigue that was threatening to take over.

"Then just put the phone beside you. I'll talk until you're asleep." Emma set the phone on the pillow next to her and drifted off to sleep as Nick told her about his day. It was sure to be the most restful night of sleep she'd ever had.

CHAPTER SIXTEEN

Friday flew by in an agonizingly slow blur. The day seemed to drag on and on, yet she couldn't remember anything that happened. She'd woken up to her phone laying next to her and a good-morning text from Nick.

She'd seen patient after patient, but everyone seemed to blend together. She checked her phone constantly, hoping for another message from Nick even though she knew he had a busy day ahead.

The girls tried to wrap up early on Fridays, and at three-thirty she sent Annie and Katie home as she finished her paperwork. Her phone chimed with a message.

NICK: Hey, Skipper. I hope you had a good day. We're probably not going to wrap up until late tonight or maybe even tomorrow at this rate. I'd love to see you when I get back into town though.

Emma's heart leaped.

EMMA: I hope it all goes well. I'd love to see you when you get home. Not to sound too eager, but I'm open all weekend.

NICK: Perfect. I'll let you know when I'm on the road and we can make plans. Have a good night, Emma.

Emma: You too, Nick.

She hadn't gotten used to him yet. She set down her phone with a giddy sigh, excited to have plans with him soon. She thought about calling Katie to suggest wine and a movie but chose instead to keep to herself and burn off some of her energy.

Emma shut down her computer, grabbed her bag from the chair by the door, locked up the clinic, and got into her car. If she went straight home, she'd have time to squeeze in a run before it got too dark. She would have preferred a release more like the one she'd experienced the night before, but a run was the only other way she'd get a solid night of sleep.

ᚔ

Nick's trip lasted a bit longer than he expected, and after the final walk-through with satisfied clients, he raced back to Boone Heights with plans to see Emma. They hadn't talked about their video call from a few nights ago but he'd been thinking of it constantly. Mostly though, he thought of how she'd fallen asleep while he talked to her. He'd sat on the bed in his hotel room, staring at her through his phone longer than he cared to admit.

Of course, he wanted to feel her—to touch her—taste her. But mostly he just wanted *her*. He wanted her with him—always—and forever.

A phone call on the bluetooth in his suburban pulled him from his daydream.

"Hi, Mom. How are you?"

"Hi, sweetie. How's your drive?"

"Halfway home. Everything good?"

"Of course, sweetheart. I just wanted to see if you could come for dinner tonight instead of tomorrow. Your sister is volunteering at some animal rescue event tomorrow, and Tyler is meeting with a new client early Monday, so he will be leaving town."

Nick hated to disappoint his mother, but he couldn't miss another night with Emma. "I'm sorry, Mom. I can't tonight. Why don't I swing by tomorrow for lunch with you and Dad?"

"I understand, Nicky. We've been fortunate to have Sunday as our day for so long, but I guess I'll have to accept it won't always work out for everyone. You all are getting older and have your own lives."

Nick laughed. His mother seemed to have forgotten that her children were all grown, and there wasn't much 'getting older' that would impact Sunday dinners.

"Give everyone my love tonight, Ma. I'll see you tomorrow."

Nick disconnected the call and turned on the radio to an eighties station—the same one he and Emma sang along to on their first date. He smiled at the thought of her.

Time passed quickly and before he knew it he was pulling into his driveway. He was an hour ahead of the time he planned to pick Emma up and hoped that the grocery order he'd placed before he hit the road would arrive soon. He took his bag upstairs and tossed it in the closet. Catching himself in the mirror, he debated fully shaving his face but sensed that Emma liked the scruff he'd had since they met.

After a quick shower and fresh clothes, he brought the groceries that had been delivered in from the porch and left for Emma's house.

On the short drive, he flashed back to her laying in her bathtub, eyes closed and head thrown back as she came in the water. He wondered how he would make it through dinner without devouring her; it was all he'd been thinking of. Then again, there was always the idea of dessert before dinner.

As he pulled into a parking spot in front of her cottage, the front door flew open and Emma came barreling down the porch stairs toward him. He'd never left his vehicle faster, bracing himself for the way she was about to crash into him. Instead, she slowed and looked at him.

He took matters into his own hands, closed the distance between them, and greeted her the way he planned to for the rest of time—with a kiss that came from deep within his soul.

Standing on the sidewalk in front of her cottage, Nick pulled her body close to his and poured the longing he'd felt over the past forty-eight hours into their kiss. Emma melted into his arms, falling weak as his tongue slipped past her lips and teased hers. A soft purr came from her mouth as her arms linked around his neck.

Before they got carried away, Nick backed away just a fraction of an inch. "It's nice to see you, Skipper," he said with a wink. Emma slowly opened her eyes and smiled.

"If this is what it's like to be seen by you, Nick Ewing, then it's nice to be seen."

"Go shut your door and we can head out," Nick said. As Emma turned to do as she was told, he changed his mind. "You wouldn't happen to be a dessert before dinner person, would you?"

Emma glanced back over her shoulder. "Depends on the menu," she said with a wink and a laugh before bouncing onto the porch, locking the door, and returning to him.

"Car, Emma. Now."

Nick barely made it down the street before his phone rang.

"Hello? Why aren't you coming to dinner tonight? And what am I supposed to do with Bo?" His youngest sister's voice filled the car. Emma looked at Nick, curious about the dinner he was skipping, and Nick shook his head in amusement.

"Sarah, just leave Bo at the Blue House. I'm heading there for lunch tomorrow. I have plans tonight that I didn't want to cancel." He looked over at Emma who was smiling, still curious.

"Nicky, Mom's going to guilt trip me for changing dinner plans if you don't come. You know how she is." His sister, while exaggerating, had a point.

"Ty can't make it tomorrow either, Sarah. Blame him." Nick glanced over at Emma again and noticed her curiosity growing.

"I just don't know what is so important that you can't come for even a little," Sarah scowled.

Emma reached for his hand that rested on the center console to get his attention. "Should we go there instead?" She whispered.

If he had to pick a moment that he knew Emma Cunningham was *the one*, it was this moment. Instead of the date he'd promised, that he'd canceled once before, she was willing to endure dinner at his parent's house with all of his siblings. He stared at her in disbelief. "Are you sure?"

She nodded and smiled. "Dessert can wait a little longer," she said, quietly enough that Sarah couldn't hear.

Wondering, again, how he'd found someone like her—someone who understood how important his family was —he agreed. "Sarah, tell Mom I'm coming and bringing a guest." He hung up the phone before his sister could ask any questions.

"You're sure? Totally sure you want to do this?"

"It seems like Sunday dinners are important to your family. I probably shouldn't have just invited myself like that, but yes, I'm sure. If you are."

"I'm sure, Emma. More than sure." At the next stoplight, Nick made a left instead of a right and headed to the Blue House for what was sure to be an interesting, and hopefully quick, evening.

Pulling up to a house that Emma could only describe as a home, the butterflies that tossed inside her the whole drive seemed to dissipate. Suddenly, she understood why they called it the Blue House. It was a house that was meant to have a name.

It was the color of the ocean—a bright blue that instantly made you feel welcome. White rocking chairs lined the front porch that was flanked with bright pink and white rose bushes. Banister planters held blooms in purples, greens, yellows, and oranges adding even more cheerful color to the home. But what Emma loved best was that the light in front of the door was on, even though it hadn't gotten dark yet. There was something about a porch light being on that gave Emma the feeling that love radiated from the home and those inside of it.

"There is still time to back out." Nick looked at her with a mischievous glint in his eye. "Technically no one knows we're here yet."

"You told your sister you were bringing a guest. There is no way we can back out now. And besides, I'm a little curious to see what your whole family is like when everyone is together."

"Well then brace yourself, Skipper. I'm sure you're about to get the full Ewing family experience."

As if Nick had spoken some magical command, the front door of the Blue House opened and an adorable retriever puppy bolted outside with Teddy close behind. At his heels was a dark chocolate lab, who wouldn't normally be considered large, but was compared to the puppy, and finally out came what Emma thought was a piglet—but she couldn't allow herself to so easily accept that was true.

Before they had time to get out of the truck, Sarah came flying through the door, followed by Ty and Nell.

"Sadie, come back here," Teddy yelled. Emma assumed Sadie was the puppy because both Sarah and Nell were instead yelling for 'Bacon', which confirmed her earlier observation that a piglet had, in fact, run out the front door.

Ty took a flying leap off of the porch and managed to wrangle the piglet into his arms, holding it tight to his chest in the hopes of calming it down. Sarah turned her focus to Sadie, who was running back and forth between her and Teddy, unsure of where to go.

The larger dog ambled up to Nick and Emma and sat at their feet while they took it all in.

"Emma, this is Bo, my sidekick." He reached to scratch Bo's ears. Emma held her hand out for the traditional sniffing before she patted Bo on the head.

"Hi, Bo. You seem like the calm one."

Nick laughed and looked like he was going to say something, but before he could reply, his mother approached.

"Emma," she said, outstretching her arms for a hug, "It's so good to see you. I'm so sorry you walked into chaos."

The trio glanced toward the front yard where Sarah was holding a squirming Sadie while Ty was still trying to calm down the piglet.

"What was that, Mom?" Nick pulled his mother in for a quick hug before gesturing toward his siblings and nephew.

Nell Ewing just laughed. "Well, Sarah brought Bacon home until he gets adopted by a farm or some sanctuary. That's where she's going tomorrow. Of course, she also brought Bo and Sadie with her tonight. Teddy thought it would be funny to see how Bacon and Sadie played together, which...clearly didn't end well."

"Well, it looks like the calm has been restored," Nick said, gesturing to Sarah, Ty, and Teddy who were heading into the house with the animals safely in the arms of the adults.

"Hey," Ty called. "Who'd have thought you'd have the most well-trained animal in the family? Sarah's been bringing home strays since she could walk!"

"At least mine were all the four-legged kind," Sarah shot back at her brother, sticking out her tongue at him.

"We have a guest tonight, kids. Let's not scare her away before she's even entered the house." Nell held out her arm, gesturing to Emma to follow the other Ewings into the house.

Sensing her hesitation, Nick reached a palm to the small of her back, urging her forward.

"Let's go, Bo," he said.

Emma crossed the threshold of the Blue House and soaked in the love that seeped from the walls. The air smelled like freshly baked cookies, just washed laundry and the outdoors. Family photos lined the walls of the entryway and she made a mental note to come back and check out photos of Nick as a child before she left. Before they made it through the hall, Teddy was in front of them.

"Excuse me, Dr. Cunningham?" *Cutest boy ever.*

"Hey there, Teddy. It's so good to see you! How's your hand?"

"It's so much better. You fixed it up so good. But Uncle Ty says girls love scars, so it's okay if I get one."

"Oh, well if that's what your uncle said," Emma laughed. "And how is Snowball? Is he still keeping you company?"

Teddy's eyes lit up at the mention of his new stuffed pet. "He's great. And he's getting really good at building with the blocks you got us. You're the best, Dr. Cunningham." Teddy threw his arms around Emma's waist and gave her a hug she would never forget. She crouched down at eye level with him.

"You know, I think it's okay for you to call me Emma when I'm here. We are friends, right?"

Teddy beamed at being called her friend. "You bet we are, Emma." He darted out of the hallway and into another room as if he suddenly remembered something. "See you later, Emma!"

Emma stood to find Nell holding on to Nick's arm with one hand and the other over her heart. "He's such a sweet boy," Nell said. "It's been a long time since I've seen him like that with a woman outside of our family" She moved toward Emma and placed a hand on her shoulder. "Thank you, dear," she said before heading into the living room.

When Emma turned to Nick in confusion, he explained. “His mom isn’t in the picture and hasn’t been for a while. He’s not usually that affectionate with women other than Mom, Sarah, and Nat.”

“Oh Nick, I didn’t realize he didn’t have contact with his mother.” Nick looked desperate to change the subject so when he cleared his throat and didn’t elaborate, Emma didn’t push. Instead, she nodded toward the living room. “You didn’t bring me here to just hang out in the foyer, did you?”

“No, Skipper, I didn’t. Let’s go see what the rest of the circus is up to.” Nick took her hand in his and led her into the living room.

Nick couldn’t remember a time that he’d wanted to bring a woman to a family dinner. He’d never actually done it. But as Emma sat next to him at the dining room table he grew up eating at, everything seemed to be falling into place.

He was glad that they decided to join so last minute. It was the most wonderfully normal dinner, and if Nell Ewing had the gift of advanced notice, it wouldn’t have been like that at all. She served her usually roasted chicken with potatoes and vegetables, and a salad. Nell Ewing was ‘known’ for how good her simple salads were and Emma reacted predictably, praising his mother for how delicious she made greens and veggies taste.

Before dinner, Emma had eased into spending time with his family. She’d taken his father’s jokes in stride and even tossed a few back at him; which earned her points with all of his siblings.

When Teddy chose to sit with her on the couch, Nick glanced at Nathan just in time to see his nod of acceptance and appreciation.

"So Emma, how long do you think you'll be in Boone Heights?" With his mother's simple question, Nick felt his stomach sink. Apparently, everyone else around the dinner table stopped short as well. Except for Emma.

"You know, when this job first fell into my lap, I wasn't really planning on anything long-term. But Boone Heights has grown on me." Emma paused to look at Nick before continuing. "The town and the people, of course." She turned her attention back to Nell. "I haven't heard from Dr. Oliver since I got here, so following up with him is, uh...well, it's at the top of my list of priorities."

Nick let out the breath he didn't know he was holding as Emma's hand landed on his thigh under the table. It wasn't a sexual touch—it was comforting. At that moment, his heart seemed to give itself to the incredible and talented woman sitting next to him.

"Boone Heights would be lucky to have you," Ross Ewing said from the head of the table. "Permanently, I mean. If Milton has anything to say about that, you just send him my way." His dad followed the direction with a wink to his girl, and Nick realized that everything felt right.

"I hear you're becoming a regular at A Novel Idea," Natalie finally spoke up.

"I'm not sure why, but reading seems like something you do in a small town," Emma laughed. "Honestly though, it's been a nice change of pace. I like having time for reading and movies— and family dinners." Emma stopped to take a sip of the white wine his mother had served. "I wasn't sure what practicing medicine would be like outside of a big city, but it almost feels bigger and more important than patching up patients in a big-city Emergency Room in some ways.

Visiting the local shops and diners and seeing patients, and getting to check in on them outside of the office is something I never thought about in Boston. But it makes everything seem...tangible. My patients were never just charts and numbers, but now they are people I actually get to see all the time. And I like that more than I thought I would."

Sarah chimed in. "I liked being in a bigger city, but there is something about coming home. I know the 'patients' we see at the animal hospital can't talk but their owners can. I love running into a dog at the dog park that we treated for something and getting to see them happy and healthy again."

"Small towns have their charms," Natalie added, "but they're also small enough that everyone is always around and knows everything. It can be hard to escape." She quickly picked up her empty wine glass and went out to the kitchen, Nick assumed for a refill.

He looked to Nate across the table in question, but his older brother just shrugged it off. Something was up with Nat and he couldn't quite figure out what. Before he could think about it any more, Tyler changed the subject.

"So are we really not going to address the pig in the room?" He glanced over at the small crate where Bacon was laying on a pile of blankets. Teddy let out a laugh.

"Uncle Ty. You know Aunt Sarah likes strays. She's never brought a pig home before, though. I hope we can keep him."

"We've had a lot of animals in this house, but never a pig. Your aunt really outdid herself this time." Ross shook his head, having resigned himself to the whims of his youngest years ago.

"Remember the raccoon she hid in her room for weeks?" Nate asked. "She thought she was so sly...bringing it food."

"Until it bit her," Nick chimed in.

She shook her head and threw her brothers a scowl. "He was hungry and I didn't feed him fast enough."

"He was a wild animal, Sarah," Natalie added as she walked back into the room with a very full wine glass and sat back down.

Turning to look at Emma, probably feeling like she needed to explain herself, Sarah continued. "It was a baby raccoon I found in the backyard. I think the mother must have abandoned it because it was so small. I brought it in and kept it in a box I found in the garage. I tried bottle feeding it at first but it wanted food. I was giving it a piece of lettuce, then got distracted. The little baby clearly got a little frustrated and chomped on my finger. I was seven years old. I just wanted to help." Sarah threw one more exasperated look at her brothers as Natalie continued to drink her wine.

"That's when Milton patched her up and told us we needed to make sure this one didn't catch rabies from a wild animal." Nell just shook her head and smiled at her youngest.

"And all these years later, still rabies-free!" Sarah pumped her fist in the air in celebration. Emma laughed.

"Well, I'm glad you've never had rabies. I assume you stopped keeping wild animals in your bedroom though?"

"I did. That's when Dad started taking me to a local rescue. In fact, that's where I'm taking Bacon tomorrow. Which is why dinner was moved to tonight."

"I'm glad it worked out this way." Emma turned to Nell. "Thank you again for dinner. This was delicious."

"You're welcome here anytime, sweetie. I make a pretty awesome sandwich from these leftovers. You don't even need to bring Nick with you."

"Hey now. The Day After Sammie is my favorite." Nick tried to pretend he was insulted, but truthfully, he loved how well Emma seemed to fit in with his family, and how quickly they'd come to like her—not that he'd expected any different.

"Before we start talking about Day After Sammies, what does a growing boy need to do to get some dessert around here? Right, Teddy?" Tyler turned to high-five his nephew.

"Right, Uncle Ty. I'm growing too."

Emma yawned at Nick's side. At a quarter after six, he was a bit surprised. The hand that still sat resting on his thigh began to move closer to his manhood, and her fingers began to trace small deliberate circles as it got closer. When she yawned again, Nick practically sprang from the table.

"Are you tired, Emma? I know you've had a long week...and I did promise an early evening."

"Oh, I'm sure we could stay for dessert. Your mom probably worked hard on it." But she yawned again, this time even more exaggerated.

"I can save you a slice of pie for tomorrow. I know you work so hard." Nell looked a little concerned, which Emma must have picked up on.

"Just a little sleepy. I'm fine, honestly. And the sugar from the pie would probably help."

"Let's just pack you two up a slice." Ross got up from the table to presumably go and do just that. "If Nick promised you an early night we won't keep you."

Ross put a hand on Nick's shoulder as he left the dining room. Everyone seemed to be missing the accusing glances Nate sent his way and the obnoxious thumbs up that Tyler was flashing less than subtly.

Ross returned with a wrapped plate, which Nick assumed held two slices of pie.

"Alright you two, off you go," Ross said. Nick made a mental note to make sure his Father's Day gift was extra special this year. Emma flashed him a look of embarrassment as she also got up from the table.

"Thank you all for such a wonderful evening. I'm sorry we're taking off so early. I hope we can do this again."

Nell reached to hug her one last time. "You really are welcome anytime, Emma. Thank you so much for coming. It was a wonderful surprise." The rest of the family got up and quickly said their goodbyes before ushering Nick and Emma out the front door. As soon as Nick heard the latch shut he grabbed Emma and pulled her into a kiss.

"I've wanted to get my hands on you all night," he whispered into her ear.

"Do you think I was too obvious with my yawns?" Nick pulled back and saw Emma's eyes shining as she asked the question.

"I don't even care if you were. Now, can we please get out of here before my family sees me ravage you? If we stay here much longer, our first time together will be right there on the porch."

Emma gasped and took Nick's hand, nearly running to the Suburban. Nick prayed he could get her home without breaking too many traffic laws because at this point his control was paper thin and dissolving rapidly.

CHAPTER SEVENTEEN

Emma's heart nearly burst from her chest as Nick drove them home. She wasn't sure what prompted her boldness at the dinner table, but she could probably thank Katie, who acted like a cheerleader on her shoulder when it came to taking what she wanted. There was something about the way his family welcomed her with arms wide open that allowed the last link of the chain she'd erected around her heart all those months ago to fall.

She looked over at Nick as he drove and noticed his tightly clenched jaw and the vice-like grip he had on the steering wheel. Even his eyes seemed to be hooded as he drove with a laser focus on the road ahead.

Smiling to herself, Emma reached over and put a hand on his upper thigh, and felt him flinch. He never took his eyes off the road, so Emma moved her hand up higher to taunt him. The closer she got to the bulge in his jeans, the more her need for him grew.

"You're playing with fire, Skipper."

"What if I like it hot?" She shocked herself again with her boldness. His growl was evidence enough that felt everything she was feeling at that moment.

"Emma." His voice was laced with heat and the promise of things to come. Pulling into the driveway of his dark gray home, which Emma would really consider a manly cottage in the woods, Nick barely put the truck into park before he hauled Emma across the center console and onto his lap.

His fingers threaded through her hair, and his lips landed on hers like they were made for him. She said his name as quietly as a prayer, fueling the fire between them.

Nick tugged on her hair, tilting her head to the side as he began to lay kisses down her neck and across her collar bones. The sensation had Emma spinning, and she pulled herself closer to Nick, desperate to feel him—and *did. she. ever.*

His arousal pressed into her bottom and she gasped at the sensation. "I need you, Nick. I don't want to wait any longer."

The driver-side door flung open and he set Emma on the ground just long enough to step out and close it behind him. He scooped her back up like a rag doll and all but sprinted to the front door.

Inside, he didn't even bother setting her down. Making a beeline for the stairs, he nodded toward the living room. "That's the downstairs. Unless you have a pressing need to see my kitchen, we can do a proper tour later."

"There are other rooms in your house I want to see, Nick." He stopped in his tracks, as if he was too turned on to keep moving, and set her down. Emma turned to face him and looked deep into his eyes, which were pools of chocolate desire.

"Show me your bedroom. Please." The air changed from lust-filled to crackling with desire and anticipation. He barely grazed her lips with his before Emma reached for more. Instead, he took her hand and led her up the stairs.

"This way, Skipper."

As they walked up the staircase, a wave of desire started at her head and flooded down through her most sensitive parts. Her body was pulsating with arousal she'd never experienced. She felt her whole body growing warmer and her nipples tightening beneath her bra. She needed the man holding her hand like she needed air in her lungs.

She stood in his bedroom at the foot of his king-sized bed with him right behind her. He slid his arms around her waist, pulling her into him before spinning her around to face him. He reached to tuck a loose curl behind her ear.

"I really want this, Emma. I want you. You're all I've thought about since I carried my nephew into your office. I've laid in that bed, night after night, thinking about you. Imagining what it would be like to have you here with me. And here you are."

Nick's words were exactly what Emma needed to hear, and worked on her like a match to kindling.

"I want you, Nick. Near me, on me, inside me."

Emma took a small step backward until the back of her knees hit the bed. She pulled the olive green silk shirt she was wearing up and over her head and then let it slide down her arm until it hit the floor at their feet. Nick's eyes were a laser on her body, targeting the pale pink bra that barely covered her breasts. Her nipples hardened under his stare.

With deliberate slowness, Emma reached for the button on the top of her linen pants, releasing them over her legs. As the material fell to the floor, she felt the heat of Nick's stare burning her skin.

Standing in a matching bra and panties in front of him, her pulse pounded in her ears, and heat pooled at the juncture of her legs.

"Touch me. Please. I need to feel your hands on me." Emma was practically panting at this point. Her words came out huskier and more breathy than she intended, sending Nick's hands racing to her. They were strong but careful as they ran down her arms and along her torso. She closed her eyes at the sensation.

"You're beautiful, Emma," he whispered before dropping to his knees in front of her. He moved closer, starting to worship her stomach with his mouth. His tongue was hot and wet as it traced circles around her navel. She didn't think it was possible to get any more soaked than she already was, but he quickly proved her wrong.

He nipped at the skin at the top of her panties and Emma felt her whole body flush beneath him. As his hands slipped beneath the waistband, Emma tensed.

"Relax, Skipper," he said looking up to her. "I've got you." As Emma looked down at him, he took the top of her panties between his teeth and gave her a wink that would have melted them right off. He used his hands to glide the lacy fabric over the globes of her ass and then kissed a trail down her leg as he removed them completely.

"Can I taste you, Emma? I need to taste you." Nick gently pressed on her stomach until she fell backward onto the bed and then tugged at both of her legs until she was spread out in front of him, bearing her most sensitive area to him.

Nick lifted one of her legs to lavish small kisses on the inside of her knee, slowly making his way up her thigh before stopping just short of her center and moving to the other leg. Again, stopping just before meeting the part of her that needed him the most.

"Nick, please don't stop." Emma was practically begging at this point. The desire that had built in her was desperate for release.

Nick must have noticed the strain in her voice. Immediately, he spread her legs even further. In the next beat, the heat from his mouth enveloped her sex. He spread her lower lips with his fingers, giving his tongue unrestricted access to the bundle of nerves that had yearned for him for far too long.

At the first pass of his firm tongue over her clit, Emma nearly levitated off of the bed. Nick placed a hand on her stomach, keeping her firmly planted on the bed beneath him.

"Stay still, Skipper. I've got you, remember?" As he spoke, the puffs of air that hit her wetness made Emma jerk with pleasure. Those were the last words he spoke before Emma heard herself let out a ragged scream. Nick began to devour her, making love to her with his tongue and the free hand that wasn't holding her down.

Emma's hands fisted the sheets, looking for something to keep her anchored as Nick's tongue had her hurdling toward a release that she wasn't sure she'd survive; she wasn't sure she wanted to. It felt like Nick was after all of her secrets as he continued his welcomed assault on her sensitive bud.

Fireworks, stars, and flashing lights danced behind Emma's closed eyes as an intense orgasm crashed through her. Nick stayed with her, lapping at her folds until the final shudder had washed over her body. It was only when Emma felt his mouth leave her that she opened her eyes.

She propped herself up on her elbows and looked down at the man who had just taken her somewhere she hadn't known existed.

Nick was sitting back on his haunches and when their eyes connected, he gave her the sexiest wink before his eyes turned to fire.

ᚔᚔ

The sight before Nick stole the breath from his lungs. He felt like he should be gasping for air, and not just because he'd spent the last few minutes devouring Emma's sweetness—the taste still on his tongue. The satisfied look on the face of the woman who was currently running away with his heart resonated with him in a way he'd never seen before.

He knew he wasn't a slouch in the bedroom and he'd always made sure the women he was with were satisfied, but with Emma, it all seemed different. Knowing he'd given her pleasure—and that he was the reason for that look of satisfaction—was enough for him.

That is until she sat up—putting her perfect breasts in full view with nipples as hard as peaks, just asking for his mouth on them. The sexy grin playing over her mouth is what caused him to snap.

He lost all control as he sprang from the floor and tackled Emma to the bed. She laughed as her back made contact with the mattress before reaching up and pulling his head to hers. As their lips met, Nick realized that Emma could taste herself on his tongue and the moan she let out stroked the fire that was already raging inside of him.

He needed to feel her bare skin on his, which required that he pull his mouth from hers. He stood and hastily threw his clothes to the floor. Emma met his eyes as he was about to slide down his boxer briefs and the hungry look she gave him made his cock jerk as the cold air hit it. She stared appreciatively, nearly making him burst faster than he ever had before.

“God, I need you, Emma.”

“Then come and get me,” she challenged him.

Urgent, but slower than before, Nick climbed on top of her. Feeling her bare skin on him was a pleasure he’d never experienced. His dick ached to be buried deep inside of her, but he didn’t want to rush through the moment—their first time. Everything that was happening between them was bigger than sex, and it caused him to pause, and take it all in.

“You’re so sexy, Emma. So sexy.” He spoke between kisses until her hands reached his chest, pushing him over and onto his back. In a blink, Emma was straddling him, her heat so close to his dick. He froze in anticipation of what she might do next.

Her hips began to make small circles, edging close to his throbbing penis before sliding away. Smiling, Emma lowered her head and dropped small kisses on his chest. Her hair fanned out and covered her face as she trailed a path down between his pecs.

Nick let out a small yelp when her tongue flicked one of his nipples but Emma was relentless. She moved to the other nipple, her hair tickling the one that she’d just abandoned, capturing it between her teeth and giving a small tug. Nick’s hips thrust forward. The slight pain was like a bolt of lightning, heating his whole body with energy to spare.

“Emma, Emma!” With a pop, she released his nipple from her mouth and Nick exhaled in distressed relief. Returning to his chest and nipping and licking at his abs, Emma made her way exactly where he wanted her. Nick knew exactly where she was heading, and so did his dick. Neither wanted to protest.

He'd been dreaming of what it would feel like when she took him into her mouth and he was starting to fear that he might have vastly underestimated it.

Nick felt her hand, soft and gentle, begin to skim up his thigh, while the other was supporting her weight as she slid even lower down him.

"Skipper, you don't have to." He didn't want her to think she had to return some sort of favor. Her hand left his thigh and pushed back her curls so she could look up at him.

"I know, but I think I'd like to," she said with an innocence that was far hotter than she probably intended. She slowly wrapped her mouth around him, barely grazing the head of his penis as her hand left her hair and circled around his shaft. Nick knew he was about to explode. When her tongue darted out to tease the small slit, Nick had to beg for mercy.

"Fuck, fuck, fuck," he hissed. He wanted to be inside of her the first time he came, but he wasn't sure he had the willpower to stop her. Her warm mouth took more of him and he reached up to grip the bed frame, desperate to regain some control.

"Mmmmmm," she hummed around him, completely undoing what was left of him. In one swift movement, he released his hands from above, reached down, and scooped Emma back up and underneath him, positioning himself at her entrance. The shock on her face turned into desire, and there was nothing left for him to do.

"I want to be inside of you the first time you make me come. I want to feel you around me when that happens." Emma shut her eyes.

"Yes, Nick. Yes."

He leaned toward the nightstand until Emma interrupted, reaching for his arm and pulling him back to her.

"I'm clean and on birth control." Nick had never been bare with a woman. He'd never trusted anyone enough—but he trusted Emma.

"I'm clean too. But I have condoms in the drawer," he gestured to the side of his bed.

"I trust you." At that moment, Nick fell the rest of the way in love with Emma Cunningham.

With one strong thrust, he found himself seated deep inside of her.

Emma gasped at his entrance and he felt her insides quiver around him. She was warm and tight and Nick nearly lost himself. Her hips rose from the bed and into him, pushing his limits.

"Holy fuck, Emma. You feel so good. Shit." Nick began to move his hips, pulling out of her and then sliding back in. He wanted to go slow and gentle, but when she moaned, begging for "more", he was gone.

Nick began to move faster and Emma matched his pace, moving her hips in perfect sync with his.

"Yes," she cried. "Please, please don't stop." Her desperation had him so close to release that he tried to think of anything that would slow him down. Before he could make any progress, he felt Emma tighten around him and listened as her breath became more labored. Her words turned into nothing but cries and moans and he knew that she was close. Nick moved faster, thrusting into her with a consistently increasing tempo. He could feel his orgasm building in his belly but vowed to hold out for her.

"Come for me, Emma. I want to feel you come around me. Come for me." His words were soft but hard—asking and demanding at the same time. The trembles he felt became stronger as Emma's hands gripped his back—her nails digging into him. He kept going, faster and harder until she shattered beneath him.

He met her release with his own, calling out her name like a prayer. Spilling into her as his body shook from the force of his climax, his hips moved until she'd milked every last ounce of him dry.

Not wanting to disconnect from her, he wrapped his arms around her and rolled so that she was on top of him, her body still shaking from her own release. They were sated, satisfied, and totally wrapped up in each other.

ᚔᚔ

Emma dosed off for a few minutes after what she would forever remember as the most intense and exhilarating sex of her life. When Nick began to stir underneath her, she tried to slide off of him but he tightened his grip around her.

"Just another minute, Skipper," he said, and she relaxed back into him. He began to rub small circles on her back with the palm of his hands and placed gentle kisses on the top of her head. When his arms finally loosened around her, she slowly lifted herself off of him, instantly missing the feel of him inside of her. She rolled to her side and found herself facing the man who had just changed everything about her.

"Hey there," he said softly, placing a kiss on her nose.

"Hi," was all she could manage. Nick started to get up.

"I'll be right back, promise," he said as he got off the bed and walked toward the bathroom. He turned back to look at her.

"Get under those covers, Skipper. I don't want you getting cold on me." With another one of his heart-stopping winks, Nick vanished into the bathroom and shut the door.

Emma quickly sat up and, less than gracefully, snuggled under the covers. She considered reaching for her shirt, or maybe one of his, but decided against it.

In the last few hours everything she'd thought she knew about sex and relationships—and as much as it scared her to admit, love—had been turned on its head. Nick Ewing was everything she didn't know she needed, but now that she'd had him, she knew she could never be without him. She didn't want to.

It had been a whirlwind of a day, more than she'd expected. She'd loved spending time with his family and was overcome with gratitude at how warm and welcoming they had all been.

And the sex? It was earth-shattering. Nick had played her body in a way a concert pianist plays a baby grand, but as their bodies had connected, so did everything else. Emma knew this was where she was supposed to be.

Not just because of Nick, but because of what this town stood for. How the residents of Boone Heights had embraced her and trusted her. In some ways, laying between the soft sheets on Nick's bed, she felt more at home than she had in her whole life.

The door to the bathroom opened and Nick stood in the entryway. Emma drank in the gorgeous man in front of her as if she hadn't just come twice in the very near past.

"I didn't want to be presumptuous, but I know how much you like to soak in the bath so there's a tub full of warm water and bubbles waiting on you in here."

Emma felt her heart explode. "Nick, you didn't have to do that." But she was so moved by the gesture that she sent up a silent thank you that he had.

"I know, but I wanted to. I even added one of those fancy bath bombs you like." The face Nick made was the cutest, like a sheepish boy who was caught bringing his first crush flowers, after he'd picked them from someone's garden.

"But chop, chop. You don't want the water getting cold." Nick motioned her toward him. It was then that she realized he seemed totally comfortable standing naked in front of her, yet she was starting to feel a little shy. She took a deep breath, reminding herself that this man had just had his face buried between her legs, and jumped out of the bed and hurried toward him.

His bathroom was beautiful and unexpected. In shades of gray with white and black accents, it was oddly soothing while still masculine enough to belong to the man who had just taken her to the stars and back. Next to the enclosed glass shower was a beautiful white soaking tub. Just like Nick had promised, it was filled with bubbles and the scent of a bath bomb hung in the air. Nick had even lit a few candles and set them around the bathroom, giving off a soft glow in the dim light.

"Oh, Nick."

"Get on in, Skipper," he laughed.

Emma sat on the edge of the bathtub and swung both of her legs over the side and into the water before sliding all the way in. Nick grabbed a small rolled-up hand towel from the counter and walked over to her. He motioned for her to sit up a bit and placed it underneath her head like a pillow.

"Aren't you getting in too?" She had never taken a bath with a man before but was more than up for the new experience.

"Not tonight. This is just for you. Soak as long as you'd like, and I'll be out there when you're done." Nick walked out of the bathroom and shut the door behind him. A moment later soft music began to play out of the speaker Emma noticed sitting on a shelf over the toilet. Emma recognized Adele's "Easy On Me" and began to hum along. A few songs later Emma was beginning to feel a tad pruney. She pulled the drain plug and as the water started draining there was a soft knock on the door.

"Towels are to your left and my closet is on the right. Grab some sweats from the shelves. My t-shirts are out here, though. I'll leave one for you at the door."

The man had thought of everything. She dried off with the soft towel he'd left for her, and began to wonder if she was spending the night. That little bit of anxiety buried itself into her stomach, giving her butterflies.

She tip-toed into the closet and grabbed a pair of gray sweatpants, rolling them up several times so they'd stay up, before hanging the used towel up on an empty hook by the shower and opening the door to Nick's bedroom. A long-sleeved Ewing Brothers' Construction t-shirt was waiting for her, which she quickly slipped over her head. That's when she noticed Nick laying on his bed in his own pair of sweats and a cocktail in his hand.

"Nick," she walked forward shyly, "thank you for that. It was so sweet of you."

"There's a glass of wine and a bottle of water on the nightstand for you. I wasn't sure which you'd prefer." He looked at her and smiled. "And you're welcome. I know it looks like I probably planned for tonight to end up this way and I'm not going to lie, I've given it a lot of thought." He paused. "I mean, *a lot*. But I would have been happy just having dinner and a glass of wine with you and spending the evening talking on my deck."

Emma picked up the wine and took a sip. The red liquid, and Nick's honesty, took away the last bit of shyness she was feeling.

"I'm glad tonight worked out like it did." Nick held up the covers on her side of the bed and Emma slid in and snuggled up next to him. "I loved spending time with your family. And the rest of it was...incredible. More than incredible."

"More than incredible," he repeated as he pulled her face toward his and placed a soft kiss on her lips.

They fell into a night full of kisses, touches, talking, and a few bouts of sleep in between. As Emma saw the sun rising through Nick's window, she knew she'd never be more content than she was here, with Nick, in the place that now felt like home.

CHAPTER EIGHTEEN

The next few weeks were better than Nick could have imagined. Work stayed busy after Nathan secured a large contract for a few historical remodels in a nearby town. Evenings were spent with Emma—either at his place or hers—sometimes out to dinner, and even Sunday dinners at the Blue House. When the sun went down, they ended up in a bedroom, just the way they liked it. Nick wasn't sure things could get any better.

Pulling into the lot at work, he found his brother already there. He grabbed the coffee cups he'd brought from Luke's and went inside, noticing the extra bounce in his step that the cafe owner had mentioned that morning.

After a quick hello to Megan at the front desk, he walked back into the massive office he shared with Nathan—who was just hanging up the phone at his desk.

"Hey, Nate, what's up?" Nick asked, handing his brother the coffee.

"I just got off the phone with Nat. Something is up with her, Nick. She's been acting strange for weeks now."

He'd noticed but was so wrapped up in everything with Emma that he hadn't made a point to check on her—at least not as quickly as he normally would have.

"I've noticed." He shrugged sheepishly, knowing there wasn't a good enough excuse. "I've been a little wrapped up in my own stuff...I haven't asked her about it. Have you had any luck?"

"So we're saying that you and Emma are a little wrapped up? Is that what we're calling it?" Nathan laughed and rolled his eyes, taking the stress ball from his desk and whipping it at his brother.

"Nope. We're not talking about that right now; we're talking about Natalie."

"What is it with her?" Nathan asked. "It started after the auction, and it's gotten worse over the past few weeks." Nick was a bit taken aback.

"You're not saying it has something to do with me and Emma, are you?" His sister had only seemed happy for him and the new light in his life. Did he have it all wrong?

"Shut up, man. You know that's not what I meant. Not everything is about you—or Emma." He said her name in the sing-songy voice that the girls used as teenagers whenever they teased their brothers about a girl.

"Well let's go over what we need to, and then I'll give her a call." Nick picked up his notebook and pen, settled into his chair, and swiveled it to face his brother. Removing the wall that separated their offices, and working side-by-side, had happened almost by accident a few years before, but it was one of the best things they'd done.

The brothers ran through the new contract they'd picked up and planned out the upcoming projects on the docket. Nathan turned to face him and they ran through the new contract they'd just picked up, other projects on the docket, and a few outstanding bids that they had in waiting. Mike McKinney, their top sales guy, was already working on the bids. They summarized the final details on the projects in progress, and that was that. They'd worked out a reliable and smooth routine over the years, and it never let them down.

"Alright, I'm going to head out to the Sampson site and see how Steve and the crew are doing. Still on for lunch?" Nate stood and stretched his neck.

"Sure. Just grab something from the diner on your way back." The boys knew each other's food and drink orders without having to ask.

Nathan nodded to his brother and tossed his keys into the air as he walked out, leaving Nick with a chance to call Natalie and dig into what had his older sister in such a fit. As the phone rang Nick thought about the timeline of Nat's frustration and realized it had started closer to the auction than he'd realized. He tapped his pen on the desk while he waited for her to answer.

"Hello?" She sounded tired.

"Hey, Nat, what's up?" He tried to sound extra cheerful

"Not much. Did you need something Nick?" The way she seemed to brush off his call had him worried.

"No, I was just calling to talk. We haven't done a lot of that recently." He knew better than to pry, but it was his responsibility as a brother to take care of her. Waiting for an explanation, he paced behind his desk.

"I guess." She was starting to sound annoyed. "I've just been busy—nothing newsworthy to report."

"Want to talk about it? We can grab a cup of coffee, or maybe some Brownie Brittle ice cream?" He knew the way to her heart.

"Who said it was anything that required Brownie Brittle?" She spat. Nat's go-to ice cream flavor was known to solve all stresses—and even heartbreaks—over the years. This was so unlike his sister; Nick was desperate for answers, even if he had to get aggressive.

"Nat, something is going on." He tried to sound gentle and empathetic, but her brothers were known to cut to the chase. "What is it? Whatever it is, you know I'll be there for you."

A quiet sniffle came through the speaker, but just as he considered that she might be crying, she replied.

"Nothing I want to talk about, okay? Can you just leave it at that? I know Nathan probably told you to call me, but it's nothing." She paused before adding quietly, "it's nothing I want to talk about."

He knew it wasn't the time to push her. "Okay, Natalie. I'll stop for now. But I know something is going on. I'm here when you're ready to talk about it."

"Bye, Nick," she said as she ended the call. The defeat in her voice was crushing, and Nick realized that this was the first conversation he'd had with a sibling over the past three weeks that hadn't revolved around him or Emma.

Emma collapsed into her chair as her mind circled with thoughts of Nick for the thousandth time that day. Her feelings for him were relentless, and though she'd made the decision weeks prior to make her move to Boone Heights a permanent one, she still hadn't done anything to put the plan into action. When she finally mustered the courage, she would need to get in touch with her uncle and see if he might consider keeping her in the clinic full-time.

She hadn't yet told Nick of her plans to relocate; he hadn't asked and she didn't feel entirely ready to share the idea—concerned in part that it might scare him off. She didn't have much confidence in gauging a man's opinion on things like that—not that Kyle had set the bar too high.

With a sudden gusto, Emma opened a new email and began to compose a note to Dr. Oliver—or, Uncle Milton. As she typed, she reconsidered how to address him, and settled on 'Milton'—personal, but not *too* personal.

Her fingers flew over the keyboard as she thanked him for the—what had become life-changing—opportunity. She shared her desire to stay in town, referencing the relationships she'd formed and how she'd fallen in love with the personal attention she was able to give her patients in the small town. She introduced the idea of staying at the clinic and asked if there was any capacity in which that might be a possibility. She ended the email with a suggestion that—when he was back in town—they could sit down and talk about why they didn't know each other. There was a story there, and she wanted to hear it from him.

Signing her email with a simple, 'Emma,' she hit send before she could chicken out. Oddly enough, she didn't feel a wild panic rise in her chest like she'd expected. If anything, she felt a sense of peace and belonging that she hadn't felt in a long time—ever since she nearly lost her ability to practice medicine, thanks to Kyle.

She closed her laptop, hoping to hear back from Milton sooner rather than later. She'd need to tell Nick about the idea to stay in

Boone Heights, and sent up a silent prayer that he'd be as excited about the idea as she was. Nick wasn't the sole reason for her decision, but he was certainly the icing on the life-change cake.

A knock on the door brought her back to the present.

"Come in," she said as Katie opened the door and walked in, closing it quickly behind her.

"What's up, buttercup?" Katie flopped down into one of the chairs opposite Emma's desk.

"Actually, I just sent off an email to my uncle," she paused and corrected herself, "to Dr. Oliver, letting him know I'd be interested in making my position here a permanent one." A squeal of glee erupted from the tiny blonde.

"For real, Ems? That's amazing. This is the perfect place for you." Katie was practically vibrating with excitement. "I've brought up filling the nursing position permanently to Annie." Her eagerness was palpable.

"You really want to stay here, too?" She'd never lived separately from her best friend and didn't want to start now. The thought that Katie might stay as well helped to soften the idea.

"I do. I've really fallen in love with this place...and the people here." She wagged her eyebrows up and down. "Gorgeous men seem to ooze out of every street corner here," Katie admitted as she sat up straight and stared at Emma. "Speaking of gorgeous men, how is Nick? Any juicy updates to share?"

Emma had shared a few details over wine and a movie but kept most of the private details to herself.

"Nothing you don't already know." She exhaled and smiled. "I really like him, Katie." If the wistful tone of her voice was a surprise to her friend she didn't show it. "I realize I don't have a ton of experience when it comes to relationships, but this feels...bigger somehow. It's like Nick is this missing piece I never even knew I needed until I found him."

"Emma," Katie eased, "you're falling in love with him."

"I think I've already completely fallen." It was the first time she'd admitted it out loud, and it was just as freeing as hitting send on the email to her uncle only moments ago.

Katie's hands raced to her heart. "I'm so happy for you, Emma. You deserve this—and more. I know we've always hated the whole 'everything happens for a reason' thing, but it almost feels like everything that happened with Kyle is what got you here—to Boone Heights, to the clinic, and to Nick."

Emma smiled, but before she could answer, her phone rang and Nick's name flashed across the screen with a selfie they'd taken laying in bed a few nights before.

"Speaking of Nick..." Emma swiped to answer the call. "Hi, you. Are your ears burning? We were just talking about you."

"Are you at the clinic?" He interrupted.

"I am. Is something wrong? Is it Teddy?" Concern bubbled violently in her chest.

"I just got off the phone with Nate. Our foreman, Steve, got hurt on a site this morning. He didn't give me too many details...but I think it's bad Emma. It's some sort of head wound."

"Oh my God, Nick. What can I do?"

"I told him to go straight to the clinic and said I'd call to let you know they're on the way. I'm heading that way too."

"Of course. Did he tell you anything else? Was Steve conscious? Any other injuries?" Emma began to put together a mental checklist of what they'd need in the exam room but Katie was already moving a step ahead of her.

"Put it on speaker so I can hear too," her friend mouthed. Emma hit the speaker button and Nick's voice filled the room.

"Honestly, Nate didn't say much—just that Steve seems a little confused. He was talking in the background, but I don't know if he was knocked out or if anything else is wrong."

"Nick, it's Katie. I'm going to go and get everything set up in an exam room and let Annie know to send them back as soon as they get here. We'll take care of everything." Katie ran for the door before turning back to add, "I'll put them in room three—it's the largest."

"Nick, I'm going to help Katie set up and I'll see you when you get here, okay?" She hated that she could hear the stress in his breath.

"See you soon." He hung up and she reached for a pair of scrubs in the drawer behind her desk. She changed quickly and left her office to meet Katie.

Nick was overwhelmed with the deja-vu he felt as he pulled into the clinic parking lot. The stressful circumstances were so similar to the ones that brought him in a few months before. His brother's truck was parked at the front door, and he parked in a nearby spot to join them inside where he found Nate on the phone in the waiting room. Everyone else must have already gone back to Emma.

Nate raised a finger to Nick instructing him to wait.

"He's with the doctor now, Martha. I sent John to come and get you from the house—he should be there any minute." Nick realized he was talking to Steve's wife of over twenty-five years. He never would have even thought to call the man's wife of twenty-five years and was grateful that his brother had the wherewithal to handle the chaos.

"Okay, I'll see you soon. I promise he's in excellent hands." Nate slipped his phone back into his pocket and ran a hand through his hair in frustration.

"What happened?" Nick asked.

Nathan fell into the empty seat next to him and just shook his head. "It was such a freak accident. One of the beams they'd just secured—it just fell. It hit Steve on the head, and I think when he fell he landed on his arm. His arm looks worse than his head, man."

"He wasn't wearing a hard hat?" Steve was known to take every safety protocol on a job site, and Nick was shocked at the situation.

"He only took it off for a second. I have no idea why. Shitty timing."

"Accidents are a risk of the job, Nate. We take every precaution we can. Emma will take care of it—he'll be alright." Nick rested a hand on his brother's shoulder. They'd never had an accident on a project, and now they'd had two in a matter of months. The idea made Nick nauseous.

"Well, I have to admit. The first aid kits you put in the trucks really came in handy. There was gauze in there that we used on his head and an ice pack for his arm." Nate seemed proud. "That was really a good idea, dude. I know I gave you crap about wasting time, but you made the right call."

Nick wanted to smile, but he didn't have it in him. He was glad he'd been so adamant about improving their safety measures after Teddy was hurt, but was frustrated that they had to use one of the kits so soon.

Annie approached the boys in the reception area with a clipboard in her hands. "Hi boys," she said gently. "I hate to ask right now but since this is a work accident, I was hoping I could get one of you to complete this paperwork and make sure your insurance is up to date." She hesitantly offered the clipboard to them. Nate took it.

"I'll take care of it, Annie. I know it needs to be done. Is it okay if I go out to the truck? I have a copy of all our paperwork in the glove box."

"Of course, sweetheart. Take all the time you need."

"You don't have an update, do you?" Nick asked as Nate walked out.

"He was awake when they got here, but there sure was a lot of bleeding. Emma's making him comfortable now, but if she needs any help, we'll have to get him over to the hospital in Frederick." Nick had assumed as much but he hated having it confirmed.

"Thanks, Annie," he said, resting his head in his hands.

"I'll be behind at the desk if you need anything."

Not much happened over the next hour. Nate came back inside with the paperwork for Annie. Martha arrived with John and was taken back to her husband. Nick ran through all the ways the accident could have been prevented but had no answers without having been there to see it happen.

Nick, Nathan, and John paced the waiting room until Annie returned.

"Alright, boys. Looks like his arm is broken. Dr. Cunningham is setting a temporary cast for now, but he'll have an orthopedic appointment in a few days. She's stitched up his head, and he has a slight concussion...but there's no indication of anything worse." The men let out a collective sigh of relief, and Nick fought the urge to high-five his brother.

"So he can go home from here?" Nate asked.

"That's what it looks like."

"Thank you so much for getting Martha here," Nate said to John. "I really appreciate you. Why don't you head home? We can catch up on site plans tomorrow."

"How about you meet us at the office tomorrow morning," Nick added.

John shook the brothers' hands and got ready to go. "Happy to help, fellas. I'll see you in the morning." Annie walked the man out the door.

"This could have been so much worse, Nick."

"I know, man," Nick answered. "We've never had any problems before. This is nuts." His frustration was clear as day.

"Well...accidents are bound to happen." A knowing look filled Nate's eyes. "This is about Teddy, isn't it?"

"Probably. I just feel like so many things could have been avoided recently."

"Nick," Nathan said, placing a hand on his brother's shoulder and looking him in the eyes. "We had everything we needed today because of all the work you did after Teddy's accident. You took something bad and made it good—just like Mom always does."

Lowering his hand and relaxing his stance, Nate continued. "Steve is going to be fine. Just like Teddy."

Nick shook his head, hoping to clear the fog that had settled over him. "You're right. It was an accident, and we were prepared."

"I'm going to head to the office and get up with the insurance company. I'm sure there are going to be questions and we need to come up with a new plan for that site. We'll need a few days' worth of repairs before we get back to it. Are you going to wait here for Emma?"

Nick wanted to, but he also didn't want to overwhelm her. "I think I'm just going to send her a text and head out. She'll call me when she can." Turning to the desk to say goodbye to Annie, Nick couldn't shake the feeling that another shoe was about to drop. He left the clinic with his brother and tried to push the anxious thoughts from his mind and focus instead on what he could control—like how he might give Emma a proper thank you later that night.

CHAPTER NINETEEN

Emma drove down Main Street and couldn't help but smile. She was sipping on coffee from one of Nick's travel mugs—which she'd made a habit of since she'd been spending so many nights at his house. They'd only missed a few nights together since she'd first slept over, and she had no plans to miss a night with him again any time soon.

Emma had seen Steve for a follow-up and he seemed to be healing well. He was scheduled to have his arm re-set in a hard cast by a specialist in Frederick a few days later, and all signs of his concussion seemed to have passed. The portable x-ray machine had seemed like overkill in their office at first but had proven its worth in just one emergency visit—saving them all a trip to the emergency room.

The next sip of coffee reminded her of how thorough Nick had been as he thanked her again last night, making sure—quite a few times—that she knew how much he appreciated her.

Being with Nick was like nothing she'd ever thought she'd experience—and certainly better than anything she'd ever felt with Kyle. Nick found new ways to impress her each day, and proved over and over again that he was a better man than Kyle ever was or would be. Nick was trustworthy and loyal and he made her—and her heart—feel safe and protected.

In fact, the entire Ewing family had opened their arms and embraced her so easily that she felt an overwhelming sense of contentment. She still hadn't heard from her uncle but decided to give it a few more days before she reached out again—especially since she didn't even know where he was or why he'd left in the first place. Hopefully, those answers would come when they finally had a chance to connect.

Emma pulled into her parking spot at the clinic, finished the last bit of her coffee, grabbed her bag, and went inside to start her day. After a few quiet days, things seemed to be picking up again. A late spring flu had invaded Boone Heights and the waiting room was full of patients feeling under the weather. By two in the afternoon, Emma finally had a chance to catch her breath and went to her office for a drink.

She'd just sat down and cracked the tab on a can of her favorite refrigerated latte when Annie stepped in.

"Do you have a moment, Dr. Cunningham?" Annie was often quiet but seemed even more timid than Emma had gotten used to.

"Of course, please come in." She offered her a seat across from her and braced herself for what she assumed was stressful news.

"Normally, I wouldn't bother you with any type of billing or insurance issue, but I've run this policy several times and I'm getting pushback from the insurance company." Annie handed a stack of papers across the desk. Emma took a quick glance at them, seeing that they were about Steve's accident.

"You know, I'm not nearly as familiar with billing in a small practice as I should be. Can you explain the issue to me?" Emma's heart started to beat faster—just the idea of an insurance issue was enough to have her flashing back to everything she'd been through less than a year ago.

"Of course, dear. It seems that there might be an issue with the boy's company plan—the worker's compensation, in particular." Annie looked to be getting more and more uncomfortable, and worry settled deep in the pit of Emma's stomach.

"What kind of issue?" She knew she had to ask, even if she really didn't want to know the answer—and judging by the silence, Annie didn't want to explain. "Annie, what kind of issue? Please, just tell me. Be direct." Emma was probably a bit more firm than the office manager deserved, but her stress was taking over.

Annie took a deep breath, seemingly to center herself before she began. "According to the insurance company, they believe that Ewing Brothers Construction has committed...f-fraud. They denied the claim on the grounds that the company did not provide an accurate count of full-time employees, and misclassified some as contract employees to save on costs. They've denied the claim, and opened an investigation."

The air rushed from Emma's lungs as if she'd just taken a gut punch from a world-class boxer. Her head was spinning.

Could this be happening again? Could someone I trusted, someone I loved, have committed fraud? How could Nick have done this? And then to bring his employee to me for treatment? Did he expect me to cover for him?

She hadn't given it much thought at the time, but the hospital in Frederick was probably closer to the job site they'd come from. Still, they had opted for the clinic instead. *Why?* Emma stared at Annie for what felt like an eternity, unable to form a response. She stayed firmly seated at her desk, despite her urge to run.

Finally, she cleared her throat. "Thank you for bringing this to me, Annie. What are the next steps for us? For the clinic, I mean." Emma wasn't just a girlfriend in distress; she had a business to run, and she couldn't allow herself to break down over a man. Not again. Not because of this.

"Typically, when an insurance company denies a claim, we send out a bill."

"Alright then. That's what needs to be done." Emma felt like a robot going through the motions. She was numb—she had to be to keep the floodgates from opening. She stood and walked around her desk, returning the paperwork to Annie. "Is there anything else you need from me?"

Annie took them and stood. "No, Dr. Cunningham. I'll take care of everything." She started to leave before turning back to Emma. "I'm sorry," she said softly and then left, pulling the office door shut behind her.

Emma collapsed into the chair Annie had just abandoned after relaying the news that threatened to shatter everything she'd been building—or, rebuilding—the past few months. Shock, anger, sadness, and confusion fought for her attention, but the only feeling she could really define at that moment was the heartbreak. She'd misread the man. *How had this happened...again?* Tears fell from her eyes and she couldn't even move to wipe them away. If she'd stopped to eat lunch that day, she probably would have puked.

This was a man who built fences for retired librarians and had care packages delivered to her after a long day at work. The man who held her night after night, sharing his thoughts and secrets with her. The man who finally made her feel something again—who allowed her to trust again. The tears fell faster and a sob escaped from her lips.

Kyle's actions hurt and angered her. But this? This felt like the worst kind of betrayal. This cut was deep and wide and she knew it was going to leave a scar that would never fully heal.

Just when she thought she couldn't hurt more, her phone buzzed with a text from Nick. *Of course.* Before the screen went black, she saw the beginning of his message and knew that she'd never be able to hear or read the word 'Skipper' again without feelings of dismay.

She laid her head on the desk and cried until there were no tears left.

Nick checked his phone *again*. Emma still hadn't replied to his text and he was starting to worry. She didn't always answer immediately, but within an hour or so he usually heard something. He thought about calling the clinic but didn't want to overreact.

He even thought about asking Nate to send him a text message just to make sure that his phone was working. The flashing cursor on his computer screen taunted him as he reviewed new bids and sent notes to project managers. But while he waited, he couldn't even remember what he'd been working on. Feeling like he was losing his mind, he stood and began to pace the space behind his desk.

Nate threw his pen onto his own desk. "Alright, I can't do this anymore. What is going on with you Nick?"

"Huh?" The exasperated look on Nathan's face was straight out of the Nell Ewing handbook, paired perfectly with the animated hand gestures he began to make. "All of this...checking your phone every sixty seconds, the pacing, the finger tapping on your computer but not actually typing. What gives?" The accusation reminded Nick to check his phone again. "That. Right there, man. What is going on?" Nathan closed in and took the phone from his brother's hand, tossing it on a nearby chair before placing both hands on his brother's shoulders with just enough force to keep Nick still and focused.

"It's nothing," Nick said, shrugging out of his brother's grip. "I just haven't heard from Emma in a while and it's not sitting right with me. She normally replies when I send her a text and she hasn't for most of the day."

"A woman. You're acting like this over a woman." Nathan's shoulders began to shake with silent laughter. "I never thought I'd see the day. Nicholas Francis Ewing all a flutter over a woman..."

"Don't be an ass, Nathan. I'm not fluttering. I just have a feeling something isn't right, and I'm not sure what to do."

"Did you call her? Or the clinic?" Nick knew that both of those were rational responses after hearing Nate say them out loud.

"I mean, I didn't want to seem obsessive."

"Well, then it's certainly a good thing we don't have cameras in our office because nothing about your behavior the past few hours has been normal."

"You're not helping." Nick stepped around his brother and went to get his phone from its landing spot. Still blank, he set the ringer volume as high as it would go.

"Just call the clinic, dude." Nathan slipped his laptop into his brown leather messenger bag and tossed it over his shoulder. "I'm going to go sit in the conference room because I'm not getting anything accomplished here with you."

As Nate left the office, Nick rolled his eyes and settled back into his chair with his elbows on his knees and his phone waiting in his hands in front of him. He pulled up the number for the clinic and called.

"Boone Heights Medical Clinic, this is Annie. How can I help you?" Nick cringed at the lack of self-restraint he suddenly felt.

"Hi Annie, it's Nick Ewing. I was just calling to see if Emma...I mean Dr. Cunningham...had a second to talk. I'm guessing you've had a busy day, so I understand if she's busy." Nick mentally slapped his forehead. He sounded like such a twit.

"Oh, Nick. Hi." The hesitancy in Annie's voice gave Nick pause, and he didn't like it. He waited silently, hoping that Annie would continue. When she finally spoke up again, her words were rushed.

"I was going to call you later today. We, uh...well, we've had some issues with the insurance billing from when Steve was in. The claim...well, the claim was denied, leaving you as the responsible party."

He barely noticed a sigh of relief when she finished her explanation. He went from worrying about Emma to being confused about the situation. Why did the clinic tell him this and not his own office manager?

"Oh...well, I'd be happy to connect you with Megan. She handles all of these things and knows how to handle everything with our insurance and billing anyway. Why were you going to call me?"

"It is a bit more complicated than a small billing issue," Annie replied in a small voice. Now Nick was just getting pissed off. The clinic had a problem with their insurance and Emma still hadn't called. None of it was adding up.

"Annie, what is going on? I have no clue what you're talking about or why you'd need me to deal with it instead of the person at my office who actually understands all of that crap. And is Emma available? You never answered my question." Nick felt his eye starting to twitch and a thin layer of sweat began to form on his temples as his heart nearly exploded.

"Nick, Emma is here but I think it's best if you just leave her be for a bit. Unfortunately, the insurance issue is far more complicated than your office manager should have to deal with." Annie paused for a deep breath. "They've denied your claim on the basis of fraud, Nick. It's serious...and much bigger than you simply needing to pay a bill with the clinic."

Confusion washed over him like the ocean was dragging him out to see in a tangle of kelp. *Fraud? Did Annie say fraud?* Nick had more questions than answers.

"Annie, I need to go. Please fax over any information you can and I'll get to the bottom of this, but I can assure you that Ewing Brothers' Construction has never—and will never—commit any type of fraud." He moved to hang up but quickly added. "And please tell Emma that I called. And tell her that I'll talk to her later today." Nick hung up and nearly sprinted from his office to the conference room in hopes that Nathan would have an idea about what was happening—because Nick sure as hell didn't have a clue.

After regaining her composure, Emma made it through the rest of her scheduled patients before leaving the office a few minutes early. Her emotion and tone left Katie confused but conveyed the message that she wasn't up for questions—and she didn't ask.

As the sun set, Emma sat curled up on the sofa in an old Jonas Brothers' concert tee and flannel pajama bottoms that she'd had since college. She sat and stared into space, swirling her glass of wine and forgetting about her pint of ice cream now melting on the coffee table.

Her mind flashed back to the days and weeks after Kyle's betrayal came to light. This feeling was familiar—too familiar—and she couldn't help but kick herself for letting it all happen again. But, here she was—and worse this time. At least after everything with Kyle she'd drank the wine and ate the ice cream, inducing a decent night's sleep.

Her cottage was quiet enough to hear a pin drop, and her tears had stopped flowing—possibly because she had no tears left to cry. Several missed calls and text messages displayed on her phone, but she'd turned off the notifications after Katie called the fourth time. She couldn't even begin to count the calls from Nick, and she didn't want to. The pain was too real and too raw. She felt as if a vise had clamped around her heart, wringing the pain out of her as it tightened.

She jumped and groaned at the sudden pounding on her door, not in the mood to deal with Katie. She knew that her best friend only wanted to help, but she'd left Katie in the dark and needed to keep her there just a bit longer. She stood from the couch and walked to the door to get Katie to stop the pounding.

Her world stopped spinning as she opened the door to find that it wasn't Katie on the porch, but the man responsible for the ache in her chest. Illuminated by the porch light, his fist was raised in the air, clearly ready to beat on the door again.

When the shock of seeing Nick on the doorstep instead of Katie wore off, Emma realized that the man in front of her was only the shell of Nick Ewing—not the man she loved. His eyes were covered in devastation and his free hand balled in a tight fist at his side. His face sat clenched in a tight hold that only highlighted his jawline, which—under different circumstances—would have been sexy as hell. The air around him, charged with anger, fear, and uncertainty, caused Emma to take a step back.

"Emma," he said curtly.

"Nick," she replied, softly as she willed herself to not cry at the mere sight of him—and especially not in front of him.

"We need to talk, Emma."

She steeled herself against the pull she felt toward him.

"I don't think there's much to say, Nick. You should probably leave." But instead of moving forward to close the door, Emma found herself taking another step backward.

Nick followed, crossing the threshold and moving closer to her. She matched him step for step, backing away as he closed her door.

"I'm not sure what the hell is going on, Emma. You ignore my texts, and then I hear from your office manager that my company is being accused of fraud—which is bullshit, by the way. But you're icing me out, and I don't know why. What is going on?"

Emma turned away. She didn't want to do this—not again. She closed her eyes but was defeated by the faded scent of his cologne, putting flashes of them in bed together into her mind. But, Nick broke her trust. He did something illegal and hoped to use her to cover it up. She refused to let the way she loved him cloud her judgment and ability to reason.

With Kyle, the happy memories never surfaced after his betrayal. Perhaps that was because her medical license was truly on the line then. Thankfully, she'd been able to avoid that this time around.

With a renewed sense of righteous anger, Emma spun on her heels to face him.

"Look, Nick. I'm not sure what exactly you're into with your business but I refuse to be a part of it." The confused look on Nick's face may have stopped her moments ago but now she just pushed on. "And beyond that, you wrapped me up in it and brought your injured employee to my clinic. I'm not sure what kind of deal you had with my uncle, or if this is just how small towns operate, but I will not get involved with fraudulent activity. I never have, and I never will." The conviction she'd felt after Kyle was caught for his crimes began to reemerge. "I trusted you, Nick. Not just to do the right thing by me, but to do the right thing in general." With a quick breath and one last wave of sadness, she finished. "And now it's time for you to go."

Nick opened his mouth to speak but, before he could say a word, Emma walked around him and opened the door.

"Goodbye, Nick." There was so much finality in those two words. She felt the onslaught of tears threatening to spill from her eyes and willed them to stay put—at least until he was gone.

"Emma," he turned around and shook his head.

"Goodbye," she repeated, forcefully.

"This isn't the end of us, Emma. It's not."

The second that he was out of her home and on the porch, Emma shut the door behind him. Only then did she allow herself to collapse on the floor, tears silently streaming down her face for the second time that day.

She had no choice but to give in to the pain and the loss. She'd fallen totally in love with Nick Ewing, only to be fooled again. This was a heartbreak she wouldn't be able to outrun. She just hoped she could survive it.

Nick stood, shell shocked, on Emma's front porch. He was nearly certain that he heard her cry out as she slammed the door, but he couldn't be sure. He wasn't sure of anything.

He still had no idea what had caused their insurance company to flag their account, but after working with Nate all afternoon and failing miserably to contribute anything helpful, his older brother had sent him home and called in their father for reinforcement.

Nick couldn't go home. He needed to see Emma. He knew that the repercussions of this accusation could be life-altering but he needed to see her—to figure out what was going on with her and why she was so upset with him instead of supporting him.

He couldn't believe his ears when she accused him of committing fraud—even worse, that she believed it to be true. The thought that she also believed he'd tried to bring her into it, to hurt her professionally, left him stunned. By the time he could process everything she said, he was being kicked out the door. Everything had gotten so out of control, and he had no idea how to stop it all. It felt like the worst type of carousel ride, and she'd just left him there to suffer alone.

As he stood with her door at his back, he felt more lost than he'd ever felt before. His slow and heavy steps back to the Suburban were dreadful, and as he turned over the engine he considered calling his brother but decided instead to go home.

How could Emma believe that I would do something like that? Had he misunderstood their connection? Had he felt something so deep for her that he had drawn an imaginary bond between them? He considered the idea that she couldn't possibly feel for him the way he felt for her. If she did, she never would have—or could have—accused him of what she just had. The idea that Emma believed he was capable of hurting her that way shook him to his core, and angered him intensely—not with her, but himself. He should be far more concerned with the ramifications of this mess on his business, his livelihood, than on a woman who clearly never trusted him in the first place.

Instead, all he could feel was the way he loved her—the way she made him feel. He'd done nothing wrong, and he was going to make her believe it. He had to.

The idea of not fighting—for the construction company or for Emma—wasn't one that Nick would entertain. He'd resolve this mess with their insurance company, and then he'd make Emma listen to him. He'd show her that he hadn't done anything wrong and that he never had, and never would do anything that would possibly threaten her personally or professionally. He would tell her that he loved her.

But first, he had to figure out why she'd reacted that way to such a crazy suggestion of betrayal. He knew her better than that, and it didn't make sense. Nick made a tight u-turn at the next intersection and started back toward his office. Going home was not an option. Fighting for everything he'd never known he wanted was the only option—and that's exactly what he was going to do.

CHAPTER TWENTY

The following week passed in a haze. During the day, Emma went to the clinic, treated patients, and went home. At night, she sat and stared into space.

Katie tried to help. She brought wine and ice cream and movies, but Emma didn't want any of that—she wanted to wake up and realize that it had all just been a nightmare. Checking the status of the bill Nick's company had with her clinic stopped her every time, confirming yet again that it was all just too much to handle.

She expected Nick to reach out to her, begging for forgiveness or some opportunity to explain himself. She expected him to deny the accusations—that's what Kyle had done. Over and over, he denied all wrongdoing. Nick Ewing, however, never even tried. Other than that first day, Emma hadn't heard a word from him, and in some ways, the silence stung even more. The idea that he could just walk away from her had her realizing that he was not the man she thought he was.

After a week of silence, an alert from the phone sent her jumping from the couch. Disappointment crashed through her when she saw that it was only Katie checking in. She reminded her friend that she was fine, and put the phone away again.

This wasn't like her. She didn't act this way when everything ended with Kyle, and they'd been together for years. Nick Ewing had only been in her life for a few months, and the betrayal was devastating. She couldn't let it continue to keep her down.

With a breath of confidence, she picked herself up from the sofa and walked to the refrigerator—the emptiness frightening. She glanced at her watch and decided that she had just enough time for a trip to the supermarket.

As she parked and glanced in the rearview mirror, she gasped at the reflection that looked back at her. Her curly hair was wild, her eyes puffy, and her cheeks stained with mascara and red blushing splotches. She pulled a hair tie from her purse to tame the curls and the emergency makeup her mother taught her to carry when she was younger to hide the darkness underneath her eyes. She didn't really care what she looked like, but she was still the physician in town and didn't want the residents of Boone Heights to see her so disheveled.

Confident that she looked acceptable for a brief walk in public, she walked inside, grabbing a cart from the corral and waving to Becky Kennedy and Bella, who stood in the checkout line.

She walked mindlessly through the produce section and grabbed a few fruits and vegetables before pacing the dry goods aisles for a full kitchen restock. She wouldn't know what she'd grabbed if anyone had asked, but she kept moving, and just went with the motions. In the freezer section, she tossed in a few extra pints of ice cream, well aware that she wasn't totally through the ice-cream stage of grief when Tyler Ewing approached.

"Hi, Emma. It's good to see you." The formality in his voice was a clear indication that he knew something had happened with his brother.

"Nice to see you too, Ty. I hope you've been doing well." Her tight grip on the shopping cart began to feel clammy as she processed the emotions of an unexpected run-in with a member of Nick's family—a family she'd grown to love as much as she loved the man they belonged to. She plastered a quick smile across her face in hopes of hiding her true feelings from the youngest Ewing brother.

Ty nodded down at her cart. "You've got the staples—ice cream and wine." He looked back up at her with a visible understanding that she was a walking heartbreak in the freezer aisle.

"Katie and I love junk food on a girl's night," she replied, hoping she'd covered well enough.

"Of course," he said with a sympathetic nod. "Well, I should head out. I promised Mom I'd pick up a few things for..." He trailed off without finishing, but when Emma glanced at the shopping basket he carried, she saw that it was filled with caffeinated beverages, protein bars, apples, and bananas—interesting essentials that were not likely for Nell Ewing.

"Of course, don't keep your mom waiting on my account. Have a good day, Ty." Before he could answer, Emma turned in the opposite direction and walked away.

She'd survived her first interaction with a member of the Ewing family—an essential step in moving forward. She'd made it through the moment but didn't want it to happen again any time soon which was more than likely in Boone Heights.

She knew that she would never get away from it all, and decided to head home to send one more email—even though she'd yet to get a response from the first.

⧻⧻⧻

Nick looked up from his computer to find Ty walking in with bags full of groceries. At the desk next to him, his father paged through documents while Nate pulled up old insurance claims from years prior. The entire week had been a complete disaster, but they worked tirelessly to get to a resolution— desperate to get to the bottom of it all. He never wanted Emma to look at him the way she did before—that is if she'd ever look at him again at all.

The hurt in her eyes had gutted him. There had to be a reason that she took the accusation so hard without giving him a chance to speak. More than anything, he hated that he'd brought up those feelings in her—even if it was all a misunderstanding.

The more they researched, the more they were starting to believe that it was all a clerical error—they just had to find it.

"This is bullshit," Nathan yelled as he slid his chair back from his desk, hitting the wall with a thud.

"We're close, Nate. We're close." Ross Ewing was good in a crisis and always served as an anchor—leveling those around him with few words and a calm demeanor.

Ty brought a few of the energy drinks he'd just gotten to the men who'd been living on them for days. The crack of a tab caused Nick to flinch. He'd been edgier than ever, and it showed.

"I just don't understand how they can accuse you of fraud in a split second, but having them review the paperwork and realize they'd make a mistake is taking so long." Tyler tried to hand Nick an energy drink but he just shook his head. He was already wired and didn't need the extra jolt from a sugary beverage.

"It's like I've always told you boys: it's not nearly as easy to put the toothpaste back into the tube as it is to squirt it out." Ross had used the same analogy with his children since they were toddlers, but it wasn't until now that Nick finally understood how frustrating it must be to actually do such a thing.

He just hoped that once the toothpaste was back—so to speak—Emma would realize that he hadn't betrayed her or done anything wrong. He was desperate to get her back. Without her, he felt empty—the colors he saw around her were dull, and he refused to accept that it would be his reality moving forward. Without her, a piece of his heart was missing.

Nick refreshed his email for the millionth time that hour and ran a hand through his hair as the inbox loaded. How much longer would they have to wait to hear from the *third* investigator their insurance company had assigned to the case? He was about to get in his car, drive to Baltimore and bang on the man's door.

Nick stood and continued to pace across the office floor. He was sure that he would have to replace the patch of flooring after the beating he'd given it recently.

Crushing his empty can and tossing it into the trash can, Nathan sat back down. "Nice shot, bro," Ty said. It wasn't the time to joke about his shooting skills, and Nathan shot his brother a look that made it clear.

"There it is," Ross said quietly. "I think this is what caused the mix-up." He held up a sheet of paper from one of the folders in front of him. "Based on what the investigator sent over, I think it was this renewal sheet that caused the problem." Nick took the sheet from his father and stood next to Nathan as they looked through the information.

At the bottom of the paper, he and Nathan's signatures showed that they'd reviewed the document. Everything on the form looked to be correct, except for one small dot that covered the last number on the page: the number of full-time employees. It was almost as if a small bit of ink had misprinted on the form, taking their employee count from over one hundred to under twenty.

"Are you fucking, shitting me?" Nick yelled. When he pointed to the error, Nathan tossed the paper onto his desk with his own string of expletives. Ty picked it up and looked over the numbers.

"Shouldn't this have meant that your rates were drastically cut though, too?" The other three Ewings looked up at him in shock. "What?" he asked incredulously, "I may not have a herd of employees that report to me, but I understand the basics of insurance, and I know that such a huge drop in employees would also mean a drop in rates."

Nate walked over to his computer again and pulled up their accounting software. For a few seconds, the only sound in the room was the clicking of his computer mouse.

"We never adjusted our automatic payments, Nick. We've been paying the correct amount this whole time, even if they had the number of full-time employees wrong." The brothers were grinning at each other like a pair of clowns.

"So clearly, this proves that we didn't try to commit any type of fraud," Nick finished.

"And that this investigation is a load of crap." Tyler always did have to have the last word, but Nick couldn't even give him a hard time about it right now.

"Print out those accounting sheets for me, Nate. I'm going to get these over to the investigator. This should be the end of it." The next five minutes passed by in a blur as the Ewings gathered the documents they needed to prove their innocence and sent them off to the insurance investigator.

And then, they waited in an eerie silence for a response. Nick hit the refresh button on his email again and again until a new email crossed the top of the screen.

"We got something." Nick opened the email and read it aloud as the rest of his family crowded behind him.

"Nick. I appreciate you sending this information over and all of the legwork this must have taken to find. While this isn't an official resolution email, I can't imagine that it will be longer than twenty-four hours before you have one. We will confirm receipt of payment in these amounts with our accounting department and dismiss all fraud charges at that time." Before he even finished, Ty was thrusting his fist into the air, Ross was clapping, and Nate slumped onto the back of his chair.

"On behalf of the company, I apologize for the inconvenience this has caused. Once we have dismissed the accusation, I'll reach out to the medical clinic regarding payment of the claim that triggered the investigation as well..."

It was done. Their business—and reputations—were safe. Until they got the official notice, Nick wasn't quite ready to celebrate. Although he did let himself start planning how he was going to win Emma back once she heard the news.

ннннн

"You're really going to let this be the reason you leave Boone Heights? I'm surprised at you Emma. Who knew you'd let a man drive you out of town." Katie flung her body down on the sofa next to Emma.

"This was never a permanent move, Katie. We both knew that." Emma knew that Katie's point was valid, but she also knew that she couldn't continue to risk emotional run-ins with the Ewing family. This was a small town, and she would be the small-town doctor. It just wouldn't work.

"Emma Olivia Cunningham, you're running away. I know that Nick wasn't the only reason you wanted to stay in Boone Heights, although I'm sure it helped make the decision easier." Katie's stare softened. "But he certainly should not be the reason you *don't* stay. If you didn't let Kyle run you out of Boston don't let Nick run you out of here."

"But I *did* let Kyle run me out of Boston. I came here, didn't I?" The truth seemed to have snuck up on Emma like a stealth lion hunting its prey.

"You needed a fresh start, Ems." The compassion in Katie's voice was back and her friend scooted up closer on the couch. Emma leaned into the embrace as Katie wrapped her arm around her shoulders and pulled her in. "This was your fresh start, not you running away. But, if you leave now...if you let what happened with Nick be the reason you go back to Boston or somewhere else—that's running away." Katie pulled back slightly. "And that's not you Emma. It's just not."

"I've made up my mind, Katie. I emailed Milton to disregard my previous email, asking about his return, and my idea to stay." Emma didn't need to admit how hard it was to send that email.

"Have you even talked to Nick?"

"Besides the first night when he came here, he hasn't reached out. Hell, maybe he had a deal with Milton all this time and that's why my uncle left. He felt the heat was rising."

"Emma," the tone of her friend's voice was firm, "do you really believe that? Do you really think that Nick had some nefarious plan this whole time? Was Mrs. Keller in on it, too? You're being absurd, now."

Emma let out a sigh, aware that she sounded ridiculous. She hadn't stepped into some insurance fraud scheme that her uncle had been trying to escape. Emma had gone back through several years of files in the clinic and saw that the company only had a few minor injury visits—certainly nothing out of the ordinary.

"I just need to leave, Katie. I can't stay here." A lump grew in her throat—the lump that she'd done so well to keep down the past few days. Then the tears began to dampen her eyes, and before she could stop them, they poured down her cheeks.

"He's everywhere, Katie. It hurts to be here, and it won't ever stop. You're right—I wanted to stay because I fell in love with the town, with the patients at the clinic, and with everything Boone Heights has. But I also fell in love with Nick Ewing, and he is so entwined in this town that I can't stay here. I can't." A hiccupping sob pierced those last words as her shoulders began to shake.

Her best friend readjusted her arms and pulled her in tight. For a small woman, Katie gave fierce hugs and Emma relished in the feeling of security as she cried on her best friend's shoulder. As the minutes ticked by, Katie held her close until the tears slowed and her breathing settled.

When the pair parted, Katie went into the bathroom to grab the tissues. Before she handed them to Emma she said, "I know you don't want to hear this Ems, but you never acted like this with Kyle. You were upset, but not like this. Kyle was a career threat, but this? This is betrayal. You're hurting on a personal level. This isn't about your job, it's about your heart. You can't fix this by running. You can't outrun heartbreak." Emma took the tissue Katie offered and dried what was left of the tears on her face.

"If I can't outrun a heartbreak, Katie, I'm afraid I won't survive it."

What if leaving Boone Heights didn't work? What if she could never stop the ache of loving Nick Ewing? Emma was desperate for clarity and wasn't sure it would ever come.

"The email will come, Nick. It's all but a done deal." His brother was far more relaxed that morning than he'd been in recent days. While Nick felt like a weight had been lifted, he still wouldn't be able to truly breathe until he fixed things with Emma, too.

"Not until we get the official word, Nate. I mean a stupid clerical error caused this whole thing to happen. I won't relax until we're told the correction is official." It was more out of habit by this point, but Nick hit the refresh button on his email inbox.

The phone on Nate's desk buzzed.

"Thanks, Megan," he said. "You can transfer him over." Nick stood, eager to hear the news.

"Hi, Jake. Nick is here, too. I'm going to put you on speaker phone." Nate hit the button and set the phone back onto the receiver.

"Hi Jake," was all Nick could manage.

"Good news, gentleman. You should be getting the official email any second now, but I wanted to call and let you know that your fraud case has been officially dismissed." The air rushed up and out of Nick's lungs as he gave Nate a high five. Jake laughed on the other end at the sound of their celebration. "I also want to apologize for the stress this has caused you both—personally and to your business. Please know that we are going to put measures in place to make sure clerical errors like this are caught well before it gets to this point."

Nick had all but tuned out the man at this point. He was back at his computer and hitting refresh for what he hoped was the last time ever in his entire life. The email Jake promised them appeared and Nick sent it straight to the printer.

Jake and Nate continued their conversation but Nick was out of pleasantries. It was time for him to get Emma back. One way or another, he was going to show her that he was exactly the man she thought he was two weeks before. He would do whatever needed to be done for her to see him that way again.

The plan that had been festering in his brain since last night began to take shape. With a wave to Nate, he grabbed the email from the printer and bolted out the door. He was going to get his girl, and he was going to tell her just how much he loved her.

CHAPTER TWENTY-ONE

Emma walked into her office the next morning and nearly jumped out of her skin at the sight of a man sitting behind her desk. She'd never seen him before but he was quickly familiar. His small, tight, smile said it all. It was her uncle, Milton Oliver.

"Hello, Emma." The tone of his voice was deep and wrapped around Emma like a warm blanket she didn't know she needed.

"Hello." She stopped, unsure of what to call the man. Milton? Dr. Oliver? Uncle Milton? No. No? No. Right? She didn't know the answer, so she just continued. "I hope I've kept your desk warm while you were away."

The joy on his face melted away her worry about what to call him. "It's wonderful to see you in person, Emma. It's been a long time, and never from this close."

All of the questions she'd been listing in her mind about the man who practically gave her a private practice came rushing to her mind, and she didn't know where to start. But the man seemed to have a window into her mind, quickly encouraging her.

"I'm sure you have questions, dear. Why don't you take a seat and we can talk."

Emma sat in a chair across from her uncle, unable to speak. Once she was seated, Milton stood from the desk chair and walked around to join his niece, turning the empty chair to face hers. She looked at the desk she'd come to think of as her own, and circled in her own confusion.

"We'll get to your emails—both of them actually—but let's do that in a little bit." Emma just nodded, still trying to process everything without actually knowing anything. "Would you like to start by asking me questions? Or would you like me to try and explain the best I can, and you can ask me about what I may have missed?"

She was desperate to know so much about this man, where he'd been the past few months and all the years of her life. But she couldn't articulate a single one of the questions in her mind. Instead, she simply said, "You can start."

Milton settled back into the chair and crossed one leg over the other—giving Emma a quick peek of his socks which were a deep navy blue with pink flamingos on them. It added a bit of whimsicality to his otherwise business casual attire and put Emma at ease.

Her uncle cleared his throat before he began. "I'm going to start at the beginning. As I mentioned, I'm your mother's older brother...but we haven't spoken in decades." He paused and Emma nodded at him to continue. "Right after I'd taken my boards, my father—your grandfather, who was also a physician—was accused of medical malpractice by several well-connected patients. As those investigations were starting, he was also presented with charges of embezzlement from his practice by two of his partners." Emma let out an audible gasp and her uncle stopped until she waved him on with her hand to continue.

"I wanted to believe that they were all false allegations, but the evidence presented against him by those involved was...well, overwhelmingly compelling. I had just taken my boards—I was finally a licensed physician, but I was also the son of a physician who was being accused of horrible things. I was shocked...and fearful, you might imagine. That fear eventually turned into anger, and I directed it all at my father."

Emma's heart began to race. How had she never known any of this? She'd gone her entire life, blissfully unaware of such a dramatic family history. She took another good look at her uncle, noticing regret cloud his gray eyes—eyes that looked just like her mother's. She spoke softly.

"I know this must be hard for you, but I'd really like to hear the rest of your story."

Milton shook his head like he was trying to clear out the cobwebs of past hurt. "Of course." He took a deep breath before continuing. "Our fight was awful...and things were said that could never be taken back. Your mother was away at college during this time, you know—she was pre-med...following in Dad's footsteps just like I had."

Did he just say that my mother was pre-med? She'd never known that about her mother. Her mother was a lawyer and always had been. She refocused her attention, ready for answers.

"Just like I was, Darra was shocked that our father was being accused of such things. The difference is, she believed in his innocence without hesitation." A wistful sound came from Milton, and she couldn't tell if it was wonder at her mother's belief in their father or regret that he hadn't. "This went on for over a year. I began to work at the practice my father had been forced to take a leave of absence from. As far as everyone was concerned, I'd replaced him and that didn't sit well with your mother. The two of us started to argue more frequently."

Milton uncrossed his legs and sat up a little straighter, clasping his hands on his lap. Emma knew she wasn't going to like what came next. "Eventually, the other partners at the practice had me so convinced that my father was guilty, I gave testimony against him to the investigators."

"Oh my gosh!" Emma's hand flew over her mouth and her eyes widened in shock. In front of her, Milton shut his eyes and his shoulders trembled slightly.

"That was the clear end of any ties I had with my family. Several months later, it was proven that your grandfather was completely innocent of every single thing he'd been accused of. I tried to apologize...I tried to make things right with my father and my sister. My own mother, who never swayed in her belief in her husband, tried to convince me to keep trying, but I couldn't do it. Too much damage had been done...and I decided that the only thing for me to do was to leave. I left town, ended up in Boone Heights, and opened up this clinic." He gestured around the room at what he'd built.

Tears filled Emma's eyes, her heart breaking for the man in front of her—for the uncle she never knew she had.

"I can only speculate on this part," he continued, "but I think your mother decided to become a lawyer to defend people—like our father—and to fight for the innocent, no matter what. Her faith in him was unwavering...and from what I can tell by the cases she's taken over the years, she's the same way with most of her clients."

Emma nodded. Her mother had always served as a champion for the underdog, always believing whole-heartedly in the clients she represented. It also became clear why her mother had jumped to her defense last fall. She refused to let history repeat itself—to allow her daughter to be dragged through the mud like her father was.

Milton sat quietly while Emma processed everything she'd heard. After a moment, he picked up where he left off.

"So, while I wasn't involved in the lives of my family anymore, I did my best to keep track of everyone and how things were going. I was a little shocked that your mother married a doctor if I'm being honest, but their engagement photos in the newspaper were just so...happy. So full of love. I could tell that she was marrying him despite his profession."

"They always talked about her work more than his, growing up." Emma wasn't sure if she was telling Milton a quick fact or if she was processing everything she'd just learned aloud.

"When I saw you'd graduated from medical school and were beginning your residency where I did my own...oh dear, I just felt a pride I didn't know was possible. I've always kept up with your career and accomplishments. I was just horrified when I saw what happened with that man's practice and the way you got caught up in the whole mess."

"That's why you reached out? You knew I'd need a change...that I would need time to heal?"

Milton leaned in close and took Emma's hands in his own. "Yes, Emma. I wanted to be there for you, and this was the only way I could think of." A smile and a quiet laugh escaped him. "You know, I was just thrilled when I got your first email...asking about staying in

Boone Heights. I was hoping we could practice together. That is if you wanted to after you heard the whole story."

Emma pulled her hands from his and sat up. "About my second email," she began. Milton interrupted her before she could say any more.

"Before we talk about the future, dear, do you have any questions about the past?" Emma took a moment to catch her breath. She needed to talk to him about the future but understood his need to clear about the history first.

She gave her uncle a gracious smile. "Actually, you explained everything very well. I can't imagine that reliving all of that was easy, and I appreciate you telling me." Relief passed over Milton's face and he let out a shaky breath at Emma's response.

"And, Uncle Milton," she said, suddenly feeling comfortable to address him so personally. "Thank you for taking care of me, and bringing me to Boone Heights. You seem to have known what I needed when no one else in my life did. I'm really grateful for that—and for you."

A tear slipped down the older man's face. "Uncle," he mused. "I never thought I'd be called that by anyone." He sniffed as another tear fell. "Thank you, Emma, for giving me something I didn't know I needed either."

Without another word, the two stood, and an uncle and niece embraced for the first time. They held onto each other for a long moment before breaking their embrace with smiles, and a wink from a proud uncle.

"Now," he began in a jokingly assertive tone. "What is this mess about you not wanting to stay in Boone Heights? Your first message made it sound like you'd settled seamlessly into life here and that you'd found your passion in small-town medicine. What changed, Emma?"

Not wanting to be any less forthcoming than he had just been, Emma tried to explain the dramatics of the past week to a man she'd just met, yet somehow felt she'd known her whole life. The whole story came spilling out faster than she thought she could speak. When she got to the part about thinking that perhaps Milton and Nick had some sort of arrangement to commit insurance fraud together, Emma stopped herself.

"Clearly, after all that you have shared with me, I know that you and Nick weren't involved in anything fraudulent together. I'm sorry I ever suspected you, Uncle Milton." And she was genuinely sorry. She'd thought the worst about someone who had given her the gift of a fresh start without needing to prove that her integrity was intact.

"Apology accepted, dear. But...truthfully, I just don't think that Nick, or Nathan, are capable of anything like that either. I've known those boys since they were in diapers. The Ewing family is one of strong moral character, Emma. Are you sure they are guilty of what they've been accused of?" The look he gave her had her questioning everything she thought she knew.

"This wasn't some hunch I had or a random accusation by a disgruntled client or partner. The insurance company filed the charges. I can't imagine they'd do that lightly or without proof. And Nick never denied it. He never fought to prove his innocence."

"And you think that this is reason enough to leave Boone Heights? To walk away from the new beginning you'd found and loved? To walk away from working with me?"

What her uncle asked was valid. Hearing it from him was different than hearing the same thing from Katie, or even from herself. Milton ran from hurt and betrayal in the past and had lived a life without a family connection. Now, Emma was more confused than before.

"I don't know how to...to be here...and not be with him. How would I get past the hurt of what he did if I stayed here?" She turned to face him with crinkled eyes. "Aren't you the one who gave me this opportunity so that I could run from a betrayal in the first place?"

"Emma," Milton fixed her with an unwavering stare. "I'm sure you can see the differences in the two situations." Before she could answer one way or another, Annie burst through the office door, seemingly unaware that Emma was with someone. She never even stopped to process who was in the room. Waving papers above her head, she screamed.

"It was a mistake, Emma! It was all a mistake!" She skidded to an abrupt halt, apparently noticing that she'd interrupted. After a moment of shock, she ran to Milton and threw her arms around him. "Dr. Oliver! It's so wonderful to see you? Are you home for good?"

Milton graciously accepted the hug but ended it quickly. "It's nice to see you too Annie, but I have to admit that I'm far more curious as to what was all a mistake." Annie looked confused for a moment before remembering why she'd come into the office in the first place. She had news to share.

The office manager turned to face Emma, pushed up her glasses—purple today, to match her bell-sleeved floral blouse and pants—and shoved the paperwork into Emma's hands.

"Emma, the insurance company just reached out. Apparently, there was some sort of clerical error, and Ewing Brothers' Construction had an account in good standing with them the entire time. All allegations of fraud are being dropped and they are paying out the claim immediately."

Emma felt the blood rush from her face, thankful to be sitting rather than standing on what were now weak and useless legs.

Did I hear Annie correctly? Nick hadn't committed insurance fraud. It was all a mistake.

"Wait, what?" She finally spoke. "A mistake?" She looked down at the papers in her hands, searching for the same explanation. Milton walked behind her chair and gently took the papers, reading them for the answers Emma was searching for. Annie crouched down in front of her, more agile than a woman of her age should be, and took Emma's face in her hands.

"Emma, apparently there was an ink stain on one of the forms the boys submitted last year, and no one at the insurance company bothered to question the drop in employees. They never even changed their automatic payment amounts...so they've been paying the correct amount this whole time. They have a huge overage in their account—one that was nearly spot on to what they would have owed if the renewal had been processed correctly."

"Well, I'll be." Milton looked up from the papers he was reading. "It's all here. What an unfortunate ink stain that was."

Relief flowed through Emma. Nick hadn't betrayed her. He hadn't committed any type of fraud. He was the man she knew him to be. But before she could fully embrace the joy she was feeling her world crashed down again.

"Oh my God," she muttered. "I accused him of awful things. I...I...," she couldn't even finish. She'd believed the worst in him so easily. She hadn't even asked for an explanation.

"He must hate me," Emma cried. What did she do now? She jumped up from her chair, causing Annie to tumble backward.

"Oh Annie," Emma went to help the woman up, "I'm so sorry."

"It's fine, sweetie. I'm okay." She said, winking at Milton. "I've got enough of a cushion that it didn't even hurt."

Behind her, she heard her uncle clear his throat. Normally, Emma would have been entertained by the banter between the two of them, but she had to get out of here. She had to find Nick. She had to explain her past to him. She had to beg him to forgive her.

"Emma," her uncle said, causing her to stop and turn. "Annie's fine. You go ahead."

"Right," she said. "Right!" Emma grabbed her bag from the coat tree by the door, tossed it over her shoulder, and nearly sprinted from the office. She almost knocked Katie down as she ran through the hall.

"I have to go find Nick, Katie! My uncle is in the office and he can see any patients I have scheduled. They'll fill you in." She quickly added, "Oh, and tell Uncle Milton to disregard my last email. The first one still stands."

"Uncle? He's here?" Katie asked, but Emma didn't take the time to stop and answer. She was out the doors of the clinic, in her car, and heading toward Nick's office.

Nick felt slightly guilty about breaking into Emma's backyard but quickly dismissed the thought as he secured the last string of lights. He smiled to himself, proud of everything he'd accomplished that afternoon—not just in the setup in the yard, turning Emma's place into a scene from a fairytale, but in the determination he had to prove everything he and Nate did with their company was above board. The way their entire family had rallied around them was something special. He knew that not everyone was so lucky, and he was grateful. He'd be sure to thank them all for their support, but it would have to wait.

He took a step back to survey what he'd done. He was beyond pleased with how everything had turned out and hoped that Emma would be too. With one final glance, he slipped through the side gate in her fence and back into his Suburban.

Assuming that Emma was still at the clinic, he went in that direction, wondering if the insurance company had paid the clinic yet. Even if they had, Nick was fairly certain that Annie wouldn't interrupt Emma during patient hours with the news, if she'd tell her at all.

The drive to the clinic felt like it took a lifetime, but finally, Nick pulled into a spot in the parking lot and breathed a deep sigh of relief. He tried to stay calm as he walked inside but knew that he was radiating the same type of energy Sadie had when she was being chased by Bacon.

Annie looked up from her desk when the door closed behind Nick.

"Nick, it's so nice to see you. We just got the notification from your insurance about their error. They're working on processing your claim right now." Her face was soft and kind and full of her own relief. "I'm so sorry this all happened to you boys, but I'm thankful it's been resolved. I knew there had to be some sort of misunderstanding, I just wish I would have pushed their billing department harder to take a closer look."

Nick approached her at the window. "It's okay Annie. We're glad it's all taken care of too. Although it seems like I lost ten years of my life this week." He dug deep to find restraint before he asked, "Dr. Cunningham isn't available right now, is she? I can wait if she's with a patient."

"Oh Nicky," Annie said gently, "she's not here right now. You missed her by about fifteen minutes."

"Nick?" He turned to find Katie standing in the doorway to the back of the office. "What are you doing here?"

"I came to find Emma," he said with a smile. "I need to talk to her...to explain everything to her."

"She's not here, Nick. You just missed her." Another voice filled the hallway and he looked up to find Milton Oliver walking out of the office Nick had come to think of as Katie's.

"Katie-girl, I'm going to go and get myself a coffee and a snack at The Roasted Bean. I've missed Luke's sweet treats. Can I get you something?" Milton saw Nick and smiled. "Mr. Ewing! It's nice to see you again, young man."

"Dr. Oliver? What are you doing here?" Nick was shocked to see the man that had been his own physician for practically his whole life coming out of what was always his office. Nick was overcome with fear. *If Milton Oliver was back in town, is Emma gone? Did Emma leave Boone Heights for good?*

"Just came back to check in on the clinic and talk about the future with Dr. Cunningham." A knowing look filled Milton's face.

"I'm just filling in for her for the afternoon, Nick. She raced out of here to try and find someone special...something about fixing what was broken." He winked at the man he'd always think of as a little boy.

Nick hadn't been aware of the air he was holding in his lungs until it all rushed out in a wave of relief. "Oh," was the only word he could manage.

"Nick," Katie said, grasping his arm. "Emma went looking for you. She wants to talk to you." Uncontrollable laughter took over Nick until he caught his breath.

"I came looking for her. I need to talk to her too." Getting control of himself, he asked, "Do you know where she is, Katie?"

"No, I don't," she answered, "but I'll find her for you. I can get her back here."

"No," Nick stopped her. "Can you get her to her cottage? Give me twenty minutes to get back there and then have her go there—please, Katie." Nick would have hit his knees and begged if he thought he needed to, but Katie was already pulling her phone from the pocket of her yellow and purple scrubs.

"I'll get her there, Nick. I'll text you once I've talked to her. Twenty minutes. Go," she waved, smiling wide. "Go now!"

"Right, right," Nick said. He stopped before turning to leave, looking back and forth between Katie and Dr. Oliver. "Thank you," he said. "Thank you both."

Twenty minutes. I'll have her back in twenty minutes.

CHAPTER TWENTY-TWO

Emma was about to attack the poor girl at the front desk of Ewing Brothers' Construction office to fess up to Nick's location when her phone alerted with a message from Katie.

Katie: Emma, listen to me and do not ask questions. Unless you are home, I need you to leave wherever you are and go to the cottage. Right now. Go, Emma.

She stopped in her tracks. The woman behind the desk looked up at her. "Can I help you?" The girl's tone was friendly and Emma was thankful she hadn't yet said anything she would have come to regret.

"I was actually looking for Nick, but I'm guessing he's not here." Emma knew she would need to explain her sudden appearance—and now, disappearance—somehow.

"Mr. Ewing stepped out for a bit but I can leave him a message if you'd like." She picked up a pen and held it poised to take a note. Emma smiled.

"I think it's better if I give him this message myself, but thank you so much." She laughed and waved, casually walking out of the door she'd just walked through and then, when out of sight of anyone in the office, kicking into a spring back to her car. Katie's message was clear enough that she assumed Nick was waiting for her at the cottage—and she had no desire to keep the man waiting.

She tried to calm her thoughts as she drove. She'd been so consumed with seeing Nick on the way to the office that she never gave a thought to what she might say when she finally got to him. She hoped that Nick could forgive her for not believing in him—for not trusting in him like she should have. She pulled into the parking spot in front of her cottage almost fifteen minutes later and saw Nick's familiar Suburban parked across the street. Her heart began to flutter as she got out of her car and walked to the front door. Before she reached the porch she saw a small handwritten sign with an arrow guiding her around to her backyard. The pathway was lined with rose petals and Emma felt the anticipation beginning to grow in her belly.

Had Katie set this up? Her friend was fast, but no one was this fast. The back gate was slightly ajar as Emma approached from the side. What she saw when she pushed it open and stepped through nearly took her breath away.

She was surrounded by twinkling lights and bouquets of the most beautiful flowers she'd ever seen in pale pinks and whites and greens. A gasp slipped through her lips when she saw Nick standing in the yard with a small white picket fence in his hands. It looked like a miniature replica of the panels they'd installed for Mrs. Keller on their second date.

As she got closer, she saw writing on the fence:

I love building fences with you Emma, but let's build them around us—not between us.

Tears began to stream down Emma's face but rather than the tears she'd been crying all week, they were tears of joy and relief.

Nick was here. He didn't want anything between them. He wasn't furious that she didn't believe him. He just wanted her—and wanted her close.

Her legs were carrying her across the yard to him before her brain had time to catch up to her heart. As she reached the man who had changed her for the better, all she seemed to be able to say was, "Nick." It seemed to be enough for him, and he laid down the fence that he held between them, reaching for Emma and pulling her in tight.

"Emma," He mumbled into her neck, healing the last bit of her broken heart before his lips crashed into hers and took in a kiss full of longing and need that had built during their time apart. Lacking the finesse he normally had, he plunged his tongue into her mouth, taking their kiss as deep as he could manage. Emma gripped his forearms in an attempt to keep herself upright, allowing herself to be completely taken by his embrace.

Nick slowly pulled his mouth from hers and began to kiss the tears that stained her cheeks.

"I'm so sorry Emma. I'm so sorry I wasn't able to explain what happened. I just didn't know." Emma placed a finger on his lips.

"Nick," she said ruefully, "I'm the one who owes you an apology. I'm the one who thought you'd done something wrong." She gestured around her yard. "And yet, you still did all of this for me. I don't know how I found you, Nick Ewing, but I never want to let you go again." She reached up and placed a small, gentle kiss on the lips of the man who completed her. "Besides an apology, I do owe you an explanation. Will you sit with me?" Emma gestured to the patio furniture near the back door.

"You don't owe me anything, Emma, but if you want to share with me, I always want to listen." Nick took her hand and led her to the small wicker couch with bright yellow cushions. As they settled, she took a deep breath and started to explain everything that happened that led her to Boone Heights, and to this moment.

To Nick, it didn't matter what Emma was about to say. He cared, and he was going to listen to every word, but nothing would change the way he felt about her, or how happy he was to finally have her in his arms again. There wasn't a chance in hell that he would let her slip away ever again.

As they settled on the small sofa, Nick realized that Emma was rattled with nerves, which was completely unlike her. He grabbed her hand and held it between both of his.

"You don't have to explain anything, Emma. You're here and I'm here. There isn't a fence between us. We're on the same side, and we always were. That's all I need." The reassurance allowed Emma to relax a bit and sink into Nick, whose heart beat stronger at her touch.

"But I want to build a fence around us, Nick. A fence that protects us from the outside world. And that starts with me telling you what happened before that led me to feel this way. Every fence needs a first post," she took a deep breath, "so this can be ours."

Emma Cunningham held his heart in her hands, Nick was certain. He knew that this was it—that *she* was it. So he nodded, encouraging her to begin.

"After I finished my residency, I joined a small family practice in Boston." Her voice sounded like she was somewhere far away as she began. Nick gave her hand a small squeeze. "My boyfriend at the time, Kyle, was a physician there, too. He and his friend opened the practice together a few years before."

Nick knew he couldn't possibly be the only man she'd ever been with, but hearing her say it out loud made him queasy. At least she'd never have another ex-boyfriend, ever again.

"Not long after I joined them, I got a letter from the medical board that said my license was at risk because charges of fraud had been brought against the practice, including all physicians who worked there." Nick tried to keep a neutral face, still not sure where the story was going. The simple fact that it involved health care-related fraud—the same type of thing he'd been accused of—forced sweat to form across his forehead.

Emma looked down as if she couldn't bear to look him in the eyes. "I was shocked. I had no idea what I was being accused of—it was the first I'd heard anything about it. My mother—remember, she's a lawyer—looked into it and a few days later she explained everything she'd learned. Kyle and his partner were being accused of insurance fraud—of falsifying medical records and charging insurance companies hundreds of thousands of dollars for treatments and procedures they never performed."

Emma stopped briefly and looked back up to Nick cautiously as if she didn't know how he might react. The pain and hurt he saw almost had him out of his seat and heading to Boston to teach Dr. Kyle a very hard and painful lesson.

"What a fucking asshole," he said instead. Emma's lips turned up in a sad smile.

"Thankfully, my mother never doubted me—not ever for a second. I never once had to tell her that I wasn't involved. She just up and started to fight on my behalf to ensure that my name was cleared from all court documents. She saw that I got to keep my license to practice medicine." Nick could feel her relax as the story went on. "Kyle and I shared a condo, and I moved out without a word. I should have known he couldn't afford such a nice place just a few years into a clinic. I moved in with my parents while I tried to figure out what to do." She inhaled and exhaled as if she'd finally admitted everything she'd kept tucked away. "That's when the letter from my uncle came. It turns out he'd been keeping tabs on me and my career, and when everything fell apart with Kyle he figured he'd offer me a break...a chance to reset."

He tried to pull her into him but she resisted. "Not yet, please let me finish." She needed to get it all off her chest.

"I hadn't planned on you, Nick. When I came to Boone Heights, I thought it would be for a month or two and then I'd move home—or maybe to another big city to start over—but then there you were. And everything made sense when I was with you. I felt things I didn't know I could feel. It felt right."

"Until I was accused of the same things as Kyle," Nick finished for her.

"Yes," she said, looking away again. "Just hearing about insurance fraud brought everything crashing back and I couldn't do it. I couldn't go through that again. I was so fundamentally changed by what Kyle had done that I didn't even think to give you the benefit of the doubt. I was convinced you were guilty without hearing any explanation from you."

"I didn't even offer you one, Emma. I should have done that—at least told you I would never do something like that."

She scoffed. "But that's just it, Nick. I wouldn't have believed you. And I'm so sorry for that. I should have stood beside you. I know the stress you just went through and I should have been there for you."

Nick couldn't take the space between them for a second longer and reached over to haul Emma across his lap, pulling her face up to look at him.

"Oh, Skipper. I'm so sorry for everything you went through—that you had to think those same things of me. I should have made you believe that I was innocent. I should have explained what we were doing to fix everything."

Emma interrupted, in surprise. "Oh my gosh! How did that even happen?"

He ran his fingers through her curls, gripping the back of her head and pulling her face to his, nose to nose. "I'll explain that mess later." Without another word, he kissed her deeply there on the sofa, before he picked her up and carried her through the back door, into the kitchen, and back to her bedroom.

He's still here.

Nick lowered her onto her bed and slipped off the heels she'd worn all day long in the office. He'd listened to her story and understood. They'd have more to talk about—like the fact that she was staying in Boone Heights permanently, or that Nick really needed to watch out for random ink spots on forms that had the potential to wreck people's lives. But for now, this was all she needed.

Nick's hands moved up her thighs as he deftly popped the button to loosen and slide her gray pants down her legs. It wasn't another three seconds before all of their clothes had landed across Emma's floor, and Nick was lowering his body down to hers.

His hard body covered hers, forcing the events of the week to the back of her mind as she focused on the sensations that ran through her body. Nick lowered his head to her neck and began to plant small kisses on the delicate patch of skin behind her ear until she moaned.

"I missed you, Skipper," Nick whispered into her ear as he pressed his body against hers. "I missed your scent and your taste. I missed your softness." His fingers found her center and pushed inside. "And your wetness. I missed feeling your wetness and your heat surrounding me. I missed doing this to you." He moved his fingers in and out, rubbing his thumb in circles around her throbbing clit.

"Nick," she said in a moan. "I need you. Please—I...I need you inside me. I need you to be closer to me." But she already felt her release rushing to break free, and Nick felt it too.

"You will, but first you're going to come for me." His soft words tickled her ear as his fingers picked up the pace, stroking her core. Emma shut her eyes to the sensation, as her whole body reacted to his touch. He closed his teeth over her earlobe and tugged, shattering her into a thousand pieces. She screamed his name as her orgasm pulsed through her.

When her senses returned to her body, Nick pressed his hardness to her center, ready to replace his fingers with all of himself.

"Yes, Nick. Now." In one thrust, Nick seated his entire cock inside of her, grunting as he reached her limits and sent her off the edge for the second time. He started to move inside of her, loving her inside and out. As soon as he pulled out, he pushed himself back into her warmth, never taking his eyes away from hers.

Just as Emma noticed the water that had pooled in his eye, he said, "I love you, Emma," and captured her mouth in a kiss that told her he'd never said anything more true in his life. His hips moved faster, thrusting into her so hard that she couldn't even respond to his declaration.

The waves of another orgasm rippled into her core and her hands reached down to grip the quilt beneath her, desperate to hold onto that feeling, at that moment, for just a little bit longer. Her pointless pursuit came to a halt as Nick's release filled her through the last waves of her climax. Instead of yelling his name, it came out as a whisper of the promise of forever.

Laying in Emma's bed, tangled up in the only woman he'd ever fallen in love with, Nick was finally beginning to understand what his father meant when he talked about finding the person you were meant to find.

"Nick," Emma whispered, raising herself up onto her elbow and running her index finger in lazy circles over his chest.

"Yes, Skipper?" He grasped her wandering finger and brought it to his lips, planting a small kiss on the tip.

"Nick, I love you." Her words made his entire world stop and start at the same moment. He looked up from his pillow and took in the shy smile on Emma's lips. "I love you so much, Nick. I kept thinking it was this town that felt like home—that it was just the charm of Boone Heights that made me want to stay here—but it's you. You're what makes this place feel like home to me." Nick sat up quickly, causing Emma to tumble onto her back. He swung one leg over her and pinned her arms above her head.

"You're staying? In Boone Heights? Did I hear that right?" Emma laughed, shaking the bed as she nodded.

"Yes, Nick. I'm staying in Boone Heights, at the clinic, with you." Nick knew this was it: the moment he could say it happened. It would be imprinted on his heart for the rest of his life. It would be with him forever.

"And you love me?" he asked, knowing the answer but desperate to hear her say the words again.

"Yes, Nick. I love you." Joy radiated from her and settled in his soul.

"Well, that's a good thing," he said more casually than he felt.

"Just a *good* thing?" He placed a small kiss on her nose, another on her forehead, and finally one on her lips.

"It's a *really* good thing, Emma, because I love you too. But it's more than that. I think I finally get it."

"Get what?" She waited for him to elaborate.

"I get what my parents meant when they talked about this feeling and the person who makes you feel it."

He pressed the expression on her face into his mind, hoping he'd never forget it. "You're it, Skipper. You're my Forever Love, and the only fences we're building now are ones that will never fall down around us."

Made in the USA
Columbia, SC
10 July 2022